PRAISE FOR WHILE THE STORM RAGES :

'A PAGE-TURNING TRIUMPH to make you
laugh and cry – it's PHIL EARLE AT HIS BEST'
JACQUELINE WILSON

'I don't think there's another writer for young people who
PACKS AN EMOTIONAL PUNCH like Phil Earle. His
prose, brutal, honest, but also deft and subtle, digs its fingers
into your heart, then squeezes. In *While the Storm Rages* he
manages to extract RIOTOUS COMEDY from TRAGEDY
AND THRILLING ADVENTURE from sadness. It's every
bit as good as *When the Sky Falls*, and that means it's VERY
GOOD INDEED' ANTHONY MCGOWAN

'A TRULY BRILLIANT
STORY of COURAGE
AND RESILIENCE
AND EXCEPTIONAL
ANIMALS. This is definitely Phil
Earle's best yet' EMMA CARROLL

'Another
STUNNING READ
from one of the most
AUTHENTIC
STORYTELLERS
writing for children today'
LESLEY PARR

'A BIG-HEARTED ADVENTURE with big-hearted kids
desperately fighting to do the right thing in a messed-up world –
the l

D0544281

WHILE THE STORM RAGES

WHILE THE STORM RAGES

PHIL EARLE

ANDERSEN PRESS

First published in Great Britain in 2022 by
Andersen Press Limited
20 Vauxhall Bridge Road, London SW1V 2SA, UK
Vijverlaan 48, 3062 HL Rotterdam, Nederland
www.andersenpress.co.uk

2 4 6 8 10 9 7 5 3 1

British Library Cataloguing in Publication Data available.

ISBN 978 1 83913 205 6

Printed and bound in Great Britain
by Clays Ltd, Elcograf S.p.A.

This book is dedicated to Lel Preston,
who passed me *Holes* and changed
everything . . .

1

The ball cut through the sky like a grenade. But there was no real explosion when it hit the water. Not at first. Not until Winn hit the canal seconds later, four paws slicing through the surface, her shaggy belly forcing the water skywards.

It wasn't a dive that was going to win medals: more a belly flop than anything else, but it made Noah and his dad laugh, just as it did every morning.

'Do you think it hurts when she does that?' Noah asked.

'Does it look like it?'

How a dog managed to smile with a ball between her teeth, Noah had no idea, but it gave him his answer nonetheless. The smile only disappeared when Winn dropped the ball at their feet, her expression changing instantly to pleading.

Throw it, please. Now.

Dad launched another throw that detonated in the filthy canal, twenty-five yards on. Same dive from Winn, same splash, same smile from all three of them.

1

It was going to be a splendid late August day. Weather-wise at least. Six in the morning, but Noah could already feel the heat of the sun on his neck, and knew that by lunchtime he'd be seeking solace in the shade. But it wouldn't just be the heat that drove him somewhere quiet. He was sure that by lunchtime the only company he'd want would be his own. And Winn's, of course.

They walked on quietly, waiting for Winn to return with her bounty.

'Penny for 'em?' Dad asked.

Noah said nothing.

'Tuppence then,' Dad added, with a sad smile, but still he got nothing in return. 'Blimey, Noah, I know you've always got a money-making scheme in your head, but I never thought you'd fleece your old man. Especially not today.'

'Don't go,' Noah said, not quite daring to look Dad full in the face as he said it. 'Please.'

Dad didn't reply. Not with words anyway. Instead he pulled Noah into his side as they walked and rested his head on top of his son's. Noah waited for the sound of a kiss on his crown, but it didn't come. It felt like Dad was just breathing him in, banking what he could before he marched off at midday.

They continued, through Wapping Woods, doing what they did every morning before the rest of the world woke.

They never tired of it, and Winn certainly didn't, though the ball was now sporting a soggy algae wig. In fifteen minutes, after another dip in Shadwell Basin, her coat would look the same, and she'd return home to the inevitable wrath of Mum and the shame of being doused in buckets of cold water.

They ambled on until they hit the Thames and turned east along the river path, saying nothing, thinking plenty, until they reached the end point: Limehouse Basin. The same place where they turned back every morning. The place that housed the boat. Dad's boat. *Queen Maudie.*

She looked glorious to them in the sunshine despite her decrepit condition. Even the rust shone as she sat, tethered to the bank.

Dad gave her flank a loving rub. She might share Mum's name (Dad's idea – to prevent Mum going off at the deep end when he bought her out the blue), but there were times when Noah thought Dad gave *this* Maudie more attention than the real one.

'Hopefully won't be long before we can work on her some more,' Dad said. 'We'll have her purring soon enough, I promise.'

Noah smiled. It was a project they both loved. The *Queen Maudie* was still some way from being truly shipshape; even short journeys had to be done slowly.

'I can keep her engine turning over, while you're . . . you know . . . not here.'

'Oh, can you now? And I can trust you, can I? For once?'

Noah pretended to look wounded: sad, furtive eyes and wobbling lip. It was an expression he'd perfected over the years to try and pull the wool firmly over his parents' eyes. 'Trust me? Of course. And, well, we don't want the engine seizing up, do we?'

'I don't want her crashing into a battleship when you get lost at sea either. So it might be best you leave her well alone, eh? Wait for me instead.'

That silenced and sobered Noah, the idea of waiting. Waiting was all he had in front of him.

Dad must have sensed it. 'Come on, son. I know me going is hard, but it's better than the alternative, isn't it?'

They'd discussed the alternative a lot. War was coming, Dad said. It was inevitable.

'Don't matter what's written on that piece of paper Mr Chamberlain was waving around, Hitler's going to keep on marching and invading. And don't be thinking the sea between us and France is going to stop him.'

'Why go now though, Dad? Can't you wait till war actually comes? Other dads aren't going now.'

'Do you think Hitler will wait patiently while we put an

army together? Course he won't. It'll come hard and it'll come fast and so we have to be ready.'

He knelt in front of Noah. It was unusual for either of them to be wearing such serious expressions. 'I have to do this, son. You might not understand why right now, but in time you will. In time, something will happen, right in your eyeline and you'll know, you'll just *know*, that you have to stand up and fight it. No matter what the fear, no matter what the cost. Because if you don't? Well, everything you know and love and recognise will suddenly look completely different.'

'But what if you . . .' Noah started, before realising he couldn't finish the sentence.

'*What if* hasn't happened yet, so there's no point giving it space in your brain. All I can think about is, if I don't fight, then how long will it be until our country isn't ours any more? Until we're taking orders from people who only know hate. Who live to make folk feel one thing alone: fear.'

What could Noah say to that? For once he had nothing. He just wanted his dad to be safe.

'Soon as I'm back,' said Dad, 'we'll *really* get to work on the boat. Make the engine run so smoothly that me, you, Mum and Winn can fire her up and point her in that direction. And we won't stop until we hit the sea. Sail her round the coast, we will, before catching our own tea and cooking it on the beach. Fancy that?'

Noah nodded. He didn't dare risk Dad hearing the wobble in his voice that might suddenly be there.

'Well, to do that, I need you to be strong, son. Because we don't know how long all this is going to last. It might be months, it might be longer. So while I'm not here you're the man of the house. You've got your mum to look after for starters. Be strong for her, don't be causing her grief with any of your madcap ideas. And DON'T be giving her any of your lip either, d'you hear me?'

A smile crept across Noah's face. There was no way he was swearing to any of *that*.

'And as for this daft beggar,' Dad said, as Winn dropped the ball at his feet for the umpteenth time. 'Don't let anything happen to her, you hear?' Dad went on to his knees and stroked Winn tenderly. 'We've been through a lot, me and Winn. And knowing that the *three* of you are safe is all I'll need to keep *me* safe. Can you do that for me, Noah?'

Noah bent down beside his dad and fussed Winn too.

'I'll do it, Dad. I promise. We'll all be waiting for you. Especially this daft beggar.'

That was enough for Dad. He pulled Noah into him, before throwing him to the floor for one final, laughter-filled wrestling match. One that Winn had to both join in on, and win.

2

'Your dog's a Nazi.'

Clem said nothing. Neither did Noah. Partly due to shock, and partly due to the fact that the words, ridiculous as they were, had come out of the mouth of Big Col.

'Did you not hear me, squirt? I said that dog of yours is a Nazi.'

Clem's mouth fell open this time, but still nothing came out.

'I mean, it's a dachshund, in't it,' said Big Col.

'Sausage dog,' Clem said hesitantly.

'Yeah, and we all know what that means. It's German. A filthy Hun dog. And dangerous.'

That was the *most* ridiculous bit. The dog, Frank, was anything but dangerous. There was little chance of him nibbling you anywhere above the ankle for starters, as well as the fact that he was probably older than Hitler's grandfather in dog years.

Frank, adorable as he was, was an arthritic,

draught-excluder of a hound who wheezed by the time he reached the end of the front path.

Big Col, though, was adamant. 'So?' he said gruffly. 'What you going to do about it?'

He was younger than Noah and Clem by months, one of the youngest in the year, but what he lacked in age he made up for in height, breadth and menace. His bulk threw the pair into shadow as he loomed over them.

'What *can* I do?' said Clem. She wasn't being clever (although she was whip smart). 'All I can tell you is that Frank's never been to Germany. We got him years ago off Mrs Shreeve on Tench Street and she ain't even been to the seaside, never mind Berlin.'

Big Col wasn't persuaded. 'Don't matter. You shouldn't be having a dog like that. Not now. Not with everything going on. My dad says Jerry dogs need shooting. It's not patriotic.' He struggled a bit with the pronunciation, but they knew what he meant.

Noah felt his insides curl in irritation at the stupidity of it all. He didn't want to hear what Big Col's dad reckoned. Why wasn't he off training to fight like *his* dad? It left Noah prickly on Clem's behalf. He stroked Winn, who was sitting alert at his side, growling quietly, and that somehow made him feel braver than perhaps he should have in front of Big Col.

'So, what you're saying is, you think Frank here – a dog – . . . is a Nazi?'

'Course he is. Every bit of him.'

'And if I can prove to you that he's not, what will you give me?'

Big Col thought about it, then pulled half a dozen sherbet lemons out of his pocket. Lord knew how old they were, but they were probably the most appealing things lurking in there.

He offered the sweets out in front of him.

'They'll do,' said Noah and he stood in front of Frank, who squinted up at him, eyes old and milky.

Clem looked at Noah too, her expression asking: 'Are you sure you know what you're doing?'

But Noah didn't care. He didn't want the sweets. He just wanted to expose Big Col for the fool he was. So, without warning, Noah faced Frank, clicked his heels together and threw his right arm in front of him.

'*Heil Hitler!*' he yelled at the dog, with a force that shocked even Big Col.

Frank didn't move or bark. And he certainly didn't raise his own front leg in a matching salute.

'See?' said Noah, pointing at the dog while looking in Big Col's widening eyes. 'How can he be a Nazi and not shout it back?'

But this did nothing to convince Big Col. Instead it lit his fuse.

'You cheeky g—' he roared, lurching forward, but Noah was no longer there. Nor were Winn, Clem or Frank. There was less chance of Frank sprinting than there was of him saluting, so Clem was now carrying him as the four of them hared down the street and out of sight.

Big Col couldn't hurt what he couldn't catch, and that was the way Noah liked it.

They only stopped when they had to. Lungs burning and foreheads pouring. The dogs were thirsty, even Frank, who hadn't run a single step, and they lapped at a puddle. Clem shook life back into her arms, Noah just shook with laughter.

'Did you see his face?' he said.

'Not for long I didn't. There wasn't time. What were you thinking, pulling his leg like that?'

'Well, he's a fool, isn't he? Reckoning Frank's a Nazi. He'll be saying Winn's a German spy next. Only spying Winn does is on Mum when she's frying sausages.'

Winn barked in agreement. She always barked when sausages were mentioned.

'Well, I don't think it's a good idea, picking a fight with Big Col,' Clem said. 'He'll knock you into next week when he sees you again.'

'He'll have to catch me first. And even if he does, Winn won't let anything happen to me, will you, girl?'

Winn growled, right on cue, though in all honesty, she wasn't much of an attack dog. She was a mongrel, a greyhound's sprinting frame covered in the thick, tangled hair of a terrier. Neither Dad nor Noah had a clue what kind exactly, nor did they care. Winn was a true original and that was one of the many things they loved about her.

'How's Winn been since your dad went?' Clem asked as Noah pulled at foliage tangled in the dog's coat.

'All right, I suppose. She's started sleeping on my bed. Sneaks up, but only once Mum's light goes out. She'd give her a good hiding if she got wind of it. Me too, probably.'

'She's never loved Winn the same way as you and your dad, has she?'

Noah thought about it, though he didn't really need to. Mum had never wanted or asked for a dog, though she'd done little more than roll her eyes when Dad had brought Winn home from the pub three years ago, wrapped sleepily in a blanket.

'At least it isn't a ruddy boat this time,' she'd sighed.

'I'll walk her, don't you worry,' Dad had said, nose red and smile wide with beer. 'We both will, won't we, son?'

Noah had nodded enthusiastically. And he'd kept his word. More than that in fact. When Winn the puppy used

11

the floor as a toilet, Noah cleared it up, no matter how awful the stink was. It was better than Mum saying 'told you so'.

'Mum likes her all right,' Noah replied. 'Winn's my responsibility, that's all. Especially now Dad's off training to fight the Jerries.'

'They used dogs in the last war. Did you know?' said Clem. She knew these sorts of things. Had a brain like a full, but well-ordered filing cabinet. 'They delivered messages between trenches, sniffed out enemy soldiers, even pulled machine guns behind them.'

'Well, Winn won't be doing anything like that. I won't let her out of my sight, apart from when I'm at school.'

'Why's that then?'

Noah's answer was simple. 'Promised my dad, didn't I? Swore nothing would happen to her while he was away. And he promised that if Winn was safe, then he would be too.'

Noah nuzzled into Winn's neck, face immersed in her fur. So immersed that he couldn't see the concerned look that swept over his best friend's face.

3

Maudie Price had the patience of a saint, which was just as well given the trials thrown constantly at her, firstly by her husband, secondly by Noah, and finally (and most irritatingly) by the damn dog, Winn.

Though her husband and son painted it otherwise, the lion's share of dog responsibilities fell to Maudie. She'd accept that yes, they *were* out with the larks every morning, walking Winn, plotting lord knows what, but even before Tom left to go to war, by half-past seven he was away to the factory and Noah had stomped off reluctantly to school, leaving her and the dog alone. It would've been almost acceptable if Winn, tired after her walk, had slept by the kitchen hearth, but in the years since she had joined the family, that had never happened once.

Instead, she followed Maudie around, twisting between her legs and lighting her fuse. Maudie wasn't daft, she knew the dog wasn't doing it out of love, but greed. Winn had worked out very early on that Maudie was the bringer of food, and that if she stayed close and sharp enough, she could eat anything that found its way through Maudie's fingers.

Only weeks earlier, Maudie had been raging, 'That stupid dog is constantly under my feet, tripping me up on purpose, just so she can eat whatever I'm cooking.'

Neither Dad nor Noah would have it, naturally. 'She just wants to be close to you,' they'd said.

'Close to me? Only time she leaves me alone is when I go out to the lav, and that's only because I bolt the door.'

'She just wants to spare your dignity,' said Dad, winking at Noah.

'We both know that's not true,' replied Mum. 'That dog was put on this earth for one reason alone. To eat anything I slave over cooking.'

'Rubbish,' said Dad, before whispering something to Noah about how Winn had better taste than that.

'Rubbish, you say?' spat Mum. 'I came back from the lav today to find her on the counter with her head in my mixing bowl.'

'You expect us to believe that?' said Dad. 'How do you think she got up there?'

'She managed to move a chair and climb up. It was there, pushed up against the cupboard.'

Dad and Noah both laughed. 'And how did she do that? She's a dog.'

Maudie felt her face flush. 'Pushed it with her nose? Built a bloomin' rope ladder? I don't know. All I know is the bowl was empty when I got back and two hours later I had several piles of flamin' dog sick to clean up. Not that you two beggars care.'

Dad always knew when it was time to make amends, and usually left Noah to cuddle Winn (who remained seemingly oblivious to the allegations levelled at her), while he talked Mum down from sending the dog to fend for herself on the streets.

Today was different. Mum was already flustered when Noah strolled in from school and sent Winn into her usual euphoric frenzy. It didn't help that Winn's exuberance saw her crash into the kitchen table and dislodge a teacup that smashed into a hundred pieces.

'For the love of God!' Mum cried, as Winn stopped barking long enough to lap up the cold tea. 'Noah, get that animal out of my sight before I take up taxidermy as a new hobby.'

Noah laughed unhelpfully, fussing Winn under her collar. 'She won't stand still long enough to be stuffed, will you, girl? No you won't.'

That was it for Mum.

'I mean it, Noah!!' she roared, before the anger on her

face collapsed into a look of sheer, undiluted despair. Tears appeared and fell so quickly that Noah did something he rarely did; he put his mother before the dog. He pushed Winn into her basket and dashed to Mum.

'What is it?' he asked, though he feared the answer instantly. It couldn't be Dad. It couldn't, could it? He'd have barely been handed a rifle by now. And anyway, he thought, we aren't at war. Not yet.

'There's been an announcement,' Mum said. 'From the Prime Minister. He said that if war is declared, then they expect Hitler to start bombing immediately. That cities will be under attack.'

A shiver of horror went through Noah. 'How's he going to do that? We're an island.'

'He has planes. Lots of them. Rita next door says there'll be nothing left of London by Christmas.'

It shocked Noah to see Mum as frightened as this, almost as much as the words she was saying scared him. But he also remembered what Dad had said. Noah was the man of the house now. He had to be brave.

'It won't come to that, Mum. Mr Chamberlain and all them generals and colonels, they won't allow it. And even if a plane does get through, we'll fight back. We will. I will. I won't let anything happen to any of us. I promise.'

But Noah didn't know what Mum knew. And when she told him, it knocked the air clean out of his lungs.

'You won't be able to stop it, son.'

'I will, Mum. I know you think I'm just a kid, but I'll fight if I have to.'

'I know you would, Noah. But it won't be possible.'

'Give me one good reason why not.'

'Because you won't *be* here. They're shipping you out to the countryside. You and all the other kids. You're being evacuated.'

4

Evacuated?

Mum looked terrible, like a vampire had leeched every drop of blood from her body. Noah felt a bit light-headed himself. Partly because he wasn't entirely sure what the word really meant.

'So, I'll have to live with strangers? Another family?'

'That's right,' said Mum.

'Who I've never met before?'

Mum nodded.

'Out of London??'

Another nod. 'Yes, love, probably a long way away; somewhere safe and far from the bombs.'

'And when will I get to come home?'

'When the war ends.'

'But it hasn't even started yet!'

'I know that, Noah, but Mr Chamberlain – well, we have to trust him, don't we? And if he says it's not safe here, then we have to do what he says.'

'But what if I don't *want* to go? What if I want to stay here with you?'

Mum turned abruptly and busied herself with a pile of his clothes that were scattered across the table.

'You don't think I want you to go, do you? That I'd want to send you God knows where to live with God knows who, with no kind of clue as to when you'll be home, if I didn't have to?'

'Well, at least you won't have to tidy up after me for a while,' said Noah, though his joke didn't make him *or* Mum feel remotely better.

'They've said we're to send you with all sorts of stuff,' she said, hands flitting from garment to garment. 'Your gas mask, pyjamas, spare this, spare that, comb, toothbrush, face cloth, handkerchiefs.'

She looked flustered now as well as sad.

'Haven't we got those things already?' he asked.

'Of course we have. But not all of them are new or particularly decent, are they? And I don't want whoever takes you in thinking I don't look after my boy. I couldn't bear that.'

She took an enormous breath. Like she was gasping for air. Noah didn't know how to respond and even Winn looked confused, preferring to bury her face in the depths of her basket in the vain hope that whatever was going on would stop.

'It'll be all right, Mum. Maybe they'll let you come and see us. You know. Every month or something.'

'Not if they send you to Cornwall, or Scotland. How on earth would I get there? And what happens if none of this ends quickly?'

'It won't be that long, Mum. Nowhere near. Hitler won't stand a chance against us. We beat the Germans in the last war, so we'll beat them again. And anyway, Dad's fighting them. He won't let them win.'

Mum tried to smile but failed. Miserably.

'I promise you, Mum. You don't need to worry. I'm not going to forget about you. Or Dad. Or home. AND I'll be in the countryside, for goodness' sake. What's the worst thing that could happen there? Even if I get chased by a cow, Winn will protect me, won't you, girl?'

Winn's ears stood to attention and she barked a swift, firm reply.

'See?' he said, but Mum didn't reply. Instead she held Noah's shoulders and eased him backwards, so she could look clearly into his eyes.

'Oh, Noah, love,' she said. 'That's just it. Winn won't be allowed to go with you. She'll be staying here. With me.'

And in that moment, Noah realised for the first time that his entire world was at war.

5

'But she can't stay here,' Noah yelled, breaking from Mum's grasp. 'She has to come with me. She has to!'

He didn't mean to be angry, or rude, but all he could think of was Dad, of the promise he'd made about Mum *and* Winn. What sort of son would he be if he let Dad down within a week? Dad had said it, hadn't he? As long as Noah kept Mum and Winn safe, then he'd be safe too. Bulletproof. So this news? Well, it was terrible. As bad as it could be.

'I'm sorry, Noah. I wish Winn could go with you too, to keep you out of trouble if nothing else, but it's just not possible. Think about how many children are going to be leaving the city. How much of a responsibility that is for the families taking them in. They can't take in every cat, dog and goldfish too. It just wouldn't be fair.'

'Fair? Well, it's not fair leaving Winn here either, is it? Why is it all right for her to be abandoned here to be blown up and not me?'

'Because she's just a dog, son.' It seemed like a perfectly reasonable thing to say as far as Mum was concerned.

21

'Not to me she's not. Or to Dad. To us she's as important as anyone else. She's part of this family. The only one who doesn't give a monkey's about her is you!'

'Noah! That's not—'

'What? True? Fair? It's both of those things, Mum. I walk her, don't I? I chop up her food and check for fleas and ticks and comb her out and everything!'

Although Noah received many of his traits from his dad, there was one that his mum had clearly passed on to him, the inability to walk away from an argument.

'And who does it while you're at school, eh?' she roared back. 'Who cleans up the sick when she vomits up what she's eaten? While you and your father are swanning about, daydreaming? Who apologises to Rita next door when Winn uses her garden as a lav? Or combs the streets every time Winn gets through the gate and goes missing?'

'She went missing? When?' If Mum was trying to reassure Noah about the idea of leaving Winn behind with her, then she was doing a lousy job.

'More times than you can count, Noah. In every weather possible. And every time she runs, I go after her, and I don't stop until I find her and bring her home. So don't stand there and tell me I don't look after her!'

Noah stormed from the room and out the back door,

slamming it behind him with venom, only stopping when he realised he didn't have his shadow with him.

'Winn!' he yelled through the window. There was no way he was stepping foot back inside. 'Come on, girl. Come on.' He didn't have her lead but he knew he didn't need it. She might run away from Mum, but she'd never do the same to him.

It didn't take Winn long to paw her way to freedom, adding to the scratches on the door with such ferocity that Mum had no choice but to set her free.

'Be back in an hour,' she yelled, at both dog and son, though if either of them heard they didn't reply. By the time Mum poked her head through the back door, the pair of them were nowhere to be seen.

6

It wasn't far to Clem's house. A three-minute run on two legs, and probably half that if you were Winn, galloping on four. The only obstacle to getting there quickly (and safely) was that Noah had to navigate past Big Col's house.

His normal tactic was to put his head down and peg it. Today though, despite wanting to get to Clem urgently, Noah didn't sprint past Big Col's. If the big thug came out at that moment, so what? Noah could handle himself. He had enough anger stored up inside him right now to fare better than normal in a fight. Plus, if Big Col put him in the infirmary, then there was no way Noah would be going anywhere and his promise to Dad would remain alive. As would Dad.

But no one was home. Or if they were, they had other things on their minds than squashing Noah's nose into his face.

So he walked on, Winn circling him excitedly, every minute spent with her boy being another adventure to be lapped up.

When Clem answered her door, she looked like Noah felt.

'You heard then?' he said to her.

'Yeah. You?'

Noah nodded.

'Do you need me to explain to you where Cornwall is?' she asked, only half joking.

'I don't give a monkey's where it is,' he replied. 'Cos I ain't going.' It felt good saying it, but it soon felt hollow. One thing he knew about Mum was that she wasn't one for changing her mind. 'They sending you away too?'

Clem nodded. 'It'll be all right though. Nearly everyone from school's going. The teachers too. It might even be fun.'

'Fun?' Noah was incredulous. 'Are you serious?'

'Well, it'll be different then. Safe at least.'

But Noah didn't want to hear about safe. He wanted to ask the important question: 'Is your mum letting you take Frank with you?'

From Clem's face it clearly wasn't something she'd even thought about. She turned and ran inside. Noah followed her.

Clem's mum, Ma Parkinson, wasn't the smiliest of women and Clem's question about Frank received a straight answer.

'Of course not. The dog will be staying here. He's too

25

old for that kind of change plus I can't trust you or your brother to look after him properly, now can I?'

And that was it, except for a dressing down for Noah who'd dared to set foot in her clean house with his dirty clodhoppers still on his feet.

Thirty seconds later, Noah, Clem and the two dogs were back out on the street, watching mothers dash from house to house, clutching pyjamas and gas masks and wash bags of all colours and sizes.

'World's gone mad,' sighed Noah as he slumped against the wall. Winn mirrored him, head on her legs, eyes staring mournfully at him.

'You think *this* is mad,' Clem replied. 'Wait till Adolf starts dropping his bombs.'

'You really think he can do it?'

'I think he thinks he can. And if it's true, then we really don't want to be here to find out.'

'But it's all right for our mums to find out? And Winn? And Frank?'

Clem sighed. 'I reckon the adults have got enough to think about, getting every kid in London out to the countryside, without thinking about animals too.'

Noah's blood still ran hot, and he answered like he was talking to his mum. 'But they're not just *animals*, are they? They're family. They're living, just like us, and they feel, just like us, in fact they get scared way more than we do. You think they're going to like it when bombs start dropping? Winn goes loopy when the postman drops a parcel through the letterbox. They can't stay here in London. They'll go mad.'

'I know,' said Clem, refusing to be hurt or wounded by the sharpness of Noah's words. 'You're telling the wrong person.'

'Well, who else am I going to tell? My mum won't listen, your mum's too busy worrying about her carpet and the only person who *would* listen isn't here, is he?'

'Is that who you're really worried about?' Clem said softly, sliding down the wall next to Noah. 'Your dad? Because I think he would understand, you know.'

'No, he wouldn't!' Noah couldn't believe she was saying this. 'Winn's safety means as much to him as mine, or Mum's.' He could feel the emotion rising in him. 'And I promised him, Clem. Told him, to his face, that I'd keep Winn safe. And I can't break that promise.'

'Why not though? I know your dad, and he'd want you to be safe first.'

'Because if I break *my* promise, then what will happen to *his,* Clem? He said if I kept Winn safe, then he'd be safe too. And I can't keep that promise if I'm two hundred miles away, can I?'

Clem said nothing for a few seconds, but Noah could see there was something on her mind.

'What?' he said. 'What is it?'

It's two hundred and sixty miles to Cornwall,' she said. 'Give or take a mile.'

7

There was nothing anyone could say that would settle Noah's mind.

Cornwall might as well have been Timbuktu it was so far away, Scotland was further, and even the Cotswolds, only a few thumb widths away on the map, was too far for Noah to contemplate. Clem tried to sell each of the places to him and, as usual, she seemed to know as much about them as an encyclopaedia. She did her best, showing him places in her dad's atlas but Noah's ears were closed to her, and eventually, with the sun dipping behind Clem's terrace, he made for home. His mood was so glum that he didn't give a second thought to walking past Big Col's, even when he heard raised voices from inside.

Instead, he rehearsed what he would say to Mum when he got home, and although he was proud in nature, he wasn't averse to apologising if it made her change her mind. It didn't even matter if his apology was an empty one. What mattered was having Winn with him. Keeping his promise.

'I'm sorry, Mum, I really am,' he said as soon as he was

through the door, though Mum didn't raise her head from her darning. If he was going to change her mind with an apology alone, it was clear he was going to have to do better than that.

'It's just, you know, well, Winn, she means a lot to me, don't she?'

'She means a lot to us all,' Mum replied, the needle in her mouth dangling like the weediest of cigarettes.

On a normal day, with Dad here, they'd argue the toss about this. How Mum was prone to resenting everything about Winn's presence, from the hairs on the settee, to the fleas that danced on her best rug. But not today. Noah knew that would be foolish, arguing would get him nowhere.

'So I reckon the best thing to do is for me to stay here with you and Winn. To look after you both. It's what Dad would want. Clem says it's not compulsory, this evacuation lark.'

'Does she now?' Mum still didn't look up. 'And how is Clem finding it? Being Prime Minister?'

'She says the pay is terrible and the hours are long, but she did say some mums aren't sending their kids away. Next door to hers, the kids are staying.'

Mum did spare him a look then. A scowl. 'Well, more fool them. If you're talking about Mrs Brining, the woman hasn't got the brains she was born with.'

'But if other kids are staying, then I could too. I won't get in the way. I'll help. I don't want you to be . . . you know . . . lonely . . . with Dad not here.'

Mum finally put down her darning, and beckoned Noah to her. Her face softened as he neared.

'You don't really think I *want* to send you away, do you?' she said, pulling him towards her. 'It's bad enough seeing your dad march off, without seeing you go too.'

'Then let me stay!'

She shook her head sadly. 'I can't, Noah. We don't know what will happen. How long the war might last, or how bad the bombing might get. The only thing I *do* know is that if something happened to you and I could've avoided it, then I'd never forgive myself. So that leaves me no choice. You have to go to the countryside. Even if it's only for a short while.'

'But what about Winn? Mum, please, I can't leave her.'

Mum sighed, though she must have known that question was coming.

'I walked to school after you stormed out,' she said. 'Wanted to speak to Mr Gryce.'

Noah felt himself shudder. It was an involuntary reaction he always had when someone mentioned his headteacher. Their relationship was fractious, at best.

'Oh,' was the most he could manage.

'I wanted to speak to him about Winn.'

Noah's next 'Oh?' sounded a lot more hopeful.

'He said the same as me. That pets will have to stay put. He doesn't know if there'll be enough space on the trains for teachers and pupils, never mind animals.'

That stumped Noah. He wanted to argue the toss, but how could he when she'd already tried like she had? No one went to speak to old man Gryce unless they had to.

Which left him . . . ? Nowhere. In the same position he was when he came back to apologise. He was leaving without Winn. And he hated Hitler for it with a passion.

'When am I going?' he asked.

'Three days, Mr Gryce reckons,' replied Mum, fighting back a sigh. 'Just about long enough to get all this darning done. If I'm lucky.'

She returned to her mercy mission, and the wounded socks in front of her.

8

Noah didn't have nightmares that night, because he didn't really sleep.

His brain whirred and fizzed, trying to come up with a plan, harebrained or otherwise, a spark that might give him even the smallest semblance of hope.

But nothing came. Winn was too big to hide in a case, and too disobedient and greedy to charm Mr Gryce (or his new evacuation family) into changing their minds. But to give up? That was unthinkable.

Instead, he rolled and cursed in his bed, dragging his bedsheets with him at every turn until they all ended up on the floor. Only Winn was comfortable, choosing the bare mattress over the rug, though her sad, mournful eyes mirrored Noah's.

When sleep finally came, it was fitful, Noah's drooping head snapping him awake with a painful reminder every time. *How can you sleep?* his brain asked him. *You've a promise to Dad to keep.*

Eventually, with the sound of the wireless seeping

through the floorboards, morning came, and Noah dressed and slumped downstairs, to find Mum still at the table, her darning pile a little smaller. There was no needle in her hand though, instead her focus was entirely on a folded booklet lying open in front of her.

'Morning,' Noah mumbled.

Mum jumped in her chair, closed the booklet quickly and tried to ram it inside a ripped envelope that sat on the table.

'Do I have to do my chores today?' Noah asked. He wasn't trying to wangle his way out of cleaning the pantry: he genuinely didn't know what was expected of him now under these new, strange circumstances, and he wanted to spend as much time as possible with Mum and Winn.

Mum's reply didn't help.

'Yes – I mean, no,' she said, booklet still in hand.

'What's that?' Noah strained his eyes to see what was written on the parts of the booklet that weren't obscured.

'Nothing.'

Whatever it was about, it looked official. He could make out the sentence 'Air Raid Precautions', but that wasn't enough to really interest him, the only bit that pricked his curiosity were the words *'For Animals'* typed underneath.

'What *is* that?' he asked again. 'That book?'

Mum looked flustered. More than flustered, speechless.

'Can I have a look?' he asked.

'I-I'm not sure,' she stammered. 'I haven't read it all myself yet.' Noah tried to take it from her, and whilst she resisted at first, it wasn't enough to stop the booklet sliding into his hands. Mum went to speak, then seemed to think better of it.

Noah read the opening line of the first page.

Animals, like human beings, will be exposed to the risks of air attack in a modern war —

Noah felt his chest constrict. He could see now why Mum wasn't keen on him reading it.

— and everyone will wish, both from practical and humane motives, to do what is possible to protect them and to alleviate their sufferings.

'Sufferings?' he said out loud, though he meant to question it only in his head. 'Mum? Who sent you this?'

'The government. Mr Chamberlain,' she said.

'Just to you?'

She shook her head. 'I shouldn't have thought so. I'm imagining everyone got one. Postman delivered it, first thing.'

'But what is it?' He flicked through. 'There's pages of it.'

'I haven't read it all, Noah. Not yet. So I'm not sure you should until I finish.'

He didn't believe her. She'd read it, or enough of it to know that it contained things she didn't want him to see. But there was no way he was giving it back to her until he had a better sense of how it affected Winn.

Not that the dog was concerned. The only thing bothering her was that her morning walk was overdue. She lingered by the back door, tail wagging optimistically.

Noah, for once, ignored her and sat at the table, going back to page one, thwarting Mum's half-hearted attempts at taking the book from him. It didn't take him long, half a page at most, to find the next line to distress him.

It should be realised that, in a hostile air raid, poisonous gas may be employed as well as high-explosive and incendiary bombs, so that wounds, fractures and burns may be complicated by gas poisoning.

Nausea rose in him and he swallowed it down.

'Did you read this?' he said, underlining the section he'd read with his finger, before showing it to Mum.

'I did,' she replied, though she found it hard to meet his eye. 'I think that will do for now.' And she tried to prise it from his hands again. But Noah wasn't having any of it and scooted away from the table, knocking the chair over in the process.

'*You're* saying I have to leave Winn here, yet *they're* saying she could end up with gas poisoning? And you expect me to stop reading?' There was an urgency to his voice now. A rise in pitch that made Winn turn to face him, instead of the back door and the freedom beyond it.

'Noah, I don't know exactly what it means.'

Noah had already turned the page and was reading on.

'It says here that it's not safe to keep animals in the city,' he said, jabbing at the page.

'I know, son, I saw that,' Mum replied.

'That they should be evacuated, wherever possible.' He looked up. 'So that means she *should* come with me, doesn't it?'

Mum made a final attempt to swipe the book from his hand, but it was too late. Noah's eyes fell on the line that broke his heart

Owners should make up their minds whether they can take their dog or cat themselves. If this is impossible they should decide whether the animal is best destroyed . . .

He couldn't read on. He couldn't. All he could see, whether his eyes were open or shut, was that one word – *destroyed.*

He looked to Mum. 'They're not saying . . .' he asked. 'They can't tell us to do that, can they? Not to Winn?'

Mum nodded slowly, painfully.

'They are, Noah. From what I can see, that's exactly what they're telling us to do. They're telling us to put her down.'

9

Noah had gone to bed the night before feeling more despair than he thought possible, only to be shown this morning that there was further for him to travel. It felt like he'd been pushed down a whole new flight of stairs that spiralled on and on.

What made it worse was that he felt alone in this new, unthinkable reality. If sides were being taken, then it felt like Mum was not on his team.

'We're not going to do what they're saying, are we?' he'd asked her.

But she'd scrunched up her face in a way that Noah didn't like one bit.

'Mum, we can't, we just can't. Look at her, Mum. Look at her. That's murder.' He'd grabbed the booklet again, devouring random words, but the more he read, the worse his despair became. By the time he reached page twenty-four, he was beside himself, and needed to sit down to read a paragraph entitled *Dogs and Cats:*

When an owner has been unable to send his dog or cat to a
safe area or to make suitable arrangements for its protection,
he should consider the advisability of having it painlessly
destroyed.

Tears pricked Noah's eyes.

'Painlessly?' he cried. 'How can it possibly be painless, Mum?'

'There *are* ways, Noah. Winn wouldn't know a thing.'

'No, but *I* would. And so would you. And Dad. There's no way he'd agree to this.'

'There's no way Dad would agree to Winn being terrified or poisoned by gas, either. You know how much he loves her.'

'And that's why we can't do what they're telling us to. We can't, Mum. How can you even consider it?!'

Noah wasn't trying to lay guilt at her door. And although there was a flush to her face as she replied, there was also a frankness that made him despair still further.

'We don't know anyone outside of London who could care for Winn, Noah. I wish we did, but we don't. I've racked my brains trying to think.'

'Then we have to keep her.'

'And risk her running riot when the bombs start falling? Noah, she wails when the milkman comes to be paid. How do you think she'll cope when there are explosions hour after hour, night after night?'

'She'll have you to look after her though, won't she?'

'Some of the time, yes. But from what I read, animals won't be allowed down in the air-raid shelters. And during the day I won't always be here.'

'What do you mean?'

'I've got to find work, son. If the war starts we'll all have a job to do, whether we like it or not. If I end up in a factory or cleaning hospitals, do you think they'll let me take Winn too?'

'But that hasn't happened yet, has it? We shouldn't be talking or even *thinking* about it when we're not even at war!'

'But, Noah, it's coming. Everyone knows it. It's like a storm. And while the storm rages, it won't be safe for any of us.'

'So we make that decision when it happens, Mum. When it's overhead and we can't run away from it any more.'

Mum said nothing.

'Please, Mum. We can't. Not yet.'

Still nothing, so Noah ran to the door and pulled Winn into him.

'Look at her, Mum. Look! She's our family. She's ours. And what's she ever done to deserve a barrel to her head?'

Mum looked, though it was clear she didn't want to. Noah said it again. 'She's family . . .' his eyes as wide as Winn's, until finally Mum spoke.

'Right. We'll do nothing yet,' she conceded. 'YET. But the second war's declared, well, we'll be doing as the government tells us. Do you understand me, Noah? No ifs, no buts.'

'I understand,' said Noah, though his mind had already moved on.

He needed space and time to think. If he was going to hold back the storm that was brewing then he was going to need one heck of a watertight plan.

10

Noah hoped that the streets would be quiet. Masterplans needed focus and space to grow.

Surely everyone would be inside packing their children's bags, ready for the trains to the countryside. And those without kids? Well, he could only wish that they had other things to busy them indoors. The world was about to end after all.

Within a dozen paces though, his hopes were dashed. The streets were teaming. Adults rushed from house to house, rounding up items of clothing or bars of soap for little Tommy or Margaret's case. He saw a boy from his class, Robbie, dragging a suitcase after his sister and mum. His mother wore a frantic expression. Robbie just looked cheesed off.

'Where you going, Rob?' Noah asked.

'Grandparents. In the countryside. Till it all blows over.'

If Noah had thought quickly enough, he could've asked them if they needed a dog. They might be farmers.

Wasn't that what everyone in the country did? He didn't know. He'd never been there.

For every parent on a mercy dash or leaving the city, there were twice as many out with their pets. And sadly, they weren't taking Bonzo on his morning stroll. These were animals being taken on their *final* walk.

Noah saw dogs, he saw cats, he saw rabbits in crates and a ferret on a lead. Birds sang mournfully in their cages as children (and adults) sobbed their way down the street.

Everyone, it seemed, had received the booklet.

It was difficult to watch, so Noah tried not to, choosing instead to look at Winn as she trotted alongside him. What if Mum saw all these people doing as they were told and changed her mind? Noah tried to walk faster, but Winn was sniffing and barking at anything and everything that interested her. Noah chose not to pull when she stopped to mark her territory every so often. How could he when the poor thing might not have many walks left in her?

Anger and confusion consumed him. At Hitler, at the Prime Minister, at all these fools following like sheep. He imagined the conversations they'd had with their kids;

This is the right thing. You will get over it in time. There will be other pets when this is all over.

He wanted to run with Winn, as fast as he could, away from everyone else and what they thought. But then he saw Clem and knew that it wasn't an option.

She was walking with her mum and Frank, but not as she normally would. Usually Clem was a watcher, an observer: she soaked up every bit of life she could. But today, her eyes were focused only on the pavement at her feet. And when she did lift her head, her eyes were wet with tears.

'What is it?' Noah said as Winn dashed to them, pulling Noah along for the ride. Though in all honesty, Noah had already guessed what was wrong.

'The booklet,' Clem wept, as her mum chatted stony-faced to a passing friend, 'from the government.'

'But your mum's not listening to them, is she?' Noah looked down at Frank, who was wheezing loudly, though this was due to his advancing years rather than any knowledge or fear of what was about to happen to him.

Clem nodded sadly. 'We're on our way to the vet's.' She grimaced. 'Are you?'

'Not yet,' he whispered. 'Managed to buy a bit of time to think. Though Mum says if war IS declared, then we have to put Winn down too.' He didn't want to ask Clem the next question, but knew he had to. 'D'you think it WILL happen?'

Clem looked at him. 'Do you want the truth?'

'Course I do.'

'War's coming, Noah. How could it not be when they've already decided to evacuate us?'

'It can't!!' he yelled, before lowering his voice. 'We can't let this happen, Clem, we can't!'

'But what can we do about it? We're just children!'

'But we can't give in. Not just like that. We need some time, Clem, that's all. To come up with a plan.'

'That's just it though,' she said. 'There *is* no time. We're off to the vet's now. Like the rest of London by the looks of it.'

They looked about them, at the sea of long, funereal faces.

'I can't believe people are doing this,' Noah gasped. 'Just cos the government say so, doesn't make it right, does it?'

'I mean, what about the cats?' said Clem. 'Without them, who's going to kill all the mice?'

'Mice. What about the rats? There's tons come up from the docks. Mum will flip her lid if she sees any!'

They walked on, as mothers spoke in hushed tones around them.

'Will you stay with me for a while?' Clem asked, and Noah was hardly going to say no. He wanted to support his friend, could only hope against hope that between them they'd think of something quickly to save Frank. Their heads whirred and crunched, but despite the urgency of the situation, nothing came, apart from one final surprise as they turned on to Wapping High Street, where the vet-turned-executioner did his atrocious work.

The surgery was at the far end of the street, some quarter of a mile away, but from his door there snaked the longest queue Noah had ever seen in his life. In fact, he didn't realise it even *was* a queue at first, though irate, frustrated people wasted no time in telling him as he walked closer to the front.

'Oi! You!' one elderly gent yelled. 'If you're here for the vet then get to the back of the queue. We've been waiting since seven-thirty this morning.'

Noah looked agog. There had to be *hundreds* of people in front of them, and some had more than one animal in tow.

'Is the vet going to put all these pets to sleep?' he said to Clem. 'In one day? There aren't enough hours. How will he sleep at night? Knowing he's murdered that many animals. Don't they take an oath like doctors do? To keep pets alive, not massacre them.'

Typically, that was the bit Clem's mum overheard.

'Massacre? That's a strong word, Noah.'

'What else would you call it?' Noah muttered under his breath.

But he went obediently, back to the end of the queue, where all he could think about was the executioner's axe falling, again and again.

11

The queue moved, but slowly. Torturously, in fact.

Noah tried to keep Clem in a positive frame of mind, which was difficult when he feared being back here himself all too quickly.

They'll never get to us today.

They'll tell us to come back tomorrow.

By then we'll have a plan. Or Mr Chamberlain will have changed his mind.

But no matter how hard or earnestly he spoke, none of these thoughts rang true. Trying to appeal to Clem's mum's better side had no success either.

'Should you not just wait a while before doing this? A few days even? It might not come to anything yet, you know.'

'And Hitler might end up being the tooth fairy, Noah,' she fired back. 'Your mother's just delaying the inevitable. Do you really think I want to put Clem or Frank through this?'

'Then let's go home,' Clem interjected, pleading. 'Please?'

'We can't. You know Frank's old. His heart won't take bombs falling all day and night. And what if there's not enough food for us, never mind dogs. They'll have to start rationing soon if the Germans stop food getting to us. I'm sorry, Clementine, but I'm not changing my mind. This is the kindest thing in the long run. No means no.'

She meant it as well, remaining tight-lipped despite the obvious pain it caused her daughter.

So they waited, largely in shocked silence. Shock at the sight of children walking past them in tears, their cat boxes empty, their dog's lead dragging uselessly along the road. Noah felt his own emotions rise. If war started tomorrow or the next day, he'd find himself here again, and how on earth was he going to go through with it? It was painful enough watching his friend endure it. He doubted he'd be able to step foot inside the surgery, never mind hold Winn as the vet injected or shot her. How could he not launch himself at the man?

Noah couldn't stand still. He moved from the line into the middle of the road, leaving Clem in the queue. He looked up and down the length of it. They'd moved a little in the hour or so they'd been waiting, but they were still nowhere near the front. And as for those behind them? Unless they'd brought a tent, then they were in for a long and uncomfortable night.

He scanned faces, every one a portrait of distress, and surprisingly many belonging to people he knew. There was Henry Williams from the year above, stroking the ear of his dog Murphy. Murphy was a shiny brute of a Lab, little more than a pup, despite his bulk. Then there was Pam Grimes, clutching a box with holes punched in its side. Lord knows what pet was in there, but every few seconds Pam was left to cling on for dear life as the inhabitant made clear its displeasure. There were more children from school and Noah's street, clutching cats and rabbits, picking up and putting down bird cages every time the queue shuffled along. No one made eye contact, not if they were a child. It was just too sad to share.

He didn't want to be here any more, but he couldn't bring himself to leave his best friend. His nerve was tested though when he spotted one last familiar face some distance behind them. Because there was Big Col, face scarlet with exertion.

'What's *he* doing here?' Noah hissed to Clem as he dived back into the cover of the queue, pulling a surprised Winn with him.

'Who?' replied Clem, looking around blindly.

'Big Bloomin' Col. Since when did he have a pet?'

'I don't know. I can't even see him.'

'He's there, towards the back. What's he carrying, can you make it out?'

'I don't know. I told you, I can't even see him,' Clem repeated and leaned outwards, only to be pulled back by Noah.

'Careful. Don't let him clock you.'

'Noah, he's hardly likely to attack us here, is he? Not in front of half of London.'

'I wouldn't put it past him.'

Noah used Clem's mum as an unsuspecting shield to get a better look. 'What's that slung over his shoulder? Reckon he's really got a pet in there?'

'God, imagine the animal *he'd* own. Probably some kind of huge wild cat, or poisonous spider from the Amazon.'

Clem finally caught sight of Big Col.

'Blimey. If it's a spider in that sack, then all of us had better start running, now.'

She wasn't wrong. Big Col had turned around, revealing a huge bulge in his brown hessian sack.

'No wonder he's sweating,' gasped Noah.

'But what's in there?' Clem mused. Noah could see her curiosity had been well and truly pricked.

'Forget it,' he said. 'We've got bigger things to worry about than that fool.'

He was right; the queue started to move again and poor Frank shuffled forwards, blissfully unaware of what he was moving closer *to*.

12

Noah could make out the lettering on the vet's sign hanging above the doorway now, though it had taken a *ridiculous* number of hours to reach that point. He wasn't sure of the time any more: daren't bother Clem's mum again after the twenty-seventh time of asking, but judging from the height of the sun in the sky, it was edging towards teatime. He should've been hungry, but wasn't; the ever-increasing nausea put pay to any rumblings in his belly. They were getting closer and he didn't have a plan to stop it. This wasn't like him. He was usually the boy who could dream up a scam as quickly as drawing breath, but not today. The scheming side of his brain felt frozen.

Maybe together he and Clem could've cooked something up, but with her mum constantly in earshot, there was no chance of that.

Ma Parkinson was shuffling from foot to foot, craning her neck up and down the queue. With every movement there was a huff, or a sigh, and although she was irritable with Noah for repeatedly asking the time, it didn't stop her checking her watch every minute.

'What is it, Mum?' Clem asked.

She shuffled and huffed some more.

'I had no idea it would take this long. And I've a list as long as my arm of things to get for you before you leave on Monday. And tomorrow's Sunday, so I can't do it then.'

Noah saw his chance and seized it. 'I can stay with Clem,' he insisted. 'I don't mind. I mean, I've waited this long with her, haven't I? And, it's going to be another hour here at least. By then the shops will be shut.'

She stared at Noah, eyes narrowing at this unusually helpful behaviour. Noah responded with his widest, most angelic eyes.

'Well,' she said, 'I could leave you here for a bit, I suppose. Just while I dash to get Clem some new underwear.'

Clem flushed and stared at the ground.

Noah cheered inside as Clem's mum hurried away, vowing to return 'in three shakes of a lamb's tail'.

'Now what?' Clem asked.

'We need to think,' Noah said. 'And think quickly.'

But for once, Clem was the impatient one.

'Think? Time for thinking's over. That ship's sailed, Noah. We need action. Now.'

It wasn't completely clear if Clem was cross with Noah

or with herself, but it didn't matter, as suddenly Noah sprung into life, moving so animatedly that it took Clem and the dogs by surprise.

'That's it!!' he yelled, squishing Clem's cheeks with joy. 'You're a flipping genius, you are. But you're wrong. The ship hasn't sailed at all. In fact, it's waiting for us exactly where it should be.'

And with that, he and Winn skipped out of the line, leaving Clem and Frank utterly bemused.

'Where are you going, Noah?'

'You wanted action, didn't you? If you stay here they'll kill Frank. Then in a day or two, they'll murder Winn too. I'm not prepared to let that happen. Are you? Come with me. I've got a plan.'

Clem paused, the thought of her irate mum large in her mind. But she didn't wait long.

Noah always did this to her. Led her into crazy adventures, making it hard to say no.

But today, he hadn't made it hard. He'd made it impossible.

So, with one final look at the queue they'd spent an eternity in, Clem dashed after her friend. Frank's arthritic little legs had never moved so fast.

13

'Wait, Noah, WAIT!'

But when Noah *did* slow down, somewhere towards the back of the queue, it wasn't because his best friend told him to.

It was because by then, he was *convinced* that his idea was not only going to save little Frank, but offer Winn the lifeline she would need when the world went to war.

As Clem and Frank panted to catch up, the plan developed still further.

When something is this good, Noah told himself, *it shouldn't be hidden away. It should be shared with others.*

As he walked down the queue, he saw more and more young faces, creased in distress, and while he knew he couldn't help all of them, he was damned sure he wasn't going to walk away without coming to the rescue of some.

So, as he approached Pam Grimes, he quickly leaned into her.

'You here with your mum?' She clutched the box tightly and shook her head. 'I'm on my own,' she said confidently.

Noah leaned in closer still. 'You don't really want to kill your pet, do you?'

'No!' she said, firmly.

'Then follow me.' And Noah walked on, leaving Pam to stare questioningly at Clem.

'Don't ask me,' shrugged Clem. 'He thinks he's the Pied Piper. We're just the rats.'

The three of them walked on, and soon became four, then five, then six as Noah invited more children and their pets to follow him.

Clem felt increasingly baffled. 'What are you doing?' she hissed in Noah's ear.

'Trying to save lives,' he replied matter of factly. 'None of these kids have got adults with them, which means there's no one to tell them they HAVE to go through with it.'

That didn't help Clem understand any better. 'But how can *we* help? We're not Battersea Dogs Home, are we?'

Noah stopped dead, just as he reached another parentless child in the queue. 'CLEM!' He beamed. 'I hadn't got that far. But I have now, you ... you double genius!' And within seconds, their merry band had grown by yet one more.

Although the fine details of the plan were still forming in his head, Noah felt indestructible. He'd done it, steered Frank away from death and given others hope too. The only thing that affected his long, happy stride was spotting Big Col, whose eyes widened and fists twitched when he saw Noah approach.

He didn't move though, the big lump; not even when he saw the rest of the disciples trot past, and it was only when they all turned the corner, without Big Col in tow, that Noah allowed himself to breathe out in relief.

'Right, keep following me, everyone. It'll be worth it, I promise. I know where your pets will be safe overnight.'

He led them through the streets, making sure to avoid the shops where he thought Clem's mum might be, and though he had to slow down a little to allow the stragglers to keep up, he couldn't stop his heart thudding with the excitement of what he was doing.

They passed their school, making assorted hand gestures as they went, and the police station too (a brave few continued sticking the V's) through Wapping Woods and around Shadwell Basin, until Noah caught sight of the river in front of them. Just as well, as the first of the dissenting voices were beginning to filter through.

'How much further is it?'

'Where are we going?'

'My mum will kill me if she finds out I'm here.'

'Not far now,' said Noah cheerfully. 'Clem? Quick, come here.'

Clem moved closer, Frank in her arms. He had long since refused to walk.

'What?' she said.

'I need your help.'

'Well, I can't help when I don't have a clue what we're doing.'

'Doing? We're saving all these animals. That's what we're doing.'

'How? You DO KNOW what you're doing, don't you?'

'Course I do. I've got the perfect place to keep them safe overnight. And tomorrow, well, that's when your bit of the plan takes over.'

Clem stopped dead in her tracks. 'Er, excuse me? My bit? Far as I remember, I haven't suggested a thing?'

'Course you have. You said it. *Battersea. Dogs. Home.*'

Clem's face remained creased in confusion. 'Oh, right. And?'

'And what?'

'Well, we don't just have dogs, do we? We have cats here too. And birds. And God knows what is actually lurking in Pam's box, but whatever it is, it is flipping angry. What if Battersea won't take them?'

Noah waved her away. 'Of course they will.'

'What are you going to do? Wrap a collar and lead around a budgie's neck? Because I'm sure that'll fool them.'

'They're an animal sanctuary, Clem. And there's a war on. Nearly. They wouldn't dream of turning a pet away, whatever it is. And they certainly won't do what the vet was going to do.'

There wasn't time for them to dwell any longer on that thought, as in front of them, finally, Noah saw their destination: the lock at Limehouse Basin failing to hide the bounty that lay behind it.

'There she is!' he yelled over his shoulder to the others, whose pace picked up in response.

They craned past him, eyes flitting along the dock, confusion on many of their faces.

'What am I looking at?' one shouted.

'My cat can't swim!' said another.

'Swim?' beamed Noah. 'Who said anything about getting wet?' and he stretched out his arms.

'So, here we are. Let me introduce you to your pet's hotel for the night. This, my friends, is the *Queen Maudie*. The finest vessel to ever sail the seven seas.'

The crowd looked at Noah's dad's boat. Whatever they had been expecting, it clearly wasn't this. They looked it up and down, at the patched-up hull and fraying rope that moored it to the bank. One lad walked up to it tentatively and stuck his entire fist through a rusty hole in its upper flank.

None of them was impressed.

'That sieve couldn't sail around our bath, never mind the sea,' one yelled, spinning on his heel and dragging his dog with him.

'Are you kidding me?' Noah replied. 'It's better than nothing, isn't it? You've seen the booklet they sent out. You've seen what they want to do to our pets. Is that what you want?'

Some shook their heads fiercely. Others walked away.

'I know she doesn't look like much,' Noah went on. 'I know she's got rust, and I know she won't be warm like your houses. But they'll be safe here tonight, I promise you. And tomorrow? Well, tomorrow we'll march them down to Battersea Dogs Home because I know *they* won't turn us away. And they certainly won't put our pets down.' He said it like he meant it. Because he did, every single word. 'So, who's with me?' No one moved, so Noah turned, and hoisted the piece of wood that served as their gangplank on to the deck. He stood on the plank, bouncing on it to show there was nothing for them to fear.

There were still frowns and smatterings of dissent. These children had believed they were marching their pets to some kind of promised land, when all they actually had walked to was a rusty tub, with the prospect of an even longer walk tomorrow.

For some it was too much. They'd rather face the wrath of their parents and turn up at home with their pets. Some had other reasons for taking their animals with them.

'I can't come back tomorrow,' one shouted. 'I'm on a train first thing to Wales and there's no way my mum will traipse all the way to Battersea from here.'

Noah felt for the boy. He really did. And he didn't stop him from walking away, as much as he might like to. He'd done his bit and given them a chance. The rest was up to them.

But just as he felt his confidence dip slightly, just as he started to feel the doubts creep into his own head, the most wonderful thing happened. Clem stepped up and proved, just as she had countless times in his life, why she was the greatest friend he could ever wish for.

'I know it doesn't look like much, this boat,' she shouted. 'It IS a bit rusty and old. But we're not going to make the animals *live* here. It's one night. One night, then we'll give them all the best chance of staying alive that we possibly can. Will your mums or mine do that if we take them home now? I don't know about yours, but I know mine won't.'

There were nods of agreement.

'I don't want to leave Frank alone on here even for a night, but I know I have to. So I'm not thinking of this as a boat, tonight, this place is a sanctuary. An ark. And not just any ark either, cos it belongs to Noah.'

Without hesitation, she put Frank on the gangplank, watched him shuffle aboard and followed without delay.

Noah smiled a big, big smile as most of the others followed suit.

14

Noah wasn't religious, but for the next hour he wished he'd actually read what happened to his namesake onboard his Ark. If he'd known how the other Noah calmed two types of every animal, then he might not have felt so hopeless.

The noise for a start was astonishing and there was no hiding from it. The *Queen Maudie* wasn't a big vessel, far from it. Granted, it had a ten-foot deck at the front and a driver's room (which was not much bigger than two police phone boxes), but the only other space was the cabin, which sat at the rear, just below deck, down three wooden steps. It was cosy enough, small in fact, with two portholes on either flank and a stove which kept it toasty warm when necessary.

The animals, however, did not find it homely in any shape or form. The cats hissed and arched their backs at the dogs who responded with howls and barks, which set off the birds, who disturbed the rabbits, kicking and rattling the bars of their cages.

The children ran from one animal to the next, but they

only ended up in each other's way, bumping and pushing and inevitably yelling at each other until Noah told all of them to go, and leave him and Clem to it.

'Be back here at eight a.m. tomorrow,' he told them firmly. 'We'll be marching to Battersea on the dot.'

After some reassurances and painful goodbyes, the other children left, creating more space in the small cabin without solving the racket. Carefully and sensitively, Noah and Clem moved between the animals, creating comfy spots on the shelves for the cats out of reach of the dogs. Noah lit the tiny stove and managed to settle the dogs in front of the flames, adding to their bliss with strokes and tickles beneath their chins. Bit by bit, the volume levels dropped, replaced by the crackle of the logs and the occasional snore which seemed to be coming from one of the five dogs.

'What are we going to do about food?' said Clem.

'I'll get my tea when I go home, although my mum will be mad I'm home so late.'

'For the animals, you fool, not you!'

This stumped Noah. He wasn't great at details. That's why Clem was such a good ally, she made up for his (many) shortcomings.

'Oh, I already thought about that,' he lied, dashing to the cupboard, where he found two tins of sardines, a dented can of spam and a tin of 'meat' casserole.

Looking at the amount of rust on the tins, he knew they were past their best, but with nothing else to offer them, Noah divided them up into too-small portions as Clem scoured the riverbank for any interesting leaves they could feed through the rabbits' bars.

It was hardly a feast, but it was the best they could do, and they knew there would be precious else until they reached Battersea tomorrow.

'We should go home,' Clem said. 'It's getting late.'

'What will you say to your mum?' Noah asked. 'About Frank?'

She looked uneasy at the prospect of lying to her mum. 'As little as I can. Hopefully she won't expect me to say much if she thinks I had him put to sleep.'

'You do realise, don't you,' he said, 'that once we leave the dogs at Battersea, it might be years till we see them again.'

'If we see them at all,' she replied, though she said it so hesitantly and quietly that Noah barely heard her. He certainly didn't answer, instead he beckoned for Clem to follow him and Winn silently out of the cabin. The animals were quiet, sedated by the warmth of the stove and the food in their bellies, and he sensed the moment to leave them for the night. With a quiet *snick*, the door closed behind them, without creating a din from inside. Noah exhaled slowly.

'It'll be all right, Clem, you know?' he said. 'We've done the hard bit now. Another walk tomorrow and the animals . . . well, they'll be alive. Nothing can hurt us, or them. Not now.'

But as they turned to leave, they realised immediately the irony of Noah's final words, as there, looming over them, was the towering silhouette of Big Col.

15

Noah swore as Big Col wrestled something huge out of his sack and into his arms. The sight of it left Noah and Clem paralysed with fear.

There, coiling itself up Col's left arm and around his shoulders, was the biggest snake either of them had ever seen.

It seemed to go on for ever, as it uncoiled and stretched.

Big Col lifted his arms out at the sides, muscles bulging at the exertion of it. The snake was longer than his wingspan, in fact it threatened to reach the floor, or it would have done had it not seen Noah and Clem. They seemed to pique its interest, its head levitating towards them, tongue flicking as if it already knew how tasty they would be.

Noah spoke again. Not a swear word this time, just a collision of consonants, with the odd vowel thrown in involuntarily.

He had no idea what to do. How could he when he felt, in every fibre of his body, that he was about to die.

Fortunately, as usual, Clem was more in control of her senses.

'Wh-what do you want?' she stammered.

Big Col said nothing, just took another, imposing step forward, edging the python's head still closer.

Clem grabbed Noah's hand and pulled him to the left, then right, but there was no way past Big Col and his pal – they filled every inch of the gangplank.

Noah looked for another way out. It was too far to jump to the bank, and although the water wouldn't have been too cold, it was absolutely filthy.

All they could do was back away as Big Col approached, only stopping when they hit the rail at their rear. Winn rallied in front of them, teeth bared.

'Don't worry,' Big Col said, mouth pulled into a sneer. 'She won't eat you.'

'Right,' said Noah. 'That's, er, that's a relief.'

'Not unless I tell her to anyway,' he added, moving his hand and therefore the python's head, closer to them both.

'What is it you actually want?' Clem repeated.

'Want?' he spat. 'I don't want anything from *you*.'

His eyes said otherwise though, and Noah spotted it.

'Then what are you doing here?'

Big Col turned his head from Noah to the snake and seemed to, well, melt, as if he were gazing on his beloved instead of a huge, ravenous reptile.

'Does it have a name?' asked Clem. Noah looked at her like she was mad. What did its name matter? All that mattered was getting away from it as soon as possible.

'Course she does,' replied Big Col.

'Well?' said Clem.

The boy didn't reply immediately. He took a half step back, face twitching uncomfortably.

'Delilah,' he said, so quietly that Noah had to ask him again.

'DELILAH!?' he chortled, before swallowing it. 'That's ... original.' He'd been expecting, well, he didn't know what he expected, he'd never met a pet snake before.

'Yeah, well. Delilah wasn't my idea, was it?' Big Col looked twitchy again, glanced over his shoulder as if someone were listening. 'She's my dad's. Well, she was.'

'Your dad's?' Noah didn't know much about even Bigger Col, except he looked like a bulkier, greyer, meaner version of his son.

'Yeah, he won her. In a game of cards. Was supposed to be money he won but the bloke was flat broke. All he had was Delilah.'

'Your dad must've been thrilled,' Noah said, loud enough to earn a dig in the ribs from Clem.

Big Col answered, but still looked ill at ease, like he wasn't sure who could hear what he had to say. 'I think he *was* thrilled at first. He liked the idea of going round with her on his shoulders. But then someone told him it was illegal to have a python, and . . . well . . . he has enough bother with the law as it is, so he gave her to me.'

'What does she eat?' asked Clem. 'Not children, obviously,' she added, with a nervous laugh.

'Whatever I can get hold of really. It's not always easy, cos, well, she's big ain't she? I mean, I set mousetraps and that, and she loves a good rat, but it's hardly going to fill her up.'

'They eat monkeys or antelopes in the wild, don't they?' said Clem, dropping back into encyclopaedia mode.

Noah had heard enough. 'I don't want to be rude or nothing, but . . . well, it's late, and my mum's already going to tan my backside for being back after dark. So, if we're done here . . . ?'

But Big Col wasn't done. 'Delilah needs somewhere to stay. Overnight.'

Noah and Clem looked at each other.

'Well,' said Noah, rubbing his chin. 'We wish you luck with that.' And he tried to lead Clem and Winn past him. To no avail.

'I know what you're doing,' said Big Col, the snake back in their faces. 'For the other kids. I know about all the animals you've got onboard.'

'Don't know what you're talking about,' lied Noah.

'Yeah you do. Cos some kids told me. Said you've got an ark. Said all sorts of animals are staying here tonight. Till you take 'em to Battersea.'

'Oh, that?!' said Noah, pulling a face that he hoped would look like he was just confused, rather than lying to the toughest kid in town. 'Yeah, it's just a few little animals. Not a big deal.'

'Then you won't mind if Delilah stays too. She won't be any bother.'

'Er . . . I'm not sure. Won't she . . .'

'Won't she what?' Big Col seemed to get even bigger in a flash. Delilah too.

'Well,' said Noah, looking for the right words, 'eat the other animals?'

'Not if they stay out of her way. She's not a monster, you know?'

Clem stepped in. Just as well because Noah had no words left, only a jaw, hanging open in shock.

'I'm not sure it works like that. You know, Delilah is . . . beautiful. But she's also a . . . well, there's a . . . wildness to her . . . and when she's hungry, well, she's going to eat. And we have rabbits and birds in there, which are, to be fair, the perfect size snack for her.'

'Then I'll leave her in another room, away from the

others.' He pointed at the small boxy captain's shelter, where the wheel and throttle sat. 'What about in there?'

'She can't sleep in there,' Noah said quickly, without a clue as to why not.

'Oh, is it not heated in there? Well, that's no use. Delilah needs it warm. She's from India.' He looked let down.

'She's the *Queen Maudie,* not the flipping *Titanic.*'

'Well, I can't take her home, can I? My ma made me swear I'd have her put to sleep. And my ma, well, she can be just like my dad. When she wants to be.' His head drooped a little. 'I know,' he said suddenly, 'I'll leave her in the sack. And we can tie it up. With a chain. Or rope, whatever you've got. She got fed this morning, so as long as we tie it tight, she'll never get out.'

'It's already pretty busy in there, and we've only just got them all quiet,' said Noah.

'I'm not asking you. I'm telling you. So you'd better find me some rope quick smart. Before I ring Delilah's dinner bell.'

Noah looked at Clem. Clem looked at Noah. They both sighed, then stared up at their nemesis.

'There's some on the deck there. Take as much as you need. Take it all in fact,' said Noah.

Big Col didn't need telling twice.

16

By dawn, Noah was sitting fully dressed on the edge of his bed, fighting the urge to sneak from the house and check that the animals hadn't somehow sunk the boat or eaten each other. In the cold light of day, his plan didn't seem such a good one.

The only thing that kept him rooted to his mattress was the fear that Mum would hear him leave. She'd been in a foul mood when he returned home and things had not gone well at all.

'Where on earth did you get to?' she'd roared, filling every inch of the doorway. 'Worried sick I've been. Racing round the streets like a fool! Well? Where have you been?'

Noah had put on his best faithful friend face.

'With Clem,' he said. 'Poor thing was queuing to have Frank put down' He paused and sighed. 'It was awful. Awful. There were crying kids everywhere. Thank God I've got an understanding mum like you.'

He went to hug her, to reinforce just how generous she was. Hoping it would sway her into a miraculous change of heart altogether.

'Noah. I'm not made of stone,' she said, holding him at arm's length. 'But I'm not a fool either. I know what you're doing.'

'Me?' he said, eyes wide and hurt.

'Yes, you. You're a caring boy, especially about Winn. But you're also as devious as the day is long. So don't think you can wrap me round your little finger. The deal still stands. As much as it pains me, if war is declared then we shall have to put Winn to sleep too.'

Noah felt something break agonisingly inside him again, but it came out as anger.

'I won't do it!' he yelled.

'You won't need to!' she roared. 'I'll take her myself.'

'You'd love that, wouldn't you? Cos you never liked her. You can't wait to find an excuse to get shot of her. Well, if you do it, you'll lose me, and then you'll lose Dad as well. Is that what you want? Well, is it?'

He turned for the stairs. Couldn't bear to talk to her any longer.

'Noah Price! Get yourself back here!'

He did no such thing. He bounded up the stairs as if they weren't there, Winn at his heels as he slammed his door behind him, a wooden chair wedged beneath the handle.

He waited for the roll of thunder to follow. He didn't have to wait long: as soon as it finished on the stairs it attacked the door, fists threatening the panels' strength.

'Open the door right this minute!'

He could picture her, a bubbling cauldron of puce and scarlet. And he knew that if he opened the door it would lead to the thickest of ears. So he sat her anger out, though it took much longer than he was expecting, nearly half an hour before he heard her slide down the wall, her voice hoarse and cracking.

'It's no good being angry with me, Noah. I'm not making the rules.'

'No,' he shouted, 'but you're following them.'

'Because I *have* to. Because none of us know what's going to happen tomorrow, never mind next week or next month. I love Winn just like you do –'

Noah couldn't stop a harrumph leaving his mouth, which Mum ignored by speaking over him.

'– but without you or Dad here, I can't keep her safe. It'll be for the best, Noah. And not just for me, before you say it, for us all. We've enough to fret about, without worrying how the dog is going to stay out of Hitler's way.'

Noah chose to stay silent.

'I'm going now,' he said.

'Where? You're locked in your room.'

'Bed.'

'But you've not eaten.'

He'd forgotten this, the worry in his belly taking up space where hunger should've been brewing.

'Not hungry.'

'I've made your favourite. Pie and mash with liquor.'

His stomach betrayed him, rumbling wildly. He gagged it with the press of a firm hand.

Why had she made him that tonight of all nights? It was a proper treat of a tea, that one.

'Gone off it,' he lied.

'I know that's not true,' she sighed. 'But it's . . . it's important we eat together tonight.'

'Why?'

'Come out here and I'll tell you.'

'No!' he said defiantly. 'Tell me now.'

'Oh, for the love of God!' she spat, the storm raging once more. 'Because tomorrow morning I've to take you to school with your case packed.'

'What do you mean?'

'We've had word through. The plan has changed, you're being evacuated first thing.'

He said nothing. Too stunned. And, anyway, he had no words to express what he was feeling.

'Noah?' Her voice had dropped again. It no longer threatened to rattle the windows. 'I know it's not what you wanted to hear, but you'll be safe and that's the only thing that matters to me and your dad.'

'Winn won't be safe though.'

'No,' she said. 'And I wish that were different, but at least I can save you the pain of taking her yourself when the time comes.'

'*If* the time comes,' Noah reminded her. 'We're not at war yet.'

'Yes, I know, Noah. *If.*'

Noah moved the chair and reluctantly opened the door.

'Where are they sending me?' he asked.

'Cornwall.'

That was a long way from London.

'I'd better eat then, hadn't I?' he said.

But their last supper was a far from joyous affair. It didn't matter how much liquor Noah added to the pie, it was still difficult to swallow. He slipped as much as he could surreptitiously to Winn, who waited patiently at his feet, blissfully ignorant of the circumstances.

'Now you promise me that you'll be a good boy for whoever takes you in? None of your tomfoolery. I'll be expecting a weekly letter, make sure you bath regularly and offer to wash up every night.'

'You're going to need to write this down if you want me to remember it all.'

'I'll tattoo it on your behind with my hand if you're not careful.'

Noah took this as his cue to rise from his seat and offer to wash up. Not to gain favour with his mum, but so he could hide several tins of food near the back door, ready to sneak them out in the morning. The animals would be ravenous.

'I'm going to go to bed now,' he said, once he was done.

'Can't interest you in a cocoa?'

Mum's cocoa was the stuff of legend, and not knowing when he would next sit to drink with her made his stomach lurch. But at the same time, he needed to be on his own to finalise his plan.

'Don't think I could keep my eyes open,' he said, with an extravagant yawn. 'Come on, Winn. Let's go.'

The dog followed him, looking over her shoulder as she went, expecting Mum to stop her as she always did.

But Mum did no such thing. She couldn't separate them, not tonight, and she held her tongue as Winn scampered away.

'I'll wake you when it's time,' she shouted up the stairs.

Noah didn't answer. She'd be wasting her time as he planned to be up and out with the larks. He didn't want to upset her, course he didn't, but he had animals to save. And war or no war, that had to come first.

17

The house was conspiring against them.

Floorboards had taken up squeaking overnight, piles of washing had thrown themselves across the landing, just to catch Noah off guard and throw him noisily off his feet. When he tripped on the rug and bounced loudly off Mum's bedroom door, Noah thought Winn would bark at him to *Shhhhhh*, but all he summoned from Mum's room was an unintelligible grunt, followed by a series of peaceful snores.

Still, Noah didn't take it for granted, collecting his food-laden jacket gingerly from the hook, not even daring to put on his shoes until he had closed the front door behind them with a gentle 'snick'.

Laced up and ready to go, he found Clem, reliable as ever, waiting for him, her pockets groaning too with whatever tins she could find in the larder.

'Have you heard about the evacuation?' he said.

She nodded.

'Will your mum go mad when she finds you aren't there?'

'What do you think?'

'I think we're both in big trouble,' Noah said. 'So we'd better not fail in getting the animals to safety.'

Clem nodded. 'Did you sleep?' she asked him.

'Doesn't feel like it.'

'Me neither. Noah, what are we doing? Disobeying our mums like this? Lying to them? Leaving all the animals on the boat?'

'We're saving them, Clem,' he said, not letting his own doubts creep into his voice.

'I just hope they're all right. With, you know . . .'

'What, a hungry python onboard?'

'It's not funny, Noah. You didn't leave your dog onboard with it.'

Noah felt his stomach flip with guilt and the prospect of what they might find. Or not find, if Delilah had got really peckish. So their pace quickened, and Noah only felt himself breathe normally when they reached the basin and the *Queen Maudie* hove into view, her rust burning majestically in the early sun.

'Can you hear that?' Noah said.

'No?' Clem wore a slightly worried look. It was a physical prerequisite of being Noah's best friend.

'Exactly. It's silent.' He grinned widely. 'We'd hear the hullaballoo from here if there was one. We've done it, Clem.

All we have to do now is wait for the other children, then get ourselves to Battersea before the queue gets too long.'

But as they reached *Maudie*, their plan quickly unravelled when they saw that the cabin door, which Noah *knew* he had closed securely, was now open, in fact not only open, but hanging drunkenly from its hinges.

'Hells bells,' mouthed Noah. 'What on earth's gone on?'

'Stampede by the looks of it,' said Clem.

They went to thrust their heads inside the cabin, fearful of what they might find, eyes struggling to adjust to the murky light inside. But as they did so, they felt the wind whip wildly and a screech split the air. Their hands flew to their faces, as claws scratched and clawed at their skin. Clem leaned over Noah, covering him like a blanket as they fell to the floor.

'Get if off me, get it off me!' he yowled.

'It's me, you fool,' replied Clem, daring to look over her shoulder as a parrot ricocheted into the light, its wings bursting into a kaleidoscope of colour as it powered towards the sun and freedom.

'Jesus,' said Noah, who still couldn't make out a thing inside the cabin, though he could hear cages squeaking as they swung off their hooks.

'What's making that noise?' Clem asked fearfully. 'Find the curtains, will you?'

All they could see in their minds was Delilah, slithering at their feet, preparing to strike with venomous intent. Cautiously Noah walked on, arms in front of him like Frankenstein's monster. After hitting the stove and more than one box, Noah finally felt the rough sacking of the curtains and pulled, raising his hands against the sudden power of the light.

But if he and Clem were surprised, it was nothing in comparison to the animals who had remained, lurking in the shadows. They were terrified, and showed it via a maelstrom of movement and noise. Feathers flew, fur whistled past their shins, there were catcalls and squawks and it all happened at such a pace that it was impossible to know not only how many animals were left, but what they actually were.

Noah however, knew two things: firstly, as the door was open, there was no way of stopping the animals' escape, and more importantly, the sack that had hung above the stove: the sack that had imprisoned Delilah safely, now sat on the floor, limp and empty.

'Get outside! Quick!' he yelled, but Clem was already on the move, bounding up on to the deck and grabbing a crabbing net which she waved around in a frenzy.

'What are you doing?' he cried.

'Trying to catch that budgie!' She pointed at a lime-green

bird perched high on the cabin's roof, but every time she made a decisive move, the bird simply scuttled away, playing with her, before flying away for good.

Clem was not deterred. She now moved the net to the floor and tried to scoop up a small rabbit with unfeasibly long ears. 'Grab it!' she hollered. 'Or at least its cage so we can put it back in!'

'I'm not stepping foot in there!' Noah yelled. 'Not till we know where that snake is.' He almost hoped (though he wouldn't admit it out loud) that the presence of the cute and tasty bunny might flush Delilah out of her hiding place. But that plan was thwarted when the rabbit dashed its way across the deck and down the gangplank until it too was truly free.

'This is hopeless,' Noah groaned.

Winn, cowering on deck, whimpered in agreement.

'Frank?' Clem yelled suddenly. 'Noah, where's Frank?'

'I've no idea,' he replied, eyes searching rapidly both on and off the boat.

'We have to find him,' Clem garbled. And she made for the cabin door, only to be held back by Noah.

'Hang on will you, for Pete's sake. That . . . thing is probably still in there.'

'That *thing* might also be eating my dog as we speak,' Clem yelled back.

She gripped the net and barged back in, but they didn't find Frank.

All they found was destruction and devastation. Cages lay upturned and open on the floor, amidst piles of cat and dog mess. The smell was horrific.

'Frank?' they called tentatively. Neither had a clue how sensitive a python's hearing was and they didn't want to test it too rigorously.

'He can't be here,' Noah whispered. 'He'd have come to you by now.'

'Shush a second, will you?'

'So let's get outside befor—'

'I said SHUSH!' Clem repeated, as she bent low, approaching the small square table Noah's dad had built in the corner, its red tartan cloth now streaked with white stains from one of the birds. With twitching, hesitant fingers, Clem reached out, her heart pounding in her ears.

'What are you doing? Don't touch that! Use the net!'

But Clem was already committed and slowly, slowly, she lifted the cloth, letting in the light, only to recoil in horror and fear as Delilah's head darted forward, tongue flicking, eyes piercing.

They swore, both of them falling backwards, feeling so much less powerful than the reptile, hypnotised by its effortless movements ever nearer to where they lay.

'WHATDOWEDOWHATDOWEDOWHATDO
WEDO?' howled Noah, as beside him Clem squeezed her
eyes tightly shut.

But just as they feared they were to become the first
casualties of a war that hadn't even begun, something else
snaked into view, a thick, slightly grubby arm, which
whisked Delilah's jaw away and over their heads, the rest of
the snake's body following suit, whipping their faces as it
went.

'What are you fools doing down there?'

They spun around to find the most unlikely of saviours.

'By the way, I know what you're thinking,' Big Col said.

'Bet you don't,' muttered Noah, who had been
wondering how he'd got through that without losing control
of his bladder.

'I do though.' Big Col smiled what seemed to be a
knowing, smug smile. 'You think Delilah ate her Nazi dog,
don't you?'

Noah felt anger rise in him. Big Col wouldn't gloat
about that, would he?

'If she has, then there'll be trouble, I'm telling y—'

But Noah didn't finish the sentence. There wasn't time,
as from behind Big Col's bulk limped Frank, tail moving
way faster than the rest of his body, his hot lolling tongue
making straight for Clem's face.

'You'd better not have hurt him,' Noah said to Big Col.

'Hurt him? The dog might be a Nazi, but I'm not. I came across him in Wapping Woods, didn't I? Panting and looking like he was going to keel over. So I found him a puddle to drink from and led him back here. There were others too. Not dogs. A couple of cats. And I think I saw a rabbit too, though I couldn't tell if they'd come from here or not.

Whilst Frank was alive and safe, it seemed they couldn't say the same for the other animals they had promised to look after.

So what on earth were they going to say to their owners when they came back to retrieve them?

18

'Tell them my snake ate 'em. I mean, what are they going to do? Thump me?' Big Col pointed at his bulk. 'Don't think so, do you?'

That part of it was hard to argue with.

'No, we'll tell them the truth,' Clem said, which drew incredulous looks from both of the boys.

'Will we?' Noah asked.

'We have to. We can't lie. After all, they knew it was risky, leaving them here overnight. And besides, they haven't been eaten by that *thing.*' She found it hard to even glance at Delilah without feeling sick with worry. 'If anything, they're free out there, aren't they? Not locked up in cages in Battersea till the war's over. Isn't it better to tell them that?'

Big Col wasn't convinced. 'You'd happily let your little Nazi dog go walkabout, would you? Cos I'm sure it'd survive for a good hour or so before someone squished it.'

Clem bristled, and Noah stepped in as peacemaker.

'Maybe we won't have to say anything at all?' he said.

'What do you mean?'

'Exactly what I said. Look at your watch. It's way past eight and the others still aren't here.'

'You mean you don't think they're coming back?' said Clem, aghast.

Big Col chortled at her innocence. 'You're so prim and proper, aren't you? Truth is, maybe them other kids didn't care that much about their pets, after all.'

'All I'm saying is,' Noah added, 'we can't be hanging around here, waiting for people who might not turn up. They might have come clean to their parents last night and ended up on the wrong end of the slipper. Or they might have been evacuated today, like we were meant to be.' He thought of his mum. She'd be awake now and wondering where he was.

Clem wasn't convinced, but as Battersea was a good six-mile walk, (not to mention six back), so they needed to get going.

'All right,' she sighed. 'But if we run into any of those kids, then we explain to them exactly what happened. No lies? Agreed?'

'Agreed,' said Noah. He didn't like the idea of explaining what had happened to their beloved pets, but they did have Big Col in tow if anyone got shirty.

Noah grimaced. Relying on Big Col was a first, and he didn't like it one bit.

19

The city bustled and thrummed. Men were boarding up windows with huge sheets of plywood and angry hammers. Any conversations, even with neighbours, were short and curt. Women in curlers and aprons humped endless sandbags into their backyards, others marched their children off to the train, refusing to carry their small, battered suitcases or mask box, regardless of the weight.

'You'll have to carry them at the other end,' one mother snapped, 'so you may as well get used to it now.' She didn't look as brave as she sounded. The rings beneath her eyes gave her away.

'Anyone would think there's a war coming,' quipped Big Col, but no one laughed.

Big Col harrumphed and returned his attention to the weight of Delilah on his back. It would be much easier to carry her without the sack: to simply drape her around his neck, but he knew that the locals weren't ready for that. There was panic aplenty already without a python adding to it.

Noah went to cross the street, but Clem pulled him back, wafting a book that she seemed to have magicked from thin air. 'Not that way,' she said.

'Says who?'

'The A to Z.' She waved it again excitedly as if it were a book of spells.

'A to what?'

'Z, as in the last letter of the alphabet. It's a map. Well, a book of maps really, it covers every road in London.'

'The long winter evenings must just fly by in your house.' Big Col looked bored to tears.

But Noah wasn't bored by it. He'd been prepared to do what he always did, and make up a route to Battersea, but if Clem knew the quickest way, then that was fantastic.

So with her guidance, they crisscrossed the streets and within thirty minutes they were in roads alien to them, punctuated only by the occasional famous landmark which reminded them they were on track. They paused intermittently, not to look in awe at the buildings, but so both Frank and Big Col could rest their weary limbs, before Clem took over again.

We must keep the Tower of London on our right.

No, it's not quicker to cut round the back of St Paul's – look, here?

By the time they crossed Waterloo Bridge, and glimpsed

Big Ben's austere face glaring from the other side of the Thames, the word *Battersea* had started appearing on signs, and as they trudged on, with Frank wilting by the yard, the mileage next to the word started to decrease. Three became two, which eventually became one.

As they got closer, Noah's legs felt heavier, though some of this fatigue was due to the worries ricocheting around his brain.

'Clem?' he asked suddenly.

'Yes?'

'It really is coming, isn't it? The war.'

'Why are you asking that now?'

'Because we're almost there. And when we arrive, I'm going to have to make a decision, aren't I? About whether I leave Winn there or not.'

Clem sighed and pondered. 'I wish it wasn't, Noah, but look around us. It's like everyone knows. It's the worst kept secret in the world. I really think there's going to be a war.'

'But how am I going to do it?' he asked her. 'How am I going to say goodbye to her? And how am I going to do it without breaking my promise to Dad?'

Clem had no answers for him, and he had none either, but in fact, as the mighty towers of Battersea power station loomed above them, he wondered if for the second time, he would have to say goodbye at all.

For although Battersea Dogs Home nestled in the shadows of the towers, the queue wrapped all the way around them and out of sight.

'You have to be kidding?' Noah gasped. Even Big Col showed some emotion, lowering the sack to the ground before bending double in disbelief.

'By the time we get inside, the war will be over,' sighed Clem.

All of them walked along the queue a way.

''Scuse me,' he asked one boy after a couple of hundred yards, 'how long have you been waiting?

'Since dawn,' he yawned. 'Some daft beggars camped out all night apparently.'

That wasn't hard to believe, though it didn't help Noah. Nor did the flustered-looking woman, working her way down the queue with what was undoubtedly bad news. Every ten yards, she would stop, look apologetic and speak before moving on again. And every time she moved, the queue did too, though not nearer to the entrance. With heavy shoulders or angry, shocked expressions, people peeled away from the line and traipsed away with their pets.

Noah didn't move. If there was something going on, he wanted to hear it now.

'Thank you for queuing so patiently,' the woman said as she reached him. She was finding it hard to look anyone in the eye. 'But I'm afraid that, well, in light of the news, we won't have space to take any more animals in.'

'News? What news?' Noah asked, confused.

The woman looked at him in surprise. 'About war being declared. Mr Chamberlain has just announced it.'

There was a cacophony of noises from those listening, a discordant swell of cries and gasps, to which the woman tried, gamely, to respond.

'I'm so sorry,' she said. 'I honestly thought you all already knew.'

'How could we?' yelled an elderly man. 'We've been stood here for hours, waiting.'

'And I'm so sorry that's the case. Turning any animal away is heartbreaking for us. It goes against everything we stand for, but since yesterday we've had thousands of people wait in line. THOUSANDS.' She looked behind them. 'And there are maybe a thousand more here now. We don't have the space inside for all the animals, and even if we did, we're scared now that we won't be able to find or afford the food to keep them alive.'

'So what do we do now?' asked Noah, panic-stricken. He'd been certain they wouldn't be turned away, but now the storm Mum had warned him about was positioned right above them.

The woman looked crestfallen. 'I wish I knew. If you

have relatives who live outside the city who could take your animals in, then I recommend you take them there. Other than that, I really couldn't say.'

Winn, ever the loving dog, chose that moment to introduce herself to the woman, nuzzling gently against her leg and licking her hand, an act of such kindness that it brought tears to the woman's eyes. 'I really am sorry,' she said, voice trembling, before starting to move down the line.

But just as the three children turned to each other, the woman stopped and returned to stand by Noah's shoulder.

'There is one last thing you could try,' she said quietly. 'It's a bit of a long shot, but . . .'

'Tell us,' Noah replied. 'Please.'

20

'There's a duchess,' the woman began, which immediately had Big Col scoffing with derision. He had no time for posh folk.

'Be quiet!' Noah and Clem snapped together.

'Her name is Nina Douglas-Hamilton,' the woman went on patiently. 'She's a distant cousin to the King, I believe, and she's dedicated her whole life to animals and keeping them safe. During the last war, she set up three veterinary hospitals for horses that were injured, and she's been a great supporter of the work we do here.'

'Blimey,' Noah mouthed.

'Oh yes, she's a wonderful lady,' she continued, 'and she's campaigned against animal cruelty for decades, about the way they experiment on them for medical research.'

'They do that?' Noah couldn't believe it.

'They do. And Duchess Douglas-Hamilton, well, she played merry hell about it. Protested for years and years in a way that other royals wouldn't dare.'

'So, do you think she might help *us*?' Clem asked, eyes widening hopefully.

'I think she might. I don't know all the details, but one of the girls here told me about something in this morning's paper. This Duchess has said that if people can get their animals to her then she won't turn a single one away. She'll feed them and keep them safe until the war is over.'

Noah could hardly keep still. 'And where will we find her? Does she live near here?'

The woman looked stumped. 'Oooh no, dear, from what I was told she lives on some estate west of London. Big old place apparently with huge grounds. Sounds like paradise for the poor animals, doesn't it?' She looked as if she were about to cry.

'Can you try and remember what it was called? Anything at all that would help us?'

But if the woman knew anything else of note, she didn't have time to tell them, as a noise suddenly split the sky in two. It was a deafening din, something between a scream and a wail that ebbed and flowed and instilled in everyone an overwhelming sense of panic. People scattered in every direction. The woman tore back to the dogs home, presumably to keep the animals there calm. Winn and Frank certainly looked scared by the din.

'Wait, missus, wait!' Noah yelled, but there was no stopping her or anyone else.

'Quick, Noah, we've got to get out of here,' said Clem. 'It's the air-raid siren.'

'What, the Nazis are coming already? But we've only just declared war. Were they waiting round the corner?'

The children hadn't a clue what to do. They were in unfamiliar territory and hadn't a clue where a shelter might be. But just as they decided to run after the nearest group of responsible-looking adults, the siren stopped wailing, though their ears didn't.

'It's stopped,' said Noah. 'What does that mean? Are they coming or not?'

No one seemed to know and confusion took the place of outright panic, until the three of them heard the same thing from several different people.

'False alarm. Go about your business.' Which was easier said than done.

'We need to find out where she lives. This Duchess.' Noah said, desperation in his voice.

'And how do we do that?' Big Col grumbled.

'We need to ask. Would they know in the library?'

'It's shut on a Sunday.'

'Oh.'

As usual, Clem's brain was already in motion.

'I don't know this for sure,' she said honestly, 'but I think we need to apply logic to the situation.'

'Go on then,' replied Big Col.

'Well,' she went on, as they walked away from the building. 'She's a royal. And where do royals live?'

'Buckingham Palace,' Noah replied.

'When they're in London, yes. But what about when they're not?'

Big Col looked flummoxed. 'I don't know, in a flipping castle probably.'

'Exactly!' replied Clem enthusiastically. 'And where's the nearest castle from here?'

Neither of the boys could help her with an answer to that one.

'Windsor!' she tutted. 'Honestly, do you not know anything? And where's Windsor?'

Again, they had nothing to contribute.

'West of London, just like that lady said. Right on the Thames.'

'So if we head to Windsor, then you think we'd find this Duchess Hamilton-wotsit?' Noah looked like he was ready to start running there.

'Well, I can't be sure, but think about it. When the old King died, where did they bury him? Windsor! And then when King Edward abdicated to marry that American woman a few months later, they gave him a new title, didn't they? Duke of Windsor. I think the place is full of all the royals who are related to the King. I don't have any other ideas, and the libraries are shut and I don't think we could find out for sure without going home first.'

'Well, we can't do that. Soon as our mothers get hold of us we'll be packed off to Cornwall. We've got to try it, Clem, it's our last chance.'

'This is all well and good,' spat Big Col, who looked far from convinced by any of it. 'But we're meant to be getting on a train to safety, remember? And I can't afford to miss it.'

It seemed a strange thing to say. Noah couldn't imagine Big Col liking the quiet of the countryside.

'How on earth are we going to get there anyway? This Windsor sounds like miles away.'

'I've no idea,' Clem said.

'Don't worry, that's the easy part. Uncle Noah's got a plan.'

Clem's heart sank at the prospect of yet another 'Noah plan'.

'You can't have,' she said. 'It will be miles and miles to Windsor, and we can't walk at more than three or four miles per hour.'

'So?' Noah replied, without breaking stride.

'So?' Clem found herself becoming a little irate. 'What

did Big Col just say? Have you forgotten what's meant to be happening to us today?'

Noah shrugged.

'Today,' Clem shouted, 'right now in fact, we are supposed to be on a train. At this very second, we are meant to be evacuated, for goodness knows how long, to live with goodness knows who. Our mums should've waved us off at school, but instead they're probably combing the streets for us, thinking we've run away.'

'Exactly!' said Noah. 'As I said, we can't go home and ask them to take us to the Duchess. If we tried, they'd frogmarch us straight down the vet's again. Now we're at war they'll put Frank and Winn and even Delilah there, to sleep. We weren't prepared to do it yesterday. And I'm not going to do it today either. And so if that train has left without us, so what? I don't want to upset my mum, or yours.' He glanced at Big Col. 'And definitely not yours, but there's a war on, Clem, and I'm not going to lose it on the very first day.'

There was little Clem could say to that except, 'We still can't walk there, Noah. It's just too far.'

But Noah of course had the answer.

'We don't need to,' he replied. 'We'll sail there. On the *Queen Maudie*.'

21

Clem didn't waste her breath trying to change Noah's mind. Instead, she spent the rest of the walk back to the boat trying to work out whether she should allow herself to be part of the plan.

Noah expected her to be, that was for sure, but she'd already disobeyed her mother by disappearing at dawn instead of boarding a train, and she knew that if she went home *now* she'd be in for the telling-off of her life. But if she did what Noah was asking? Well, despite whatever he said, it seemed unlikely they could sail down to Windsor and back quickly. They'd be runaways, fugitives almost, and she knew her mother would be apoplectic.

Two miles from the boat, Frank decided he'd gone far enough, and began begging to be picked up, wrapping himself around Clem's leg so many times that it was easier to carry him than waste time and effort not falling over him.

She felt Frank sag as soon as she held him to her, a long low sigh of pleasure escaping his grey muzzle. It was a sigh that soon became a snore and that was when Clem knew that whatever adventure Noah was about to embark on (and she felt, instinctively, that it wouldn't be a smooth one), she would be going with him.

For as she looked down at Frank, and felt and saw the trust in him, nestled deep into her chest, there was no way she could hold him as a vet put him to sleep. She knew that any time she saw a dog, from that point on, all she'd be able to think of would be Frank and what she had allowed to happen.

She knew this choice would upset her mother, knew that it would worry her more and more with every second she was missing, but she also knew that in time, her mother would forgive her. Could she forgive herself if she ended Frank's life? No, she could not.

'Is the boat up to the job?' She frowned. It had never looked in any way impressive before.

'Course she is. If we . . . you know, take it slow. Me and Dad have been working on her.'

Clem frowned. 'Hmm, and is there a map onboard?'

'Enough maps for us to sail to flipping Zanzibar,' smiled Noah.

'Windsor will do, thanks.'

'Fair enough,' he replied. 'But we need to hurry. It's high tide now and we need to set off or we'll run aground.'

'Aye aye, Captain!'

'And that reminds me. I'm wearing the captain's hat. All right?' He flicked a glance at Big Col, who was showing no signs of leaving them for home.

So no one mentioned it, and certainly not when they arrived back at the *Queen Maudie*. Because their attention was taken by something else entirely: a new large shape in a hat standing tied next to the boat. A shape that appeared, occasionally, to be moving.

Noah's first thought was that it was Mum. That she'd caught on somehow to their plan, and had arrived to drag him home. But after another look, he realised that wasn't possible, not unless Mum had taken to standing on four legs instead of two. For what they were looking at, unless they were mistaken, was a donkey. And a big beast at that.

'Who's tied that up there?' Clem asked.

'No idea,' replied Noah. 'But it had better not kick *Maudie*. The rust on that flank means her hoof would go straight through.'

'Donkey as big as that one could sink that boat if it wanted to,' added Big Col.

They hurried, only slowing down when they came closer to the beast. It was a hell of a size, with hooves like buckets.

The only thing that softened its brutish looks was a

wide-brimmed, slightly battered straw hat, with holes cut out for its ears.

'Why's it wearing that?' asked Clem.

'Stops the flies getting in his eyes probably,' suggested Big Col, unaware that this was the most intelligent thing he'd ever said to his companions.

'Never mind that, what's it doing here? Look! Some cheeky beggar's actually tied her to the boat!'

They had as well, a thick knotted rope adding to the *Queen Maudie*'s moorings.

Noah moved quickly towards the donkey, as he'd spotted something, a folded scrap of paper tucked into the brim of the hat.

He reached for it, only to be nudged forcibly away by the donkey's head.

'Leave off, will you?' Noah tutted, not wanting to admit he was a little scared of the power in the beast. 'Or I'll feed you to *his* snake.'

'Think even Delilah would struggle to eat him in one go . . . though she'd probably give it a whirl.'

Clem though was running out of patience. 'Oh for goodness' sake,' she huffed, and marched purposefully up to the donkey's head, before repeatedly blowing gently up its nose.

'What on earth are you doing?' said Big Col, who'd

never seen anything so bizarre in his life, and he owned a python.

'It calms them,' she said, without looking away, 'makes them realise you aren't a threat, but a friend.' Big Col laughed, and Noah might have too, if it hadn't worked enough to let him get at the piece of paper without further assault.

'What does it say?' asked Big Col, suddenly all interested.

'You're not going to believe this,' Noah said to them both.

'Oh, with what I've agreed to today, I think you'd be surprised,' Clem replied.

'It says, *I hear you're saving animals. Here's another for your collection. His name is Samson. He likes eating grass.*'

'Is that it?'

Noah turned the paper over and found nothing. 'They were hardly going to leave an address, were they?'

'No name either?'

'No, but the strange thing is, it doesn't look like a child wrote it, see?'

It was true, there was no spidery writing, just the clear copperplate hand of an adult.

'What are we supposed to do with him?' Clem asked. 'We can't take him as well!'

She felt sure Noah would agree with her. No one in

their right mind would add a straw-hatted donkey into the equation.

But she was wrong.

'Course, we can,' said Noah with a smile. 'We can't just abandon it here.'

'Why not? You read the note. Samson's clearly not fussy about a varied diet, and there's enough grass in Wapping Woods to last him for months. Let's take him there. We do not need to take him on the boat with us!'

But Noah wasn't having any of it. 'Leave him here and this donkey won't live a week. Target as big as him, Hitler will snuff him out on his first raid. That what you want, Clem?'

'Of course it's not.'

'But that's what will happen if we leave him here. It'd be as bad as abandoning Frank, or Winn.'

'Or Delilah,' added big Col, in what he (mistakenly) thought was a helpful interruption.

'So, what you're saying,' Clem said, wanting to make sure she'd fully understood, 'is that you think we should tempt this huge, surly donkey onboard your dad's decrepit ship and sail it down the Thames, along with two dogs and the world's hungriest python?'

'It's a boat, not a ship,' shrugged Noah. 'And yes, I do. I don't see what could possibly go wrong.'

Clem at that point should have gone home. But she didn't, of course she didn't.

'You do realise, don't you, Noah, that the donkey's called Samson and the snake's called Delilah?'

'Er . . . yeah. So?'

'You never did read the Bible, did you?'

He shook his head. 'Course I didn't. None of it's true. It's all just stories, isn't it?'

For once, Clem *really* hoped that her best friend was right.

22

There are many moments in life when books are priceless, fonts of knowledge and wisdom.

But this was not one of those times. Clem's walls were lined with huge tomes, but Noah knew with certainty that none of them included a chapter on how to lead a stubborn donkey onboard a riverboat.

So the children improvised. They had to, as Samson made it clear very quickly that a sailor's life was not for him. He was perfectly happy on dry land. The children began by trying to lead him down the gangplank, but soon gave up when Samson didn't blink, let alone clip clop onboard. They offered handfuls of weeds and dandelions that they collected from a nearby stretch of wasteland, but sadly those lacked the flavour or freshness needed to tempt him from his spot. Big Col suggested slapping his rump with a stick, but when Noah handed him a weapon he strangely went off the idea. Nothing to do with the size of his rear legs of course, and the fact that to hit him, Big Col would have to stand in range.

In the end, they paused, frustrated and defeated.

'I'm hungry,' Noah said.

'Me too,' agreed Big Col.

'We can't eat yet,' warned Clem. 'Who knows how long the rations will have to last. And we've the animals to feed.'

'I'm thirsty too,' Big Col added unhelpfully.

Noah was tempted to point at the river and tell him to help himself, but thought better of it.

Instead he told Big Col that Dad kept a tank of water in the cabin for brewing tea. It was hardly fresh, but it was cleaner than the Thames at least.

Clem plodded up the gangplank after him, fetched a tin of sardines from her coat pocket and pierced it with her penknife, before swinging her legs over the side of the boat.

'Come here, Frank,' she cooed, 'lunchtime.'

But it wasn't the slow padding of the dog's aching paws that filled her ears. One whiff of briny fish was all Samson needed to galvanise him into action. All of a sudden, the *only* place he wanted to be was onboard the *Queen Maudie*, and he practically galloped up the gangplank, making the boat wobble furiously, almost knocking Clem overboard.

'Don't move, Clem!' shouted Noah, wild-eyed with excitement.

'That's easy for you to say,' Clem shouted, as she backed away from Samson. He had the look of a donkey who would devour her hand whole so as not to miss a scrap of sardine.

'Lead him to the bow,' Noah went on. 'In front of the captain's cab.'

Clem did as instructed, though it was far from easy. Samson's heavy hooves made the deck pitch and sway as though the boat were already navigating the fiercest of seas.

Clem had heard of tempting animals with carrots and sticks, but frankly this was ridiculous, and she was nothing but relieved when the donkey finally sucked up the fish from her palm before rooting in her pockets for more.

'Tie him up, will you?' she told the boys, and Noah did the honours, grinning from ear to ear.

'There you go,' he said. 'Not so bad, was it?'

'Apart from my palm's covered in donkey drool, no.'

'Well, wash it quickly, will you? Now Samson's onboard we should get moving, before he changes his mind.'

'That's not the only thing that needs washing,' said Clem. 'The cabin stinks after what happened last night.'

'Well, there's buckets and a cloth over there. You and him will have to sort that out cos I'm the only one who knows how to sail *Maudie*, aren't I?' He gestured to Big Col and then raced back into the small captain's cab, which was little more than a tiny wooden shed with a wheel and hole where a window once sat.

'You lazy git. All right, I'll clean up down there, Noah Price,' Clem shouted after him. 'But that's it, do you hear? I'm not on this trip to be your skivvy!'

Noah chuckled. 'Right,' he said. 'Now, how did Dad do this again?' But he said it too loudly and Big Col heard through the broken window and was far from impressed.

'You don't know how to start up this wreck?' he shouted. 'You are kidding me!'

'You know you *can* get off if you want to?' Noah spat back. 'I don't actually remember anyone inviting you along.'

'Yeah, well, go on then, try and send me packing. Because I'll tell you something, you're going to need me at some point along the way. Couple of wimps like you.'

There were plenty of things that Noah could've said to that, but knowing how long a broken nose took to stop bleeding, he said none of them, his attention turning to Winn, who had appeared at his feet, with something unexpected in her jaw.

'What's that, girl?' he asked, before grinning widely.

Dad's captain hat. A shabby peaked affair that he'd inherited when he purchased the boat. Dad loved it. He wore it every second he was onboard, whether the boat was moving or not. So wearing it now? Well, it felt good. Kept Dad close.

Not that the other two saw it the same way.

'Oh, that's better,' scoffed Big Col. 'No doubt in my head now that you can steer this wreck.'

'Unless that hat contains magical navigational powers, Noah, I think we should start with a map, don't you?' added Clem.

But Noah disagreed with a dismissive wave of his arm. 'We can look at it as we go,' he replied. 'The captain knows which way is west and we need to set off now while the tide is high. That's all we need to think about at the moment.' And with as much certainty as he could muster, he reached for the ignition, which coughed and spluttered, without ever threatening to start.

'Give me a second,' he said, without looking up. He tried again, and again, but there was nothing; the only life was the heat rising in his cheeks. 'Always takes a while . . . come on, *Maudie, come on*!'

He could feel their restlessness beside him. Even Samson on the deck looked slightly agitated, slamming his hoof hard on the ancient deck.

Noah tried the choke, then let the engine rest, not wanting to flood it and risk never getting started. But whatever he did, the engine simply refused to catch.

'Where shall I hit it?' said Big Col.

'Hit my boat and I'll hit you straight back.' Noah couldn't help it, he was flustered and frustrated.

That was all the encouragement the bully needed, aiming a kick at Noah that would've impressed Samson himself. But whilst Noah was smaller than Big Col, he was way quicker, and seeing the kick coming, he swivelled out of the way, leaving his attacker's foot to thwack against the steering column.

There was a metallic bang, then a rumble, and what sounded suspiciously like a belch, which made Noah jump back in front of the wheel, turning the ignition one, final, frantic time.

And that was it, the *Queen Maudie* awoke, announcing it to everyone within a one-mile radius.

'Quick! Clem, untie her. Now!!'

The *Queen Maudie* roared a throaty, smoky greeting that was matched by Noah, as he cautiously opened up the throttle and felt the water part either side of the boat's flanks.

Noah whooped, the dogs barked and Samson brayed in what they all hoped was delight.

They were moving, already feet closer to Windsor, the Duchess and hope, but within seconds they reached their first obstacle. Limehouse Lock, which separated the basin from the freedom of the Thames, and a rotund, pock-faced man who stood guard there.

23

'Who on earth is that?' Big Col asked as the boat pulled closer.

'That,' sighed Noah, 'is Tipsy Nev.'

'What sort of name is that? And what's he doing there?'

'He's the lock keeper, isn't he? And as for his name? Well, you'll see, soon enough.'

Noah closed the throttle as *Queen Maudie* pulled up to the lock. Big Nev leaned forward, squinting. 'Who's that then?' he barked, voice thick with tobacco. He leaned still further, unsteady on his feet, the wooden pillar in front of him the only thing stopping him from tumbling headfirst into the water.

'Is he drunk?' Clem asked, although Nev clearly was.

'Drunk?' replied Noah. 'At this time of day. No, Nev's just tipsy. Like he always is.'

'Who's that then?' Nev repeated, his eyes two bleary bloodshot slits.

'It's me, Nev, Noah Price. You know, Tom's boy.'

'Tom? Tom's not here. Marched off to sock Adolf a

couple of weeks back.' He threw a clumsy punch that saw him lurch against the pillar for a second time.

'Yes, I know, Nev, and I'm his son. You remember me, don't you?'

'Course I do!' the man chuckled. 'Whass your name again? Nick, is it?'

'Noah. Like the man on the ark.'

'Ah yes, yes, course.' Nev's face remained blank, clueless. 'Where you off to then?' He tried to look the length of the boat, his eyes widening when they happened on Samson. 'That an 'orse?!' he gasped, rubbing at his eyes.

'Oh no,' Noah replied. 'I'd never take a horse on a boat. This is a donkey. It's a completely different thing.'

Nev burped, like Noah's statement had caused a tiny explosion in his brain. He knew he should say something back, he was a responsible lock keeper after all, but he couldn't think what it should be. So came up with something else.

'Your dad know you're taking his boat?'

'Course he does.'

'S'just . . . well . . . you're a kid, aren't you. Not sure I should be letting you loose on the river with a beast onboard. Ain't safe, is it?'

'We're not going far, Nev. Just to Woolwich and back.

Need to get this donkey to a field down there, you know, before the bombs start.'

Nev snorted and staggered. 'S'hardly the safety of the countryside, is it?'

'Are you kidding me?' joked Noah. 'The Nazis won't bother dropping a bomb on Woolwich. It's a wreck already.'

That brought a drunken hoot from Nev. It was working, Noah thought. He'd open the lock in no time. But then Nev seemed to sober up a touch.

'Very funny. But I can't let you out, can I? Maritime rules.'

'Come on, Nev. We'll only be an hour. Two at the most!' And by then, Noah thought, by then you'll be too drunk to remember we even exist.

'Rules . . . is rules.' Nev smiled, like he'd said something incredibly profound.

'I understand, Nev,' Noah sighed, feeling Clem and Big Col's eyes burning into him. 'It's just, well, Dad left you a gift, to say thank you, because he knows how . . . well . . . professional you are. I'll just go fetch it.'

Noah dashed from the cab and into the cabin. Nev weaved and lurched on the jetty. Clem and Big Col just looked confused, until Noah returned, holding a half-empty, dusty bottle.

'This is for you,' he said, thrusting it into Nev's fist.

'Courtesy of my dad. Half a bottle of his finest, famous Moonshine.'

Nev's eyes widened, his pupils a murky green and the rest pure bloodshot red. He gasped, and pulled the bottle to his chest, cradling it like it was his first, precious grandchild.

'My dad was always very grateful to you,' Noah said, laying it on thick. 'And, well, this was his last wish, before he went off to fight. *Get Samson to safety,* he said. *That's all that matters to me.*'

Noah had no idea if Nev had heard him. He still seemed lost in thought, enthralled by his new booty. But just as Noah thought he'd come up short, the man turned, set the bottle down with utmost care, before turning his hands with surprising dexterity, to the lock's mechanisms.

'It's working!' Clem whispered. 'What is in that bottle?'

'Water,' Noah whispered back. 'But he's legless, isn't he? And before he realises, we'll be long gone.'

As soon as they chugged slowly away from the basin and on to the Thames, Clem went for the map, concertinaing it out until it filled the cab. Her pupils dilated, swimming in the vast sea of knowledge that the map held, her brain drawing an instant line from where they were, to where she thought they needed to be.

Noah, though, had challenges of his own to consider, namely the busyness of the river itself.

He had lived by the river his entire life, and so knew this stretch pretty well, but he'd never seen it from this vantage point: never been steering a boat down it. And if he was honest, it was all a little bit much. Everywhere he looked there were boats, some large, some small, but all seemed to be belching the most furious acrid smoke into the sky, which lingered over them, nipping at his eyes and scratching his chest.

If that wasn't bad enough, everything seemed to be moving much faster than them, and more aggressively, taking advantage of the high tide. It was like the world was about to end in mere minutes and everyone needed to get home before it did.

Tugs surged to his left and right, some of them hauling vessels that were ten times the size of theirs: their wake alone threatening to capsize them. There seemed to be no order to it, who went where and who waited for whom. Noah knew how it worked on the road: you drove on the left and gave way to the right, but here? Well, it was a free-for-all.

Panicking he decided to veer back to portside, to hog the bank, thus avoiding the bigger vessels, but as he did so he merely earned a savage blare of a horn from a boat behind, which made him veer right once more.

'Flippin' Nora,' he moaned, heart pounding. Whichever way he steered he saw obstacles or trouble: a bobbing buoy to his right, a sandbank to his left. He had no idea whether it would be best to open up the throttle and push on, or creep along, hoping that if he crashed slowly, it would do less damage.

What didn't help was Clem wafting the map too close to his eyeline.

'Leave off with that, will you?' Noah huffed.

'What, and not know where we're going?'

'I can't flipping see where we're going because you're waving that thing in front of my face!'

He grabbed at the map, pulling it roughly from her hands and throwing it over his shoulder, before realising he had steered too close to the bank again. A swift, stern turn of the wheel saw *Maudie* veer quickly right, too quickly, drawing a stiff rebuke from Big Col, and an even stiffer one from Samson, who turned and brayed his disapproval. If Noah didn't know better, he could've sworn the donkey tutted at him, before turning its head away in search of luscious grass to pine after.

'Noah, what are you doing?' Clem snapped.

'Trying not to crash because of you and your obsession with maps!'

'It's not obsessive to want to know where we're going. It's not obsessive to have a PLAN!'

'Why do we have to have a plan?' Noah sighed, 'Why can't it be, I don't know, an . . . adventure!'

'Because I want to know how far we're going and when we're likely to be back.'

'Why? What does it matter?'

'It matters to me, Noah.'

'Will we see the Houses of Parliament again?' interrupted a voice from behind them both. It was the first time in his life that Noah had ever been pleased to hear Big Col's voice.

'Course we will. Once we reach Waterloo. But we've only just left home.'

'Oh. Right.' It didn't seem to make much sense to Big Col, even though they'd practically passed it on the way to Battersea earlier. 'And Tower Bridge? What about that?'

The excitement looked odd on his usually aggressive face, and for the tiniest split-second Noah saw a slightly different side to him.

'Tower Bridge is ahead. We'll sail right under it soon.'

Clem saw his enthusiasm as an opportunity, grabbing the map and smoothing it on the floor in front of Big Col.

'Look, here's Tower Bridge, and here's the Houses of

Parliament and we, well, we're somewhere around here.' She jabbed her finger slap bang on top of Wapping.

Big Col looked like this was all news to him. 'And Buckingham Palace. That's over here, isn't it?' His finger went too far north, so Clem patiently put him straight.

'Haven't you ever, you know, walked round London with your mum and dad? Seen the sights?' She wasn't judging. It just seemed like the most natural thing in the world to do. Why live in the capital if you weren't going to go out and explore it?

'Dad works. Mum too.'

'But Sundays, maybe?'

Big Col shrugged but seemed to retreat inside himself, like he was remembering his Sundays and wasn't too keen on what he saw.

'There'll be other landmarks on the way too,' added Clem. 'Hampton Court Palace maybe. And the maze.'

'Thought you didn't like getting lost,' Noah interrupted, trying to make a joke. But there wasn't time to answer.

'Is there somewhere warm I can put Delilah?' Big Col said, stroking her gently.

'Warm? It's bloomin' boiling today already!'

'Not for her it's not. She's from India. She needs it like a furnace. Sleeps in a box near the stove at home.'

Clem looked concerned. 'And what happens to her . . . if she gets too cold?'

'Dunno really. I only usually take her out for a bit, until she seems to go a bit still. Then I pop her back in the warm again.'

Noah didn't like the sound of this. He was hardly a vet, but he didn't know if they could keep Delilah as warm as she needed to be. And if she got sick? Then he didn't want to see how Big Col would react. He clearly loved the snake enormously.

'Stoke the stove in the cabin. That's your best bet. With the door shut it'll soon heat up. You can tidy up while you're down there.'

'It better had warm up,' Big Col replied, his voice suddenly like it had just been sharpened. 'I'm trusting you.' And with that, he thudded from the cab, leaving Clem and Noah alone.

'Never mind him,' said Clem. 'But we do need to look at the map and work out exactly where Windsor is and where we can moor the boat.'

Noah gave in. 'Fine, just do it on the floor and not in front of me. I need to concentrate on all this traffic!'

So she did and he listened occasionally, when he wasn't too stressed, tuning into the bits about distance and tides and times, tuning out when it veered away from the essential into a geography lesson.

'So I think if we're going about ten to fifteen miles an hour, we should be there about seven o'clock tonight. Hopefully the Duchess will let us in at that time and then we could come back tonight or sleep on the boat and make an early start in the morning –'

Noah interrupted her, hollering 'TOWER BRIDGE!!' at the top of his voice as it loomed imperiously into view, though Big Col didn't seem to hear. Or if he did, he suddenly wasn't interested.

'Lord,' Noah thought to himself, 'Please don't let Big Col be below deck, resuscitating a snake with hypothermia.'

Noah had his own things to worry about. The bridge brought a new wave of boats, weaving left and right, jostling for the quietest passage. The smoke intensified too. Made Noah think about what it would be like if bombs *did* start to drop on their city. Is this what it would be like? Foggy and miserable and scary?

He tried to stay calm, but it felt like there was menace and threat everywhere. Not just from other boats, but from the cranes that seemed to suddenly loom over them out of the smoke. It looked like they had sharpened their claws, ready to pick them out of the water and abandon them, broken, on the shore.

It felt strange. All of it. And a more sensible child might have realised they were suddenly out of their depth.

But that wasn't Noah's way. There was a dog nuzzled up against his leg and a donkey in a sunhat obscuring his view, not to mention the others. He had a mission to fulfil, and he told himself repeatedly that he couldn't give up.

24

So, they veered tortuously slowly towards central London, belching dirty clouds of their own and drawing strange looks as they went.

The looks had less to do with *Queen Maudie*'s mechanical limitations though, and more to do with the donkey tied up to the bow of the boat. It wasn't rare for vessels to have elaborate figureheads carved into them, but Samson and his straw hat had passing sailors rubbing their eyes in wonder.

It didn't go unnoticed by Clem.

'Do you think there will be bobbies patrolling the river? You know, in boats?'

'Policemen in boats,' laughed Noah. 'Why?'

'Well, because they'll stop us if they see us. I mean, three children and a donkey steering a clapped-out tub down a heaving river on the first day of war?'

Noah was affronted. 'Oi! *Maudie* is not a tub or clapped out. And she's named after my mother. So, if you insult one, you insult them both!'

'Noah, I'm serious. We'll be in real trouble if the police

stop us, and that's before they discover the man-eating python in the cabin.'

Noah looked around him. And she did have a point. The river *was* teeming: a jumble of boats of different sizes and lengths, though none of the vessels seemed to be out for pleasure. Everyone was carrying something. Fruit boxes piled high, burlap sacks packed so tight it was a wonder their decks weren't sagging beneath the drink. One larger boat looked like it was carrying some sort of gigantic gun, which unsurprisingly, piqued Big Col's interest, as he came out of the cabin.

The one thing they all had in common was that every other vessel was manned by an adult, not by a twelve-year-old child.

'At some point, someone is going to see it's you, a boy, driving this boat, and when they add in Samson, well, they're going to be suspicious.'

'It'll be fine, I'll just pull Dad's cap down a bit.' He did so, before realising that he couldn't see a thing.

'Noah, your dad is six foot tall at least. And well, you're not. Clearly.'

'Good things come in small packages,' he replied, quickly. His dad had said it to him enough times.

'*Children* come in small packages. Which is why they get arrested for driving boats that don't belong to them.'

That shut Noah up.

'Of course. We could let Big Col drive. He is much taller,' continued Clem.

Big Col *loved* that idea. Course he did, making noises like a racing driver, which spurred Noah into action. He told Clem to grab a wooden crate and a long oilskin mac that had been thrown in the corner of the cab.

Then, while keeping half an eye on the traffic around him, he rummaged in an old tin box, palming something long and wooden, before jamming the box under the steering wheel and the heavy coat over his shoulders. Standing tall on the crate, he shoved an old pipe into his mouth and beamed the smuggest of grins.

'There!' he said. 'Now I'm six foot two. And thirty-five years old.'

'Smoking will stunt your growth,' Clem said, deadpan.

'And you don't look old. Just ugly,' guffawed Big Col, 'but then again, you always did.' He yanked Dad's hat further over Noah's skull. 'There, that's perfect. Don't ever take it off.'

Even Clem laughed, which riled Noah. He asked them in the most colourful language possible to leave him well alone. He needed some space if he wasn't going to crash, or try to throw them both overboard.

*

It continued that way for the next hour, with the river busy and the three children giving each other a wide berth. As wide as the *Queen Maudie* would allow anyway. Each of them seemed content enough with their own company. Noah gave his focus to the steering of the boat and the avoiding of bigger, faster, angrier vessels. He had taken the decision to stick close to the bank again but worried they might run aground, whilst the wake from the other boats made steering difficult, as the water not so much lapped against the sides of the *Maudie* as slapped them. It gave the impression of being at sea, rather than on the river.

Clem sat out front, nervously watching Frank and Samson get acquainted, which boiled down to the little dachshund cowering arthritically every time the donkey showed any interest in him. One unfortunate, misplaced hoof could easily mean curtains for the old dog, and he seemed to know it. Samson knew it too, and he did his best to put the dog at ease by rubbing his head gently on Frank. Sadly, it wasn't long until Frank sought the safety of Clem's lap, where he remained, breathing heavily as he slept.

'You are a silly thing,' she cooed to him. 'Could you not see Samson was trying to be friends?'

But Frank slept on and Clem instead took the opportunity to take in the landmarks as they passed. This was her city, the only one she'd ever known, yet here on the river, it was like seeing it anew.

She felt herself shiver as they rolled past Big Ben exactly on the hour, hearing its chimes ring out. It was like everyone around them, no matter how big or small their boat, stopped to take in the noise. Like it was the only thing that mattered. With every landmark Clem's brain flicked to stories she'd read about them, whether it was the plague or the Gunpowder Plot, and if the boat's engine hadn't been so loud then she would've tried to pass the stories on to the boys – not that she imagined they'd be interested for a second.

Big Col had positioned himself too far away to hear, at the stern of the boat, sometimes on his own, sometimes he brought Delilah out of the cabin and talked quietly to her, as the python slid and slithered its way around every limb he owned. It was like Big Col's entire upper body was swathed in snakeskin, like he was wearing the most decadent jacket. Two minutes later and his trousers seemed to have been tailored by the python.

Noah saw this and shivered. Not with cold, but fear. There were times when Delilah seemed to be squeezing tighter than was comfortable, Big Col's hands or even neck turning slightly scarlet, before the snake moved on and gripped him elsewhere. If it bothered Big Col in any way, then he was mighty good at hiding it, though Noah made a note to stay well clear until Delilah had been fed something substantial, like an elephant.

He shook the image from his head and turned his attention back to steering a route down the river. The Houses of Parliament stood judgementally behind them now, and he could see the towers of Battersea Power Station ahead and beyond it the west of London.

They were doing this, just like he said they could. And all right, he might not be a particularly good navigator, and Windsor might not be round the next corner. But it wouldn't be long. It really wouldn't.

Only then, the engine went bang.

25

It wasn't a bomb-like bang. But it was enough to shock them all, Samson in particular, who threatened a stampede up and down the deck.

'What the blazes was that?' Clem shouted as she and Big Col piled into the cab. Noah was still dressed as his dad, but lacked a captain's composure. The skipper's cap was pushed askew and he looked out of his depth, a boy lost in his dad's mac, as much as he tried to hide it.

'It's fine,' he gasped, pulling hard on the wheel. Too hard. Or so it felt to Clem.

'Go the other way!' she yelled unhelpfully. 'That's starboard. We need portside!'

These weren't new terms to Noah. He'd chugged up and down the river with his dad enough times to have heard them on plenty of occasions. He thought he had the hang of them too. But now, with smoke billowing from below deck, all that went out the window. At that moment in time, he would've been flustered by *forward* and *back*.

'What do you mean?' he yelled.

'You're steering us into the middle of the river. LOOK OUT!'

Noah might not have been a bona fide skipper, but he didn't need to be to see the biggest boat yet speeding towards them on their right. Fifteen times the size of *Queen Maudie,* any kind of contact would've seen the vessel act as a tin opener, leaving the boat, AND them, well beyond repair.

'Portside! Portside, NOAH!' She yelled. 'LEFT! LEFT!!!'

That was an instruction he *could* follow, and he pulled hard and left with his whole body, so much so that the cap fell from his head, demoting him instantly from captain to cabin boy.

Queen Maudie howled and cried in pain, sending more smoke through the floorboards, but her cries were drowned out by the oncoming boat's horn, blaring its condemnation as it passed on the starboard side, closer than anyone wanted, the wake from the river making *Maudie* tilt and rock like a rowing boat on the high seas.

'You idiot!' Big Col roared. 'Don't you know your left from your bleedin' right?!?'

Noah couldn't believe what he was hearing. '*You* can talk! You didn't even know where the King lived, did you, genius?!'

'That's enough!' Clem barked, stepping between them. 'Noah, get your eyes on the river and us over to the bank! Big Col, just . . . well . . . just stop it, will you???'

Big Col, much to her surprise, did exactly that, storming from the cab and slamming the door with such force that the whole boat shook again. Noah swore under his breath as he quickly steered Maudie to a mooring before any more damage could be done.

'Help me tie her up, will you?' he said to Clem, and as she jumped ashore, feeling her legs tremble at the sensation of being on dry land, Noah killed the ignition, before lifting the trapdoor to the engine.

The result was instantaneous, smoke billowing into his face like he was standing over a factory's chimney. It was a relief to see only smoke and no flames.

'What's going on?' yelled Clem, standing behind him.

'Just overheated, that's all.'

'You sure?'

'Course I'm sure. I practically rebuilt this engine with Dad, you know!'

This was partially true. He'd lost count of the number of tools he'd passed down to his father as he tinkered and hammered and spannered the boat back to life. Not to mention the number of cups of tea he'd made. Without those, Dad would've overheated, never mind the boat.

'So what do we need to do to fix it?'

'Nothing for now. She's just not been used for a while, Dad had been . . . tinkering with the engine before he left.'

Clem knew Noah well enough to understand what that meant. 'You mean it was broken before we even set off?'

Noah jumped up from his knees and shushed her, paranoid that Big Col would hear and demand answers.

'No!' he hissed. 'It wasn't broken. It just wasn't, you know . . . finely tuned.'

'You mean it wasn't working properly?'

'Well . . . parts have been harder to get hold of lately.'

'So you led us onboard, and sold us the idea of sailing all the way to the Duchess' estate, when you knew full well that this rusty old bathtub was never up to the job?' She was furious now.

Noah hushed her again, like he was afraid the boat herself would hear and take umbrage. 'I knew no such thing. And there's nothing wrong with *Maudie*. She could go to China if we asked her. She'd just have to do it . . . slowly.'

'Slowly because we'd have to swim in front and tow her behind us!'

Their argument had attracted not just the attention of Frank and Winn, but Big Col too, who reappeared, arms out like a scarecrow, with Delilah draped across them. There was very little space in the cab as a result.

'Why don't you get Samson in here too. We can turn it into a proper East End knees-up!' moaned Noah.

Big Col, though, wasn't one for sarcasm. 'Are they the towers we saw this morning?' he asked, pointing back to Battersea Power Station.

'Yes, that's right,' said Clem. 'That's Battersea.'

'So you mean we've been travelling all day and we're still in the same place?'

Noah felt his fists clench and he swallowed down the reply he wanted to give.

'How long we stopping for?' continued Col.

'Long enough to let the engine cool. Then I'll top up the water and oil and we can set off again.'

'Right,' said Big Col. 'Good. Cos it's definitely time to eat.'

Noah looked at Clem, and Clem looked at Noah. Both of them gulped in fear.

They didn't like the way the snake was looking at them.

26

The engine did not cool quickly, and nor did Big Col's hunger. In fact, there was soon a red-hot longing for food in each of them that couldn't be satisfied by the tins they'd found onboard or scavenged from the larders at home.

There was barely enough sardines or spam for the dogs, never mind the humans. Samson was easily enough pleased – there was grass aplenty in Battersea Park, though Noah brought it to the donkey in a bucket, rather than trying to lead him ashore. Samson was so stubborn and the grass so lush here that they doubted they could tempt him back onboard a second time. As Noah brought him the bucket, Samson gently rubbed his enormous head on Noah's arm, as if in thanks. It made Noah glow, craving contact with him, feeding him directly from his hand as he scratched behind his ear.

And as for Delilah, she continued to unsettle them by doing very little really. Her presence even for the shortest periods, before being returned to the warmth of the cabin, was enough to set their nerves on edge, though that probably wasn't helped by the agitation hunger brought with it.

'I'm still starving,' Noah moaned, looking longingly at the empty tins. He'd have run his finger round the edges for stray flakes of fish had the dog's tongue not already done it.

'Stop moaning,' Big Col snapped. 'You should be more like Delilah. Makes her food last, she does.'

'Probably because her last meal was a pony,' replied Noah. 'And she probably ate the rider on its back too.'

'You two are paranoid. She's not going to eat you. She's not going to be hungry for days.'

'What do you mean?'

'Well, exactly that. She'll often go five or six days between meals. 'S what snakes do.'

Noah looked at Clem, outraged almost. 'Did you know this?' he said.

'Thinking about it, I reckon I *did* read about it somewhere, yes.'

'Then why didn't you tell me? I've spent all day worrying that this . . . thing was going to eat me while my back was turned.'

This did little to impress Clem, who like everyone, was now both hungry and irritable.

'You know, Noah, I'm getting a little bit sick of being your walking encyclopaedia. If you want to know things, why don't you start finding them out yourself, because the last time I checked you had eyes for reading too.'

'What's that supposed to mean?' Noah bristled.

'Do I need to explain it twice? Or are you lacking a brain as well as eyes?'

Both of them were on their feet now, fingers pointing and eyes flaring. Even the dogs were agitated: facing each other as they stood at their owners' feet, teeth bared and snarling.

It was a moment that could've derailed their entire friendship never mind their mission, had help not come once again from the most unlikely of sources.

'Does your dad fish?' asked Big Col, a question so unexpected it dragged them from their stand-off.

'What?'

'It's a simple question. Does he fish? When he's on the boat?'

'Er, yes. Sometimes.'

'Where's his rods then? In fact, just point me. It'll be quicker. And the quicker we fish, the quicker you two will be full enough to stop arguing.'

Noah and Clem looked at each other, still riled, but also slightly ashamed to have been caught bickering by Big Col.

Noah mumbled something and pointed him to the cabin and the rod Dad stowed there.

'Hmm,' said Big Col, a look on his face that Noah didn't recognise. Usually if the bully was concentrating, his face had a look of constipation about it, but minutes later, as he handled the rod, he actually looked like he knew what he was doing.

'Line's tangled,' Big Col said. 'By the time we unravel that it'll be 1940 and you two will have either killed or eaten each other.'

And with that, he pulled a knife from his pocket, which made Noah gulp. He'd no idea Big Col was carrying it, nor why he thought it necessary.

'What are you doing?' Noah said.

'Nothing for you to fret about. In fact, in about an hour, your stomach will be thanking me. So shut up and watch.'

Noah did exactly that, out of both fear and interest. He watched as Big Col cut the line free, removing the spool of twine altogether, before putting the rod back in the cupboard carefully.

'Don't you need that?'

'Nah. Prefer to do it my own way. Besides, Dad would never let me near his fishing rod. We had words when I used it once.' Noah saw him flinch and rub at his arm before heading outside and down the gangplank.

Noah stood at the doorway and watched him on the bank. If there was something bothering Big Col, then he soon shook it off, dropping to all fours, head down in the long grass, almost doglike, sniffing something out.

Noah wanted to ask what he was doing but held his tongue, snapping his fingers to get Clem's attention instead. 'What's he up to?' he mouthed quietly, before realising he was doing what he always did: asking his friend for the answers.

Clem hadn't a clue anyway, so they both watched silently, until . . . after a good few minutes, Big Col jumped to his feet.

'Aha!' he yelled, delightedly, holding not a snake this time, but a long, wriggling worm. 'This one's a beauty.'

Bounding up the gangplank, he waved the worm in their faces, making them worry this was tonight's menu.

'What are you waiting for?' he said. 'Get on the bank there and get a fire lit. Give me half an hour and we'll be ready to cook. You have my word.'

They didn't move, not straightaway. Instead, they watched the boy cut the worm into multiple pieces, before attaching a piece on to the twine he'd cut from the rod.

Leaning over the side of *Queen Maudie*, he cast the line into the river like a professional.

Only then did he realise he was being watched. 'You do *know* how to make a fire, don't you?' he asked.

Clem and Noah nodded and backed away to the riverbank, hungry enough to place every ounce of trust they had in the fists of Big Col.

27

The smell was otherworldly. Like something from a dream.

They'd had fish, plenty of times, but had never watched it be caught, gutted and prepared like Big Col did it. His thick stumpy fingers seemed to take on a life of their own, all deft and precise like a surgeon's.

When his line twitched the first time, they'd thought it was a fluke, and then they watched, expecting (but not hoping) him to fail the second time around. But ten minutes later another fish lay twitching on the deck, then a third and a fourth.

Big Col didn't make a fuss about it, or show off, nor did he take any delight in putting the fish out of their miseries. Instead, he talked to them quietly, apologetic after the deed had been done and then set to work filleting them.

He didn't step away from the cooking either, though he did moan about the size of the fire, putting that right effortlessly before frying the fish in an old pan of Dad's, without the flesh ever sticking or burning. The only noise he did make was a long low burp that escaped his lips as he lay back sated, and it bounced off the trees that lined the riverbank.

'Well,' said Clem, full but suddenly tired, 'that was delicious.'

'Yeah,' agreed Noah, who still found it hard, despite the feast, to say thank you to his nemesis, 'it was . . . needed. Thanks. Who taught you to do that? Your dad?'

Big Col lay there, hands behind his head. ''I've watched him fish a lot, but teach me? That's not really him.'

'Well, you were obviously a good watcher then,' said Clem.

Big Col side-eyed her, not sure if she was trying to get a rise out of him.

'No, I mean it,' insisted Clem. 'I thank you. Noah thanks you. And our stomachs definitely do.'

But Noah had done with the niceties, pulling himself to his feet and unexpectedly kicking dust on to the dying flames to put them out. 'Delicious as that was, we haven't got time to pat ourselves on the back. Windsor is still further away than I'd like, and it'll be dark soon. Be good to have London properly behind us before that happens. Can't help thinking I'm going to turn round and find my mum running towards us with her rolling pin in her hand.'

If ever there was an image that was going to stir them

into action, it was this one, and they gathered everything back onboard.

'You sure this old sieve is up to it?' asked Big Col.

'You do the fishing and leave the boat to me,' replied Noah tersely. 'Besides, I topped her up with water, so she should be much cooler again.'

'Till next time,' huffed Big Col, not caring who heard.

Noah swallowed his irritability, donned his skipper's cap and mac once more and took a deep breath before turning the *Queen Maudie*'s key, feeling his confidence return when she roared into life without the slightest complaint, or even worse, smoke.

'Full steam ahead then,' he said, and with Winn happily perched on the box beside him, he pulled nervously and slowly back out into the traffic.

It may have been their full bellies, it may have been the repetitive rumble of the engine beneath them, but the next hour or two passed without incident or concern. The traffic on the river thinned somewhat, as did the buildings on the banks. At the start, in Wapping, it had been all warehouses and cranes, followed by the big, obvious landmarks, but now, in West London, it became more about houses, but not the sort the children knew. There didn't seem to be rows of terraces, simple two-up two-downs, these were glorious, four-storey town houses, some semi-detached, others standing proudly on their own. Noah found himself slack-jawed, wondering how anyone could ever afford such a thing? Did these people own banks or simply rob them? It seemed alien to him, even the football grounds out here seemed grander. Once they sailed under Putney Bridge, they saw Fulham's Stadium, Craven Cottage, perched on the riverbank to their right. Although there was no game playing, Noah could imagine the roar of the crowd.

A quick, stern warning toot from a passing tug soon pulled him from his daydream and forced him to concentrate once more.

Bridges loomed then passed: after Putney, there was Hammersmith, Barnes, Chiswick and Kew, with fewer big commercial boats around and more rowing boats appearing. The children mentally marked off the bridges, another landmark down, another step closer.

The approach to Kew Bridge had even brought a new landmark: one that Noah hadn't expected, in the shape of an island, sitting proudly in the middle of the river.

'Is that what I think it is?' he asked.

'Depends what you think it is,' said Big Col, deadpan. 'Cos it's not the Duchess' estate, you know.'

'Obviously,' Noah scoffed. 'I just didn't know there were islands in the Thames.'

Cue Clem and her encyclopaedic knowledge. 'There are nearly two hundred of them.'

The boys looked at her like she was mad.

'What? There are. Do you never listen in class? Honestly.'

Noah thought she must have been in different lessons to him. He concentrated in lessons. Sometimes.

'I think this must be Oliver's Island,' she went on, reaching for the map. 'SO many birds nest on there. Herons and geese and cormorants.'

But that wasn't the thing on Noah's mind. 'Which side do I stay on? Left or right?'

'Left,' Clem advised. 'Tide's not as high now, is it, so don't veer too close to shore.'

Noah did as he was told, Clem's wildlife lesson continuing on deaf ears as he tried to keep his focus purely on the river ahead, burning orange as the sun set. He had to get them there in one piece because he knew, KNEW that at the end of it, was the Duchess' estate and the animals' salvation. He'd even managed to force the thought of his mum and her certain anger from his mind.

Yes, she'd be cross, he thought, crosser than ever before, but surely she'd be proud as well. And as for Dad? Well, this would be the story he'd tell down the pub when he returned, never mind what he'd done on the battlefields.

Know what my lad did?

Saved animals from death. Single-handed.

Sailed the Maudie *down the Thames and back. Not a scratch on her or anything.*

Noah felt a glow fill him up. It would be all right. More than all right. Dad would be safe, and they'd fetch Winn from the Duchess the day war finished.

But just as the image seemed as real as it could possibly be, he was dragged back to the here and now.

'Here, Noah,' Clem called, from the bow of the boat. 'Look at that boat there. To the right. The little one.'

Noah tilted his cap back. There wasn't much to see. It was little more than a rowing boat to be honest, and as it was in no danger of crashing into them, he was ready to dismiss it.

'What about it?'

'Well, shouldn't there be someone onboard, given that it's drifting down river?'

Noah frowned. She was right; although the river was quieter it was still wide and fast-flowing. How had he not noticed that?

'Maybe they're having a sleep?' he offered weakly, but Clem was having none of it, putting one foot on *Maudie*'s rail to make herself as tall as Big Col.

'It's empty, I'm telling you. There is literally NO ONE onboard.'

But, unexpectedly, as soon as the words left her mouth, Clem realised she'd got it wrong. As above the bow of the rowing boat poked one, then two small heads, kitten heads with their fur stuck to them, making their eyes look as round and fearful as they could possibly be.

'Cats!' yelled Clem. 'Two of them. Look! They can't be more than a few weeks old.'

It was a bizarre sight, and it rather paralysed Noah, staring at them blindly instead of easing off the throttle.

'What are you doing?' shouted Clem. 'Slow down, will you?' Which was enough to engage Big Col into the conversation.

'Why? 'S not our problem, is it?'

'Neither were you or Delilah, but here you are.'

Big Col swore under his breath, then was nearly thrown off his feet when Noah eased off the throttle entirely. 'Watch it, you idiot!' he yelled. But Noah only had eyes for the rowing boat, plotting its course and feeling his heart race when he saw it approaching a sandbank laid bare by the lowering tide.

'It's going to run aground, look. They'll get stuck,' he shouted.

'Good,' huffed Big Col. 'Least they won't smash into another boat.'

'Yeah, but what about the kittens, you fool?' Noah said the last two words under his breath.

'Not much we can do about them, is there?'

'Not much we can do?' Noah felt his cheeks reddening. 'What sort of answer is that?

'Well, they're not ours, are they?'

'Neither's Samson and he's got the best seat on the flipping boat!!'

Noah looked to Clem for moral support, but surprisingly found her siding with Big Col.

'He's right, Noah. I don't know what we can do.'

'What? This boat has got reverse, you know?'

I know,' said Clem, 'but get too close to that sandbank and we'll end up stranded too. People passing might help a couple of cute kittens, but do you really think they'll get close enough to rescue three kids, two dogs, a donkey in a straw hat and a python?!'

Noah wanted to swear. Why did she have to do that? Be so sensible ALL THE TIME?!

'So that's it? We just sail on and do nothing?' he ranted. 'Then why even bother telling me about them?'

'Calm down, Noah, please.' Clem moved towards him, palms outstretched in peace, but Noah was in no mood to be pacified. He was fed up with people telling him he was wrong, that his boat was a rusty bathtub, and he was especially tired of people telling him his plans were rubbish.

He shut down *Maudie*'s engine, and slung aside his captain's mac and cap before marching to the boat's stern, tossing his vest and shirt behind him too.

'Noah, what are you doing??'

'The wrong thing, I expect,' he replied. 'As per usual.' And with that, his shorts hit the deck too, leaving him resplendent in a pair of underpants that had once been white.

And that was it. With a jump on to the stern's rail, he stood, like a grubby Tarzan of the Apes, before diving (less gracefully than he thought), deep into the Thames' embrace.

28

Reactions on board were mixed.

Big Col laughed, not quite believing what he'd seen, whereas Clem, while she might have wanted to bury her head in her hands in disbelief, chose not to. She was too worried.

'That boy belongs in the asylum,' hooted Big Col.

'If he's not careful he'll end up in the blooming morgue,' she replied.

'It's only a river.'

'Yes, and until we get to Teddington this river is tidal and has strong currents. You can't go swimming in the tidal part of the Thames. You just can't. It's too dangerous.'

'Poppycock,' sniffed Big Col. 'Look at it. Smooth as anything and the sun's been on it all day. It'll be like being in the bath.'

Clem chose to ignore him. She knew what she knew. Sun or otherwise, it could be cold under the surface, and the current could change in a second. It wasn't like Noah was a strong swimmer, or if he was he'd certainly kept unusually quiet about it.

She hung over the side of the boat and told him again and again to turn back. Not that he listened to her. But if *her* reaction was one of worry, then Winn's was frantic, trying to use Clem's leg as a ladder to find out where her master was.

'It's all right, Winn,' Clem said reassuringly, bending down to pet her. 'Noah's just gone for a little swim, that's all.' She wanted to tell her he was being a damned fool, but the dog was so much brighter than its owner, Clem was worried she would understand.

Either way, Winn was neither reassured nor silent, and scratched again at Clem's leg, whilst whimpering and crying.

'I know, I know,' said Clem. 'He doesn't listen to any of us.' Not that Noah could at the moment anyway, as his head was in and out of the water while he thrashed gracelessly closer to the sandbank.

The water was *not* as warm as he'd expected it to be; in fact it was freezing, and despite his exertions, his finger ends were already a little numb. But still, he could see the bank and the boat were getting closer, and as he finally made contact with the sandbank, he could hear the kittens crying for help.

But the sand? Well, it wasn't like being on the beach at Margate. It was thick and cloying, and he realised very quickly that if he stayed still on it for too long, then it started to grip and swallow first his ankles then his calves. If he panicked and paused further it'd be edging up his knees, and if that happened, it'd take something a lot stronger than two soggy kittens to get him out. So he ploughed on, ripping his leg from its clutches, not stopping until he gripped the side of the rowing boat and pulled himself, breathless, into its tiny bow. The mud let go with one last, reluctant slurp.

He must have looked a state, this boy in baggy Y-fronts, caked in mud and smelling none too pleasant, and the kittens were far from overjoyed at seeing him: one hissing venomously while the other hid fearfully under the bench.

'It's all right,' he whispered. 'Nothing's going to hurt you now.' But as he reached out, he was rebuffed with a swinging claw that might not inflict much damage, but still remained a shock. It was at odds with the kittens' appearance, as they were the very epitome of chocolate-box cute. Their eyes appeared way too big for their faces, whilst their fur, despite being sodden, still shone the most vibrant tiger orange.

'Noah!!' came a voice from the distance. 'Are you all right?' It was Clem. He turned and offered her a thumb, but looking back across at the boat he felt a little nervous. Once he calmed the kittens, he would still have to navigate both the sandbank and the current back to the *Queen Maudie*. He couldn't even try to row the boat back, as the oars were missing.

For now every attempt he made to befriend the kittens failed miserably. Eventually he tried a different tack, sitting on the floor of the boat, not moving or looking in their direction, until slowly, the more timid cat appeared from beneath the bench and gingerly approached his big toe, sniffing first, then batting it with its paw as if it were prey. Noah did nothing. Move too quickly and he risked scaring the kitten away, so he waited, and waited, only wiggling his toe back when he sensed the kitten wanted to play. A quick bat with its claw, followed by an energetic pounce and then the kitten ignored his foot, rubbing itself along the length of his calf, despite the mud caked there, until finally, it allowed itself to be stroked, nestling its soggy fur against Noah's chest and fingers, purring gently.

It was a victory, he knew that, but there was still the second cat to win round. But as he pondered how best to do that, the strangest thing happened; the spitting kitten retracted his claws and trotted up to Noah, demanding the same attention as his brother or sister.

It took Noah by surprise, and reinforced his opinion

of cats. They could be very cute of course, but unlike his beloved dog, they were contrary and fickle and troublesome. That said, he still couldn't leave them to starve, so he took a deep breath, stood tall inside the boat and worked out the best route back to his friends.

It was only then, that the flaw to his genius plan revealed itself.

How on earth was he going to swim while his hands were full with two, unpredictable kittens?

29

Noah avoided the worst of the quicksand by entering the water from the other end of the boat, where the bow met the river itself, but the second the kittens realised what was going on, they panicked, writhing and squirming so ferociously that Noah lost grip of them altogether and they were left to paddle for themselves. This increased their panic, one of them sliding under the water altogether, saved only by Noah's quick reactions as he scooped it back up, treading water to stay buoyant.

It didn't take long for Noah's lungs to burn from exertion, and this was before he'd even attempted to move. His hands were redundant as paddles, full as they were with kittens, which left him with just his legs. But if he tried to kick towards the boat, it was impossible to keep both his own head and the kittens above the water level. He felt trapped, helpless, and the others felt it too.

'What can we do?' asked Big Col, in an unprecedented display of sympathy. 'He can't swim like that.'

'Do you think we can get the boat closer to him?' Clem replied, scanning the water between them and the sandbank.

'I dunno. Doubt it. We'll run aground. And you know it might not just be sand under the surface. Might be rocks too.'

Clem doubted it, but shared his worry about getting stranded. The sun was setting now and the traffic on the river reduced to practically nought. If they did run aground, how would they get off, let alone lead all the animals safely to the Duchess. But as much as she wanted all the animals to be rescued, this was her best friend in the water and he urgently needed her help.

If Clem were concerned though, it was nothing compared to Noah's other true companion, because although Winn couldn't really see what was going on, she sensed, *knew*, that Noah needed her. So with every yard of run-up that the deck allowed her, she suddenly leaped into the river, front paws using the rail of the boat as a springboard. The effect was breathtaking as Winn cut through the darkening skies, soaring with such grace that it felt as if she would only hit the water when she landed beside her master. As she burst into the Thames with her customary belly flop, she cut it in two, ignoring any current or undertow that might dare to conspire against her. Within a minute she had reached Noah, and seeing her master flail and panic, she took the scruff of one kitten's neck between her jaws, before turning, and paddling her way back.

The effect on Noah was immediate. The kitten may not have weighed any more than a bag of sugar, but his hand, now free of the load, was able to paddle, and he turned on his side, one arm swimming furiously, the other keeping the second kitten just above the water.

'Keep going!' yelled Clem from the deck. 'Quick. Grab something we can use as a pole to fish him out,' she screamed to Big Col.

'Like what?'

'I don't know. Anything. And bring your fishing line and a basket or box, something like that?'

'What for?'

'Just do it!' she shouted firmly.

Big Col scuttled off, returning with a fishing rod, line and a battered old wicker basket that had held kindling for the stove.

'This do?'

'Fine, great. Now rig the line to the basket so we can winch the kittens up when they get here.'

Big Col didn't need telling twice and fashioned a hoist in time for Winn's return. The poor dog didn't look as spritely now as she had when she left the boat.

Quickly, down went the basket, and although Winn was

a dog, who wanted nothing but a simple life of walks, food, warmth and strokes, she knew immediately what to do. She dropped the kitten into the basket before turning to swim back for the other one.

Later, Noah would feel emotional about what happened in the water that day: the devotion his dog showed in saving him not once, but twice. Because by the time Winn returned, Noah was exhausted from battling the current, and close to giving up. The more he swam towards the boat, the further away it seemed to get. But as soon as Winn took that second kitten in her teeth, Noah banished those thoughts, and although he ached and burned with tiredness, he forced himself to swim behind his dog. If she hadn't given up, then neither could he.

Winn was swimming along with the current, not trying to battle through it. And it seemed to be working. After a while they were able to find a passage beyond the worst of the currents and make their way back to the boat, Clem and Col shouting encouragement all the way.

Noah refused to get out of the water before Winn was safely back onboard, using every last bit of energy he had to hoist her towards the outstretched arms of Big Col, as his own legs kicked below the surface. It was a struggle, and Winn didn't think much of being handled in such an undignified way, but finally, finally, everyone who entered the water, had exited it again, and everyone, whether they had been swimming or not, lay on the deck of *Queen Maudie*, panting with exhaustion or relief. All except the two kittens, who were already asleep, nuzzled deep into Winn's coat. The dog might not have liked it, but at that moment in time, she was too tired to do a single thing about it.

30

The sun finally gave up and hid below the horizon. There was no way they'd reach the Duchess' tonight. Big Col did not take it well.

'What do you mean we're going to have to stop for the night?' he moaned.

'Exactly that,' Clem replied in her firmest teacher voice. 'If you looked at the map, you'd see we're not even halfway there yet.'

'Why not?'

'For a number of reasons. Perhaps the boat hasn't been quite as fast as we expected . . .'

Noah flinched, expecting to be blamed for that.

'. . . plus, the river has been busy, and we've stopped twice, haven't we?'

'Well, I say we go on,' the big lad spat.

'Just as well you're not the captain then,' Noah interrupted. 'And anyway, why are you in such a rush? Do you *want* to be evacuated or something?'

'You would too, if you had a family like mine,' Big Col

muttered, but Noah didn't hear him, and he had his own reasons for stopping. Wanting to rest *Maudie*'s tired engine for one. 'In a while we're going to start hitting locks – there's a big one at Richmond, and I reckon three kids trying to get through it in the middle of the night might just draw attention from the lock keeper there, don't you?'

'Well, where are we going to sleep?'

'In the cabin. Unless you'd rather stay on deck?'

'No chance. Besides, Delilah needs to be warm, doesn't she?' And he stomped below deck, presumably Noah thought, to grab the best spot to bunk down.

'Any thoughts on where we could moor for the night?' he asked Clem, who was trying to read the map in the dark.

'Course I have,' she replied. 'Old Deer Park. It should be coming up on our left.'

She wasn't wrong either, as despite the absence of light, they could still make out a vast rolling meadow, beside a bank that would be simple to moor against.

'I hope the deer here aren't old,' Noah joked. 'Because they're the only ones that Frank and Winn would probably bother chasing.'

'Oh, I think they've had enough excitement for today,' Clem added, before folding the map precisely and carefully. 'Now let's get to land before anything else goes wrong.'

Noah didn't need telling twice, feeling tension in every

part of his body until *Queen Maudie* was secured and he could turn off the engine for the night.

It wasn't especially cold on the riverbank once they'd disembarked, but the day *had* been warm, and it had spoilt them. Now that the sun had gone, they missed it and felt keenly the disappointment of not being as far along as they should be. Their mission was still so far from complete.

Noah was the coldest of them all. He still hadn't shaken off the effects of his dip, and while Winn had the bravery to edge to the very fringes of the fire they'd lit on the bank, Noah liked the hairs on his legs to go unsinged. His tiredness made his thoughts messy and difficult to order, and as a result he felt an array of difficult emotions: confusion, doubt, loneliness, as well as a lingering, stomach-churning fear that he had never experienced before in his life. Fear that he couldn't possibly succeed in his plan, fear that he had embroiled others due to his bravado, but most . importantly, fear for what would happen to Dad if he fell short. This took him to a place that was as dark as his surroundings, and he sought to distract himself by picking up the last of the fish, and chewing slowly, before offering it to one of the kittens. Again Big Col had not let them down, setting about his fishing task with gusto. The only time he had shown any sense of irritation was when anyone offered to help.

'Do I look like I need a hand?' he said, affronted, when Clem offered.

'Clearly not. I just thought if you taught me, then we could all eat even quicker.'

'Yeah well, think again,' he'd replied, before mumbling something derogatory that Clem thankfully didn't hear.

He was right though, single-handedly delivering fish after fish with startling regularity. Noah watched with irritation as well as deep gratitude.

'What do you think your mum will be doing now?' he asked Clem.

'I don't like to think about it,' she replied. 'She'll probably have gone to the police. What about yours?'

'Same. Plus pacing, swearing and cursing.'

'We shouldn't have done it, should we?' Clem sighed. 'Or we should at least have left a note, so they didn't worry.'

It was hard to argue with that. But Noah tried anyway, despite the horrid images of a distressed Mum looping in his mind. 'Could we have managed that? Really? They'd probably have followed us to Battersea and caught us, seen the dogs were still alive, had them put down and THEN given us the rollicking of our lives.'

'It'll be nothing compared to the one we get when we finally go home.'

Noah shuddered. Especially as Dad wouldn't be there.

He always managed to dampen Mum's fire when it was raging at its most savage. 'What will *your* mum be doing?' he asked Big Col.

'Mum probably won't have realised I'm not there. Not if there's still gin in the bottle.' He said the last bit quietly, without looking up, but Noah and Clem heard it all the same.

Big Col picked at the bones of a fish before letting a kitten nibble his fingers.

'We should give them names,' he said.

'Who?'

'The kittens, idiot.'

Noah thought about it. 'Wonder what their owners called them.'

'I doubt they called them anything,' said Clem, 'if they abandoned them in a flipping boat.'

'No owners. Not even any parents,' mused Big Col.

'Must have been an immaculate conception,' laughed Clem, which sparked Noah's imagination.

'Well, that makes naming them easy,' he said. 'That one's Joseph, and the other's Mary.'

They all laughed.

'But we haven't checked what sex they are, have we?' said Clem.

'Does it matter? It's not like they're staying with us. We

just have to keep them safe and fed until the Duchess takes them in.'

'If we ever get there,' said Big Col.

'*When* we get there,' corrected Noah, making himself say it. 'There is no if.'

But did he believe that? Not as much as he wanted to, but it *had* been the longest and most tiring of days.

'We'd better put the fire out before it attracts attention,' Clem said.

'What, from bombers or the police?' Big Col asked.

'Either. Both. I don't have the energy to run from anyone right now.'

They slept. Fitfully, though they had done their utmost to make the cabin feel as cosy as they could. The stove glowed all night, to keep Delilah warm rather than them, though the dogs took advantage too, stretching out like they were by the hearth at home. Noah watched as Frank laid his aged, grey muzzle on Winn's flank, noting how rapidly the dachshund's ribs rose and fell in comparison, like even resting was tiring for him. Noah worried about the little dog. He may not have been his, but he still cared for him, and could only hope against hope, that this journey wouldn't be too much for his ageing bones to cope with.

He could see it was on Clem's mind too: she glanced in

pity at Frank while she laid out old, musty blankets to lie on and folded the oversized mac into a pillow for Noah, not that he would accept it, slipping it by her blanket while she wrestled with an old tin of powdered milk for the kittens.

'Do you think this will be all right for them?' he asked. It looked old, the tin rusted and the lid reluctant to let them inside, as if in warning.

'We don't have any choice,' Clem replied. 'If we want them to sleep we need their bellies to be full. I don't think I could entertain a hungry kitten all night, could you?'

Noah shuddered at the thought and fetched the water from Dad's cannister, shocked as he saw how little was left inside it.

'We're going to be out of water by tomorrow,' he said grimly, though he didn't ration it for the poor kittens. He watched as they drained every drop from the bowl, and if he needed evidence that he was doing the right thing, here it was in front of him. It made him take a walk outside, to check on Samson, and found him in a happy mood, head thrown back in joy as he saw the boy approach. The joy turned to ecstasy as Noah's fingers scratched behind the donkey's ears, feeling Samson push his neck further into his hands, as if telling him to press harder. How could anyone abandon such a beautiful animal? Noah thought to himself, and Samson seemed to read his mind, braying softly in agreement, before rubbing his head against the boy's face with clumsy affection.

By the time he eventually left Samson and padded inside, the kittens had settled, balled up together against the warmth of Frank's belly, and the sight of it made the pressure of expectation build in him again. They had a long way to go, and he couldn't let any of them down, whether they were animal or human. When he slept, finally, he dreamed of wrong turns and dead ends: and of serpents rising from the Thames and threatening to swallow them whole.

Little wonder then, that he was already awake when Samson decided to do his finest cockerel impression, braying incessantly as the sun rose. As alarm clocks went, it was effective, but very annoying.

'Put a cork in it, will you?' Big Col yelled. Even Delilah seemed annoyed, tail thrashing in her sack.

Noah made himself see it differently, positively, pulling himself to his feet and rubbing the sleep from his eyes.

''S'perfect,' he said.

'Are you soft in the head?'

'Not a bit. Means we can get moving while the river's quiet.'

'Cos no one else is stupid enough to be up yet.'

'Yes, but think about it. By now my mum, Clem's too, they'll definitely have been to the police. They'll be looking for us, and if they realise the boat's gone too, well, it won't take long till they're on to us.'

Clem didn't like what she was hearing, but she had another thing on her mind too. A rather important thing. 'We are going to have to wait a while though, Noah.'

'Why?'

'Low tide,' she replied flatly. 'Look. Set off now and we'll run aground.'

Noah could have kicked himself. Why hadn't he thought of that? He was the sailor round here allegedly, but had left himself wide open to abuse from Big Col, which came quickly.

'Call yourself Captain?' he ranted. 'You are absolutely clueless. If we listen to you, we'll sink before the day's out.'

Fortunately, Clem turned the argument around.

'This means you can go back to sleep though, doesn't it? Without the engine keeping you awake. And while you do that, me and Noah can tend to Samson, then walk the dogs, tire them out so we can make better progress once the waters rise again.'

Big Col moaned and tutted, but wasn't going to turn down the chance of more sleep, which left Clem to pull Noah and the dogs out into the early dawn sunlight.

It wasn't seven o'clock yet, but there was already power in the sun, the kind that made it not only hot, but sticky.

Noah was struggling to remember when the clouds had last emptied, but knew it couldn't be long till it not only rained, but poured.

'You hungry?' he asked.

'Not for fish. Not at this time.'

Clem had a point, so they walked slowly around the park, enjoying the dogs' innocence as they smelled every bush and tree they passed. They enjoyed the absence of Big Col's complaints even more, Noah walking on with Winn, when Frank's legs chose to take him no further.

By the time he reached *Queen Maudie* again, he was relieved to see that the water levels had risen, along with Big Col, whose mood was just about bearable. 'Where've you been?' he asked.

'Tea with the Queen,' Noah replied. 'She sends her regards.'

'I think you should have your disguise on if we're going to get going.' Clem smiled, passing him his dad's mac. The thought of the mac's heavy material against his already clammy arms made Noah feel uncomfortable, and his face showed it.

'Or, I could drive for a while?' Clem added, perching the hat on her head. Noah rammed his arms speedily into the coat. This was his dad's boat, which meant no one was captain apart from him.

But as his skin stuck to the material, and his scalp sweated beneath the retrieved cap, he realised it might not just be him overheating soon. He worried *Queen Maudie* would soon be protesting beneath his feet again, her belly groaning and straining.

'Do you think you could work out exactly how many miles it is to Windsor?' he asked, without trying to sound perturbed.

'I thought you didn't want details, just an adventure.'

'Well, maybe I've changed my mind.'

Clem smiled. 'I can try,' she replied, mind already whirring, but it will be a guess at best. Sorry.'

Noah felt his throat tighten. Guessing, when they were in a boat that was already struggling, felt like one heck of a gamble, and unless they learned how to walk on water, he doubted they would cover the remaining distance in the way they were all expecting.

31

Noah was wracked with nerves, his grip on the barely opened throttle so tight that it felt like the engine wasn't even engaged. They seemed to bob on the water rather than part it.

'Are you planning on getting us there today?' Big Col demanded.

'Course I am.'

'Well, you might think about speeding up a bit then. There's people on the bank *walking* quicker than us.'

Noah looked to land and saw Big Col was right. There were a couple of young lads taking great delight in not only their own speed, but the *Maudie*'s lack of it. Noah pulled his cap down lower as his cheeks burned.

'Well?' Big Col prompted. 'Are you going to do something about it?'

'Not if we're going to hit Richmond Weir at the right time,' said Clem, swooping to Noah's rescue.

'Richmond *what*?'

'*Weir,*' she went on. 'Because we're getting to the end of the tidal part of the Thames.'

Big Col shrugged ignorantly.

'So, they installed a set of gates over the river, which close to monitor the water levels.'

'It's like being back in school!' he moaned.

'Which *means,*' Clem said, exasperated, 'that the gates are only open around two hours either side of high tide. What Noah is doing, is timing it so we hit Richmond when the gates are open. Time it wrong, and we'd have to go through the lock.'

'And what's the problem with that?'

'Well, it may be busy, for starters, which would slow us down. Plus the lock keeper might ask too many questions about why we don't have an adult with us. Not everyone's going to be as drunk as Tipsy Nev.'

That seemed to shut up Big Col for a while, and bought Noah more time to ease *Maudie* there, rather than risk her overheating so early in the day. They passed Isleworth Ait, Clem naming birds as they circled and landed, and as the island fell behind them, they caught their first glance of Richmond Lock and Weir, Noah's chest filling with joy when he saw that Clem was right and the barriers stood open, allowing them to flow through. He even left the throttle open slightly, paranoid that as they approached, the gates would fall and trap them, slicing Dad's beloved boat in two. Only when the bridge was behind them, did Noah truly relax, wiping the sweat that had pooled beneath his captain's hat.

Clem could see the nerves he was carrying.

'You know, at some point, you're going to have to tell Big Col the truth,' she said.

'About what?'

'About the fact that the boat isn't up to the job. I mean, there will be other locks we can use as an excuse to slow down, but you have to be honest, we're crawling along here and it's already taken longer than we thought!'

That was it. The mixture of heat and nerves and pressure was too much for Noah.

'Is there somewhere else you both urgently need to be?' he spat. 'Would you rather be on that chuffing train being sent to God knows where for God knows how long? Cos if you would, then leave Frank and Delilah with me and I'll drop you on the bank.'

'For goodness' sake, Noah, why are you so defensive? I *know* this isn't a racing car, but look at what's happening. We've not been sailing an hour and listen to the noise it's making? We were going much faster yesterday. That's all

I'm saying. So if you'd rather *I* left, then I will. Me AND Frank.' She made to make a dramatic turn, before realising she had more to say.

'But don't forget you need me, Noah. You might not realise it, and you certainly won't admit it, but you do. You might *think* you have all these big ideas, but it's me, it's always *me* that makes them actually *work*. So if I leave now, it's on your head. You'll either be shipwrecked, capsized or arrested by the time the day is out.'

Her words were an arrow to Noah, puncturing him immediately. And he knew deep down that she was right.

'You know I don't want that,' he garbled, before she could move any further. 'It's just . . .' he checked over his shoulder to make sure they were alone. Aside from two dogs, two kittens and a behatted donkey eyeing them through the window, they definitely were. '. . . well, you're right. I think she *is* going to blow again. Listen to her. You can almost hear her moaning.'

Clem listened, but heard nothing except the same guttural roar that had filled her ears since they first started her up.

'Do you think there's anything you can do to fix it?'

'Only by giving her continuous rests. She's overheating. Can't remember the last time we took her this far.'

'She's not actually alive, Noah.'

Noah covered his ears in mock horror. 'Shut up!' he hissed. 'If she hears you she'll really throw a tantrum.'

But Clem's mind was already whirring, forming contingency plans for how to invent rest periods whilst keeping Big Col calm, but also what they would do when the boat did give up entirely.

'I know what you're doing,' Noah sighed. 'You're imagining how you're going to dig me out of whatever's going to happen. Even though it hasn't happened yet.'

'Somebody's got to,' she smiled, her voice disappearing beneath *Maudie*'s growl. But it didn't matter that Noah couldn't hear. He was thinking too, trying to work out what Dad did whenever the boat overheated. He wouldn't have just pulled over and waited for it to cool. That wasn't his way at all. Dad would've sorted it. So why couldn't he do that too? He was made of the same stuff, wasn't he?

But no matter how hard he thought, inspiration was nowhere to be found.

All he knew was they couldn't pull over yet, not without a mutiny from their most volatile crew member (and his snake). So, tentatively, Noah made them chug pathetically onwards, much to the *Maudie*'s throaty disgust.

Lord, it was hot. By early afternoon there was no air. It felt like they were sailing down the Nile, not on the outskirts of

Twickenham. Their clothes stuck to them, tongues lolled from mouths, even Samson was still. The only movement the occasional whip of his tail to remove a particularly obstinate fly. They didn't even get excited by the sight of Eel Pie Island to their right. Clem tried to enthuse them, telling of the slimy pie served there in the nineteenth century that gave it its name, but despite their hunger, the boys didn't respond or show interest.

The water cannister had been empty since lunchtime, though it didn't stop Frank shuffling to it every ten minutes to see if anyone had mysteriously refilled it. His face every time he found it empty was one of disgust and despair.

With the heavy mac and hat on the heat addled Noah's brain, his worries grating against each other, new ones fighting for space too. The river was slightly quieter today, as Central London shrank slowly behind them, but he remained standing on the box, in full captain's attire. He couldn't be sure if his disguise was fooling anyone though, as every vessel that passed slowed down to stare. First at the donkey, then at the dogs who inevitably barked and hollered, whilst the kittens walked the deck's rail like a couple of drunken trapeze artists. Then the spectators turned their attention to the driver, and Noah would turn his collar higher, pull his cap lower, and feel the sweat glide down his back.

'Do they realise we're kids?' Noah asked Clem, each and every time it happened.

'Who knows? It didn't trouble them enough to stop us, did it?'

'Suppose not.' But in his mind he fretted that they were already planning to find the nearest bobby and report what they'd seen.

Noah scanned the horizon, a haze hugging the surface of the river, but he could still make out a copse of trees overhanging the water on the northern bank, and movement and noise coming from them. As they neared, Noah spotted what was going on: there was a rope swing dangling from one of the branches, much to the delight of a gaggle of children about their age, who were plunging again and again into the coolness of the river.

Noah felt envy instantly, but Clem saw an opportunity. One that would give the boat some respite.

'You look *so* hot, Big Col,' she said. It was true; the boy had spent half the morning in the overheated cabin with his snake and was now slumped over the side of the boat sweating heavily beneath Delilah's embrace.

'You really are *smart*, aren't you?' he replied sarcastically.

'Gosh, imagine how great it would be if we could stop, even for a few minutes, to do what they're doing.'

'I thought you said it was dangerous to swim in the Thames.'

'No, that was the tidal bit. There's no current here. Just cool water for swimming in.'

Clem waited and watched, sighing every few seconds, noticing how Big Col couldn't take his eyes off the children now. By the time the boat was fifty yards from them, it was too much to bear.

'I reckon we should stop and swim,' he announced suddenly. 'Not for long. Just to take the edge off. Besides, I can see the dogs are hot too.'

'Oh, I don't think we can do that, not when we've been making such slow progress,' Clem said, mock innocently. 'Besides, what would we do with Delilah and the kittens?'

'Delilah won't mind being in the cabin keeping warm. And as long as she's in her sack, then the kittens can be in there too.'

Noah looked at Big Col, aghast that he wanted to stop after moaning so loudly about their progress, but as he went to speak, Clem dug him in the ribs.

'Say nothing,' she whispered. 'We can rest the boat without him realising it was his idea.'

Noah did as he was told, pulling over where Big Col

told him to, killing the engine gratefully as Clem moored the boat in the shade by the rope swing.

Their arrival was greeted with hilarity and intrigue, especially when Samson was spotted. The local children, of course, wanted to know everything about what the threesome were doing, so Noah, getting carried away, concocted the shaggiest dog story he could. It didn't matter that not all of it was true.

'We're runaways,' he bragged. 'From our parents, the police AND the Nazis.'

None of them believed him, which suited Noah, but he allowed them to stroke Samson as he fed himself grass on the bank, and before long they all found themselves in the river, thrashing and ducking and plunging with such delight that they forgot everything else.

It was like the war hadn't even started, they were children again, without the pressures of saving animals or their dad's boats. They played until they were tired, saying goodbye to the others before drying themselves on the deck.

'Do you think the rest will have done *Maudie* good?' Clem whispered once they were dressed and casting off.

'Can't have done any harm,' Noah said, feeling the paranoia return as he gradually opened the throttle and they spluttered from the bank.

But as it turned out, the boat was for once the least of their problems, as suddenly, from nowhere, Noah heard a voice behind him. It didn't belong to any of his crewmates, and the tone of the question made him jump.

'Afternoon, all. And where do you think you're going then?'

32

Noah's instinct was to accelerate away. Surely only one type of person asked a question like that, and if the police *had* tracked them down, then he wasn't going to surrender peacefully or quickly. If they wanted him to go home without achieving his mission, then they'd have to handcuff him and drag him there kicking and screaming.

But before he accelerated, he looked to who had spoken and saw it wasn't a policeman at all. It was a man who had pulled up alongside in a small boat. He was about Noah's dad's age, with a threadbare beard and a skipper's hat of his own, grubby and frayed, a good three sizes too small. It sat at a curled angle on his head, like a comma on a page, and although the mouth below the hat was smiling, the eyes were not. They were furtive, darting, surveying everything onboard, like the man was totting up what it was all worth.

'I said, where you all going on your own then?' he asked again, revealing fewer teeth than expected. The ones that still sat in his gums seemed to be hanging on for dear life.

'Oh, you know, nowhere special,' Noah replied without lifting his head. He kept his voice low and slow but succeeded merely in sounding like the boy he was.

'Youngest skipper I've ever seen.'

'Yeah, well my dad, he's . . .' But the answer wouldn't come.

'Sleeping downstairs,' Clem suddenly offered.

'Sleeping? Mid-afternoon? Been on the drink already?' The man laughed.

'No, he's just unwell. He's . . .'

At that moment Big Col made an appearance, swaggering up with Delilah coiled around his upper body and three dead fish in his grasp. The man stumbled backwards in his boat, eyes wide and unblinking.

'He's eaten a dodgy fish,' Clem said quickly, using Big Col's catch as her inspiration.

Big Col, unaware of the situation, saw only a slight on his fishing skills.

'Whose fish are dodgy? And who's taken sick?' He couldn't work it out. Noah was standing right there, at the wheel like he always was. And, anyway, there was nothing wrong with anything *he'd* caught. Every single fish had practically jumped straight from the line into the pan!

'You know?' Clem said, turning her back to the man so he couldn't see her eyes, imploring Big Col to play along.

'Noah's dad. The only reason Noah's driving is his dad's having a lie-down. Isn't that right?'

But the boy wasn't great at picking up signals: he was all sledgehammer and no subtlety.

The man however, was no longer interested in a queasy dad. Now he had recovered his balance, he only had eyes for Delilah and probably the money she would make him if she happened to find her way into his possession. Any thoughts he might have had though about wrestling her from the boy were soon squashed by Delilah herself, who without warning, lurched towards the man, fangs extended, a long, sly hiss slithering off her tongue.

'You need to control that thing!' the man said, clearly terrified. 'Put it in a cage or something.'

Normally, Clem would correct the lunacy of his statement: that bars would do little to contain a python, but Delilah answered herself. Another lurch forwards, a ferocious one this time, that almost pulled Big Col off his feet. It was a reminder, and a scary one at that, of the raw power she held. He might have been on the relative safety of his own boat, but the man had seen enough.

'I don't know what you lot are up to, but you're clearly trouble. Especially you!' he spat, though it was unclear if his words were pointed at Big Col, or Delilah. 'You want to be careful, though,' he added, 'threatening a fellow sailor with a snake. Things like that have a way of backfiring. So I'd watch your flipping back if I were you.' Except he didn't say flipping, he said something ruder, before opening his engine and moving off.

'Well, that worked,' sighed Noah in relief. 'Even if you didn't mean it to.'

'Why were you on about your dad? ' said Big Col.

Noah thought about explaining, but he was hot, and he was tired, and he was trying not to get distracted by the idle threats of a drunken fisherman. He had to keep his mind on the mission in hand: sail the boat to the Duchess'. Deposit the pets safe and sound. Don't blow the boat's engine up. And don't get arrested. If he could manage that as well as not being eaten by a python, it would be a job well done.

33

'Why are you slowing down AGAIN! We'll be going backwards soon, and I've already seen Richmond once today!' yelled Big Col. He yelled something similar, on a number of occasions.

'I thought I saw a heron,' would be the reply from Noah. Or kingfisher, or otter.

Noah did nothing but fret and worry about the state of *Queen Maudie*'s engine and went as slowly as he could to keep her temperature down.

There were other excuses on offer too, thankfully.

The next lock, at Teddington, proved a lifesaver in more than one way, for as they waited for the water levels to even, Clem spotted a tap on the side of the keeper's house, and bundled on to the bank to fill as many bottles and cans as she could find. As she busied herself, *Queen Maudie* rested, welcoming the minutes on offer, until the lock gates could be opened.

But as they spluttered forward into the lock, with Big

Col pushing them closed behind them, they hit a new problem. The prying eyes of the man in charge of it.

'Bit young to be sailing a vessel like this, aren't you?' he said suspiciously.

Their feeble retelling of the '*ill father below deck*' story was met with a raised eyebrow and more questions, especially about Samson.

'Have you not heard about what they're doing to animals?' Noah said. He didn't have to act to put emotion in his voice. 'Killing them. Thousands of them. All cos of bloomin' Hitler. But my dad's got a brother, out Windsor way, with a field. I mean, it wouldn't be fair to put a healthy beast like this to sleep, would it?'

The man looked momentarily sympathetic. 'That's all well and good,' he said, 'but young uns like you shouldn't be left in charge of a boat like this.'

'We're not. Not really. Dad'll be up in no time.'

The lock keeper pulled at his beard and shook his head in doubt, but as he was about to demand again to talk to the responsible adult, he was interrupted by a loud tuneless horn from behind them. As they turned, Noah saw a boat much bigger than their own, manned by men in soldiers' uniforms. His first instinct was to check for his own dad there, but then realised it was foolish, as an officer yelled over them.

'Can you get a move on?' he demanded. 'We've

important cargo to get to Reading by end of day. We've no time for idle chat.'

He spoke with an authority that exceeded that of the lock keeper and everyone knew it, especially the lock keeper himself.

'I've some stupid children here, with no adult on board. Can you back up so they can reverse out?' he stammered.

'Our boat don't work in reverse,' Noah blurted.

The lock keeper looked appalled, but not as appalled as the soldier on the boat.

'We haven't the time for this!' he roared. 'For pity's sake, let them through so we can be on our way. Do you hear me?'

'Right,' the lock keeper blustered, throwing Noah the meanest of looks.

Picking up his wrench he turned to the mechanisms, spinning his tool so quickly that his arm seemed almost to blur.

Almost instantly, the children felt the difference. The water around them seemed to drop and the *Maudie* began to drop with it. It was a strange feeling, unsettling, yet the lock keeper didn't look concerned, only angry, muttering under his breath for the next four minutes until the water level on the other side of the lock was identical to their own.

Pushing the gates open, he offered them a final, parting shot.

'Get out of my sight, quickly. And don't be thinking you can come back through my lock without an adult at the wheel, do you hear me?'

Clem thanked the man and told him that she was sure their dad would be well again by then.

'You heard the gentleman, Noah,' she went on. 'Let's go.'

So Noah did, though he knew, as the soldiers' boat breezed past them minutes later, that they had had not one, but two lucky escapes in a very short amount of time.

The episode left them rattled, the relaxation of the swim entirely forgotten, and after a short while, Noah was almost pleased that Frank and Winn started to demand another break in their journey.

The *Queen Maudie* was not a big boat, far from it: the dogs had grown tired of its confines and began to whine. There wasn't enough of interest left to sniff. They wanted to breathe in other animals, to cover and mark their scents, as well as run and chase and hide in the long grasses that lined the riverbank.

'We will stop soon, I promise,' Noah told Winn repeatedly, but when that promise wasn't kept quickly enough, the dog took matters into her own paws, and with a run-up, leaped effortlessly over the edge of *Maudie*'s rail, into the cooling water of the river.

The splash was a huge one, and any wildlife in the vicinity soon turned and fled. Winn barked her pleasure all the way to the riverbank.

Frank, back on deck, was furious that his friend had jumped ship without him, but no matter how hard he tried, there was no way his little, arthritic legs were going to clear the rail.

Instead, he looked at Clem with pleading eyes and a tilted head.

'Frank, if you think I'm throwing you into the river, you've another think coming. You can't even swim the length of the bath without wheezing.'

Frank barked his feeble disagreement.

'The dogs need a run,' Noah said, trying to sound disappointed despite knowing a break was exactly what *Maudie* needed too. 'Winn's made that clear. And if we don't do the same for Frank, then he'll start protesting all over the deck.'

'All right. I think we must be near Hampton Court now. Maybe those fields there are part of the grounds, it's hard to know for sure.'

'Doesn't matter,' Noah replied. 'Any field is good enough to wear them out a bit. Let them do their business.'

Big Col didn't like it, of course, but he also didn't like the thought of watching his every step for whatever gift the stupid Nazi dog might leave on deck either. So he didn't complain quite as loudly as normal, choosing an icy glare and a simmering rage instead. Noah knew he was cross about it, but at that moment, he really didn't care.

As much as Noah wanted to reach Windsor as quickly as possible, he was ready for the break. His hands ached from holding the juddering wheel of the boat, and it was a blessed relief for his ears not to be battered by the protesting engine.

But there was one thing he couldn't escape, and that was his exhaustion.

It might have been nearing teatime now, but it felt like midnight to Noah. After tying the boat up securely against the bank, he tried to relax with a quick paddle, which was fine, but as soon as he stood, his bones felt heavy once more.

'Why am I so flipping tired?' he moaned at Clem, after gingerly leading Samson on to dry land.

'I can't think why. It's not been a busy couple of days, has it?' she replied with a smile, before watching Samson try to adapt to a different type of terrain. 'Do donkeys get seasick?'

It obviously wasn't a question she'd considered before,

but if she had to hazard a guess, she'd say yes. For Samson seemed to be weaving drunkenly, each of his four legs quivering, trying to work out why the earth suddenly felt different under his hooves. Clem also didn't know if donkeys were prone to vomiting, but knew she didn't want to be too close if they were.

'We don't really know a single thing about him, do we?' she sighed.

'Apart from his name and his terrible taste in headwear, no,' replied Noah.

'I mean, who would just abandon an animal like that? What if we hadn't brought him along. What would've happened to him?' She thought about it a while. 'I know people will say it's only an *animal*, but he still deserves a decent life, doesn't he? Just like we do.'

Noah nodded and the two friends sat with their elbows on their knees watching the donkey from the shade. Once the beast shook off his sea legs, his movements became much more energetic. Winn and Frank, who were in their element exploring the riverbank, started circling Samson playfully, yapping an invitation for him to chase them, darting between his legs, making him perform a clumsy dance that made the children laugh. Frank looked like a puppy again, which made Clem teary.

The play didn't stop there, and within minutes Samson

and the dogs were running laps around the field, chasing, howling and braying with excitement. The kittens tried to join in too, ploughing through the long grass and comically failing to keep up with their older friends. It didn't put them off though or stop them from trying to hitch a ride on old Samson's tail, their claws clinging on for a second or two before he swept them back to the floor for another try.

Samson was a truly strong beast. His legs propelled him at great speed and there was incredible power in his hind quarters. Irritated by an itch after running so much in the heat, he backed himself into a tree to scratch, and despite it being no mere sapling, the trunk bent and swayed under his power.

'You think he used to pull a cart?' asked Clem.

'I think it was more likely one of those new tanks they've built for the war.'

At that moment, as if he'd heard, Samson cantered over to an apple tree, delivering a kick with his rear legs that would have astounded the karate masters of the Far East.

The tree shook and shuddered before relinquishing (much to the delight of the other animals) almost every apple that clung to its branches. They rained down to the floor and Winn and Frank fell on the bounty with glee.

And Noah and Clem? All they did was sit, and watch in silence, recording every moment in their minds, their hearts swelling with both pride and resolve. Pride that they had done the right thing in saving these wonderful animals, and resolve that now they had come so far, they would never give up. Not until their fight had been won.

34

They ate, grateful to Samson for putting a little bit of variety on the menu.

They were thankful for Big Col's fish of course, but as this wasn't their first serving of the day, the foraged apples slid down a treat, and the donkey practically shuddered with delight at the neck scratches he received from Noah as they digested their meal. Samson's discovery had inspired Clem too, and she scampered into the nearest hedgerows to Noah's bemusement.

'She probably needs the lav,' laughed Big Col, only for him to eat his words when she returned with handfuls of the sweetest, ripe berries.

'I wouldn't have thought of it if it wasn't for Samson,' and she offered the donkey one, which he sniffed at, nibbled, then sneezed out in disgust.

It was amazing what a full belly could do to improve the outlook. The berries managed to be both sweet and tangy, and the juice in them made them momentarily forget that they would soon be out of clean water to drink. It was enough to allow them to sit a while and reflect.

'We should plough on,' Noah said eventually. He could see though that tiredness was setting in, most of the troupe looked exhausted. The kittens were the only exception: they seemed to want to do nothing but play. It may have been their increasing familiarity with the children, but they were definitely showing a more mischievous side to their personalities: one that was difficult to control.

As Big Col reluctantly made to stand, one of them launched himself at his backside, grabbing on to his shorts and making the boy recoil so violently it was clear that its claws had made contact with flesh. It would've been comical had Big Col not been so angry, swinging his hips from side to side as the kitten hung on for grim death. Finally dislodging the cat didn't help either, as the second one saw this as their opportunity to join in the fun.

'For Pete's sake!' screamed Big Col, his face such a collage of scarlet and crimson anger that Clem and Noah felt compelled for their own safety, as well as the kittens', to help. Not that they did much good. It merely stirred the devil up in the kittens and they skittered around the bank, avoiding every attempt to round them up. Not even the lure of the fish bones was enough to bring them under control. By the time they were, finally, back in hand, all three of the children were saturated with sweat.

Noah had a thought. Big Col actually said it out loud.

'Are we really going to take these blasted cats all the way with us?'

'We don't have a choice, do we?' Noah replied. 'They're just babies.'

'They're a flipping nuisance, and unless you can control them, it's going to be a nightmare, you mark my words.'

'It won't be that bad,' Noah said, though he didn't believe it after what he'd just experienced. 'Anyway, it can't be that far now.'

'How far?' It was clear Big Col wanted answers and straight-talking, so Noah did what he always did when facts were needed, he looked to Clem, who sighed before making some mental calculations.

'Hard to say exactly . . .' she pondered.

'Why is it hard?' said Big Col.

'Because the boat's going slower than I expected . . .' Noah glared at that. 'And I don't have a ruler to measure the exact route, and even if I did, we know where Windsor is on the map, but not the Duchess' estate.'

The colour in Big Col's face escalated from livid to

volcanic, despite the fact that he already knew this. 'This isn't going to work,' he ranted. 'Not when we don't even really know where she lives.'

'Not in terms of the map, we don't,' Noah interjected. 'But we all agreed Windsor was the most likely place. As we get closer, there'll be people we can ask.'

'What? Like policemen? Why don't we just turn ourselves in now, eh?'

'Why don't you just clear off now instead?' Noah roared back. 'Do us all a favour!'

He looked to Clem for support, but didn't get it.

'Calm down, both of you!' she said, one palm pointing peacefully at each of them. 'This is getting us nowhere. NOWHERE. What we need to do is not argue. Split up, and we're useless. We may as well all turn back. But stick together – and well, there's nothing we can't do, and nowhere we can't reach.'

She turned to Noah. 'You're the ideas man.' Big Col coughed sarcastically. 'All right, they might be rough and ready sometimes, but more often than not, there are diamonds there that just need a bit of polishing, that's all. And as for you . . .' she turned to Big Col as Noah crossed his arms, defying her to find something positive to say. 'If it wasn't for your fishing skills, well, we'd be even grumpier than we are now. You might not like it, but we all need each other. And there's a big enough war going on elsewhere without you two adding to the hostilities!'

Clem stopped and waited. She didn't want to resort to banging their heads together, but if it came to it, then she'd blooming well try.

'I'm not shaking his hand,' was the best Big Col could muster.

'Suits me,' replied Noah, and after slapping Samson's rump gently, he led the way back onboard. The others followed, Frank as always huffing and puffing at the rear.

Noah didn't hesitate to resume captain duties, while Big Col returned Delilah to the warmth of the cabin. And Clem? She breathed a sigh of relief, and allowed herself a moment of respite, fussing Frank as he muzzled her legs affectionately.

Back behind the wheel Noah was not as relaxed, because from the second he powered up *Maudie*'s engine, he knew something was wrong. Seriously wrong this time. For starters, the engine didn't catch first time. Instead, there was a short sharp yelp, a noise Noah hadn't heard before, whether on this journey or any other. And so he had no idea how Dad would cope with it. Open the choke and try again? Or wait a minute for fear of flooding the engine?

Out of panic, he tried the engine again and again, until finally, finally, it caught. But it wasn't right. It was pained, panting almost, and it didn't improve as they started to edge down the river. He could see Clem watching him, concern etched on her face but he tried to ignore it. In fact he ignored everything, concentrating only on the boat and willing it along. He didn't so much as look up when Clem pointed out Hampton Court Palace and started trying to tell him and Big Col all about Henry VIII and his six wives.

The next twenty minutes were tortuous. Noah felt his panic and temperature rise, so much so that he wondered if he was coming down with something. His body ached from the tension he was holding in his muscles and then his other senses started to trick him too. His head throbbed, his fingers tingled, but most weirdly he started to smell burning, like his insides had caught fire.

He tried to shrug it off, to tell himself not to be so silly, but the smell would not go away, in fact it got worse, so bad that it wasn't just him who could smell it.

'What is that stink?' grunted Big Col, appearing for a moan. But it was Clem as usual who got to the root of things.

'SMOKE!' she cried, pointing to the deck in front of the driver's cabin, as a plume slithered between the planks, thick and noxious.

'What's going on?' shouted Big Col fearfully.

'It's pretty simple – we're on fire!!' she replied.

'So what do we do?'

But neither Noah nor Clem replied. They were both already moving in the same direction, to the metal buckets sitting at the cramped bow of the boat. It was tricky to get past Samson without agitating him, and he was already shuffling nervously at the sight of the smoke, but they couldn't be deterred, not if they wanted to stay afloat.

'We need to bail water on to the engine, and we need to do it quick,' Noah yelled. He couldn't believe this was happening, could kick himself. He'd known all day that the engine wasn't right, but he'd done what he always did and made rash decisions, and now? Well, he risked sinking something his dad held dear, so dear that if he *did* make it home from the war, he'd probably disown Noah anyway.

'Fill this up!' he said, throwing the bucket at Big Col.

'Where from?'

'Are you serious? We're on a river, you bloody fool! Clem, back Samson up, and keep him CALM!' Noah yelled, ripping open the hatch that led to the engine and releasing a new thunderous cloud of black smoke. 'Soon as the buckets are full, pour them on here. Then get more! Quick!'

He wasn't barking orders out of laziness, he'd already dived behind the wheel and was steering hard to portside, so hard that he felt the *Maudie* lurch, sending both Clem and her full bucket skittering across the deck.

"NOAH!!!' she yelled.

'I can't help it. I have to get us to the bank before she bursts into flames!'

The plan in his head was remarkably clear. If the smoke became flames, they needed to abandon ship, and quickly. They would have seconds, not minutes, and whilst it was fair to assume that most of the animals could jump and swim to dry land, Noah couldn't imagine Samson leaping the rail. And as for Delilah? Well, snakes weren't known for their breaststroke.

Noah knew he was responsible for everyone being on *Queen Maudie* in the first place, and so he was going to do everything he could to get them off safely too.

But whatever his plan, he was going to have to execute it quickly, as through the deck, the first orange flame poked its fingers, and waved the most sinister of greetings.

35

They were surrounded by water. In front, behind, underneath, it was everywhere, but they couldn't they get hold of it quick enough.

It was a stretch for Big Col, never mind Clem, to reach the river from the side of the boat, and even when they managed it, too much was spilt before they reached the fire. As Noah had feared, the flames were spreading rapidly, devouring the planks of the deck, throwing the animals into a blind panic. Winn had leaped on to the cabin's roof, barking incessantly at the flames, as if she could scare them away, whilst Frank could only scrabble at the cabin's wall, his little legs and ageing lungs letting him down as usual. The kittens, though, had found a more unusual sanctuary, clambering up Samson's tail like it was a rope in a gymnasium. Joseph was now sitting on the donkey's back, claws dug in for maximum purchase while Mary had gone even further, not stopping until she was perched on Samson's hat.

Samson wasn't happy about it; in fact, the poor beast was the most terrified of all. He started braying wildly, rearing on to two legs which tested the kittens' balance, hooves stamping in the most futile fashion, trying to quash the flames that danced closer and closer.

All Noah could do was hang off the steering wheel, pulling left as hard as he could. He'd had to kill the power already, terrified that a running engine would only fan the flames further, or even worse, cause an explosion below deck, sinking not only *Maudie*, but everyone on board.

The world seemed to slip into a strange dimension where time stood still, the only thing moving, still growing, was the flames. Clem and Big Col did their best, but their buckets seemed like thimbles, and the fire almost laughed at their pitiful attempts to extinguish it. It was then that Noah knew his plan was in tatters.

'Get the gangplank ready and the animals too,' he yelled, hands white as he gripped the wheel still harder. 'Soon as we're in range, you need to wedge it on the bank and get Samson off the boat.'

'And what if he won't go?' Big Col shouted back.

'Ride him down it, pick him up and carry him. Do whatever you have to do to get him on land. Do you hear?'

For once, Big Col didn't argue. He nodded, before putting the sack with Delilah already in it, next to where the gangplank would sit. While he did that, Clem gathered Frank, Winn, Joseph and Mary by her side, though keeping them there wasn't easy. The kittens in particular, hissed and spat their disapproval.

'Brace yourselves!!' Noah yelled as the riverbank finally approached. Even if he'd had a brake, he wouldn't have hit it. He wouldn't have dared: not with the flames roaring their presence now.

When contact came, it was still a shock, knocking all of them, apart from Samson, off their feet. Noah heard and felt a crunch, then a crack. He was terrified. It was the noise of something breaking irreparably.

'Go, GO, GO!!' he yelled, jamming Dad's skipper hat on to his head, but forsaking everything else that lay around him.

Big Col didn't hesitate, hoisting the gangplank like it were a toothpick and jamming it into position.

'Clem, get the dogs and kittens off first,' Noah yelled, and she did as instructed, none of the animals needing any encouragement.

Samson however, was a different matter. Donkeys are, of course, known for their stubbornness, and as the cramped deck where he stamped was now dominated by flames, he was paralysed with fear. He wasn't moving for anyone, or anything.

Big Col pulled hard at the rope around his muzzle, but Samson wasn't listening, never mind obeying. Instead, he raised his head back sharply, almost dragging Big Col headfirst into the flames. If they didn't get the donkey moving quickly, then it would be surrounded by fire in no time. Noah ducked back into the driver's cab, grabbed Dad's mac and dunked it into the river over the side of the boat.

'Here. Quick,' he shouted to Big Col as he dashed to his side, 'we need to spread the coat over Samson's back.' Samson was so big, there was much more chance of the flames catching hold of some part of him. And if they did? Well, with all that fur, Noah feared for the donkey's life.

Big Col did as he was told, and the coat seemed to be working, with sparks disappearing the second they hit the mac. Getting him to move however, was still a serious stumbling block. They begged, pleaded, pulled and swore at Samson to move, but nothing worked, sending Noah's anxiety spiralling still further. What else could they do? The answer simply was force, though Noah knew he couldn't get too close to Samson's back end if he wanted to spur him on. One kick from his powerful hind legs wouldn't just mean an end to their mission, but to him remaining conscious. He needed something, anything that would help him keep a healthy distance.

And there it was, slung in the corner, Dad's fishing rod. Without hesitation, Noah grabbed it, and after apologising to Samson for what he was about to do, he delivered a firm whack to the donkey's rump.

The effect was instantaneous. Like a thoroughbred, spurred on by his rider's crop, Samson drove forwards, dragging Big Col along with him, arms wrapped around his head to shield himself from the flames' finger ends.

'That's it!' roared Noah in delight, following closely behind, not stopping roaring until four hooves and four legs had negotiated the gangplank and were standing on dry land.

Then, and only then, did the horror of the situation reappear, as they stood, together, looking back at *Queen Maudie*, as the flames ate her alive.

Tears slid slowly down Noah's face. He couldn't believe what was happening, couldn't imagine what Dad would say when he finally found out, or cope with the fact that all of it was his fault. But he tried to tell himself repeatedly they were lucky to be alive.

'Is everyone all right?' he asked, turning to the others.

Clem nodded. Big Col coughed yes.

'And the animals?'

His eyes scanned them, as if he were taking a register. Two dogs? Tick. Two kittens? Yes. A donkey? Yes, though the straw hat was singed and charred.

Which left only one.

Where was Delilah?

Noah's eyes flitted quicker than a snake's, but no matter where he looked, there was no sack to be seen, and neither was Big Col wearing her as he often did.

'Oh no,' mouthed Noah, before Big Col did the same.

'On the deck!' the big lad screamed. 'The sack is on the deck! Why didn't you grab it?'

But Noah had no time to listen to accusations. He was already on the move. Back up the gangplank.

Clem screamed, but Noah didn't hear her.

All he could hear was the blood pounding in his ears, and the welcoming, warning roar of the flames as he jumped, flush, into their arms.

36

'The problem with you, son, is you jump constantly, from the frying pan to the fire.'

The line had often been repeated (by Mum, mostly), but seldom heeded. If it had been, then he wouldn't have found himself here, the living embodiment of her warning.

But Noah couldn't help it, not just on this occasion, but always. If an idea flashed into his head and it seemed like a good one, then what was the point in delay? He wanted to grab the thought, seize it by the scruff of its neck and make the most of it.

Sometimes it went wrong, but even when it did, he usually found a way to wrestle some kind of positive from the result. It was just what he did.

But at that moment, surrounded by fire and smoke and the remains of his dad's beloved boat, Noah wondered if his impetuousness had finally caught up with him.

The power of the flames seemed to be shrivelling his skin, and no matter which way he moved, it worsened. The smoke too, was thick and acrid, making him hack so hard that he thought his lungs would burst. And with watering eyes, it felt impossible to see.

'Delilah!' he yelled, though he had no idea why. The snake was hardly likely to call back. In fact, he only found the sack by accident, tripping over it as he groped instinctively. As his feet made contact with the hessian, he felt the lump inside it kick back. Was she trying to bite him? Noah wasn't scared though, only relieved. Relieved that Delilah was still alive, because if she wasn't then he had no doubt that Big Col would kill him as well, regardless of who was to blame.

The next problem was how to get both the sack and himself off the boat. The flames were incessant now, so high and vicious that Noah had no idea which way the gangplank lay. He strained into the fire, trying to get a view of something, anything that offered help, even if it were a glimpse of the river on the wrong side of the boat.

But it was fruitless. All he knew was that he was surrounded, and the only thing he could do was take a guess and hope for the best.

As he tried to lift the sack, he realised the next of his problems. It was too damned heavy. It may have been the smoke in his lungs affecting his strength, it may have merely been his own puniness, but no matter how hard he strained, he could not lift the sack on to his back.

How had Big Col done it? He'd carried it halfway across London and back for Pete's sake, so surely Noah should be able to lift it? What was wrong with him?

He tried again, and again and again, but whilst he might have raised it past his knees, he simply could not get the leverage needed to hoist it on to his back.

Once more, he thought, *ONE. MORE. TRY.* But as he strained, a new flame erupted from below deck throwing Noah on to his front, and on to the sack, and causing Delilah to hiss through the hessian.

Noah screamed, he couldn't help it. How long did he have? How long till the flames hit the fuel line or the oil in the engine? How long till he was blown heavens high?

It wouldn't be long. Seconds maybe. So if he was going to do this, it had to be now. NOW!

He pulled himself to his feet, and planted them either side of the sack. Where the idea had come from, he had no clue, he just knew that if he couldn't *carry* the sack, then he had to at least try to *throw* it.

He'd seen athletes do it on the Cinema newsreel, those Scottish hammer throwers, veins practically exploding from their necks as they cast the lump of iron further than was humanly possible.

He didn't have to throw the sack *that* far. All he had to do was clear the flames and *Maudie*'s flank. Even if the sack caught the flames a touch, then the river would douse it before any kind of damage was done to Delilah.

He could do this. He had to.

With every bit of strength he had, he gripped the sack and, ignoring the flames and sparks nipping and biting at his exposed skin, he hauled it to shin level and began to spin.

It wasn't easy. He was tired, and dizzy and flustered, plus there was precious little space on the deck that wasn't already alight. His lungs burned, as did his skin, but he didn't stop, he couldn't, he daren't, all he could do was build every bit of momentum he had, until, dervish-like, he spun so hard that his arms and the sack were at a right angle to his body.

He had no idea if he had enough momentum, not to mention strength left in his body to do what he needed to do. He had no idea if Delilah could possibly survive the shock of what he was about to do, or even the sudden drop in temperature, but he couldn't think about that. He was simply giving the animal the best chance of survival that he could.

This was it: the moment, do or die, so with one final spin and a cry that rumbled deep from the depths of him, Noah let go, and the sack (and Delilah), went flying.

37

Temperatures on the riverbank were far from cool either.

Neither of them could believe what Noah had done. Big Col had been wide-eyed in shock as Noah raced aboard the boat, and had to hold Clem back from following her friend. Clem in turn, had enough about her to grab Winn's collar, as she knew the dog would follow her master anywhere and everywhere, regardless of the danger.

All they could do, was stand and yell, imploring Noah to 'get off' and 'come back', though Big Col peppered his demands with somewhat stronger language.

'What is he *doing?*' Big Col demanded.

'Saving *your* pet!' Clem replied tersely.

'I didn't ask him to.'

'No, but you didn't run back on there yourself either, did you?'

'He didn't give me the chance!'

They bickered on, temperatures soaring, Winn barking madly and Frank joining in howling as well. The kittens, sitting on Samson's back still, dug their claws into the donkey in worry, which started him braying as well.

In fact, the only thing to break them from their noisy quarrelling, was the incongruous sight of Delilah's sack, one corner smoking furiously, cutting through the flames before plummeting into the river.

Despite the shock, it galvanised Big Col into action. He kicked off his boots before sprinting towards the river, and belly flopping gracelessly into its depths.

As his head emerged, coughing and spluttering, he saw ripples on the surface some twenty yards away. Thrashing wildly, he made progress, desperate to reach the sack before Delilah breathed her last. But as he edged nearer, and his lungs burned with the exertion, a bomb fell from above: a bomb in human form, arms and legs flailing, voice squealing as Noah landed on Big Col's back, sending them both plummeting.

Disorientation followed. Which way was up? And where was the sack? It was way too murky to make anything out, and as Noah and Big Col both broke the surface, their heads spun furiously for a sign of the sack.

'Left, left, LEFT!' yelled Clem, pointing the way, and Noah kicked on, arms windmilling until he found himself on top of the ripples, Big Col still some yards behind. Noah didn't wait though, there wasn't time, and after a huge gulp of breath, he broke the surface one final time, vowing not to return until the sack was in his grip.

The river surface kicked and spat back, then went quiet, the only noise from Big Col as he caught up, panting, his sodden clothes threatening to pull him under whether he liked it or not.

'Where is she?' he shouted uselessly. 'Where's Delilah?'

But Noah could neither hear, nor see from beneath the surface. It was too dark for a start, and the water too grubby. All he could do was flail his arms in every direction in the hope of striking lucky and brushing the sack.

Panic rose in him, and also in Big Col. It had been too long. He had no idea how long a snake could breathe underwater. Big Col did the only thing he could, which was keep himself above water, because if Noah *did* make it up, he had to be ready to help.

Seconds dragged by; Big Col tried dipping his face into the water but felt nothing but panic and claustrophobia. If he couldn't manage the briefest of moments, then it was stupid to expect a miracle from someone else. In fact, maybe he shouldn't be worrying about his pet at all, but hoping that Noah himself was all right. Suddenly there was an eruption beside him. So close and so volatile that he was submerged briefly himself. As his eyes opened and stung,

Big Col was left with the most wonderful of sights: two outstretched, dripping wet arms raised to the heavens. It didn't matter that the head they belonged to was still underwater. All that mattered was that the hands attached to the arms were holding Delilah, or as much of her as was humanly possible.

Big Col gasped.

'Is she alive?' he shouted, though Noah's head remained underwater. He looked for a sign. Was she breathing? He couldn't tell? Moving even? She wasn't. Her tail fell limply back into the river. It wasn't even as though he could look for her blinking, as he knew full well she had no eyelids. Despair seized him instantly, until . . . he saw it! A flick of the tongue. Small, but definite. She was alive. And tasting the air. Her head turned to him feebly and she flicked again, like she knew he was nearby.

At that moment Noah managed to force his head above water, his chest hacking and ejecting everything he'd swallowed. He felt disorientated and faint, but he daren't let his arms bend or relax. The snake had been underwater too long already, and he feared what would happen if she was submerged again.

'Take her!' he gasped, arms levering towards Big Col. But despite his exhaustion, Noah still saw the expression change on the other boy's face. The joy and relief that Big

Col initially wore seemed to slip from his face the second he held Delilah.

'What do you think you were doing?' he spat breathlessly. 'Throwing her overboard like that?' He seemed hysterical to Noah. 'I mean, you know she's sensitive to cold temperatures. And pythons can't swim, you fool!'

Had Clem been in earshot, she'd have put him straight: told him that *actually,* some species of pythons waited in shallow water to catch their prey. But Clem remained on the riverbank, her attention torn between the boys in the water and the frantic animals beside her.

'I thought you'd be pleased!' Noah said, flabbergasted.

'Pleased? That my pet nearly drowned?'

'That's not my fault. It beats being burned alive, doesn't it?'

'Neither would've happened if you hadn't put us onboard that death trap of a boat!'

There were so many replies that Noah could've given at that point. That he should be grateful either way. That the boat had safely transported them a long, long way towards their destination. Plus the most important point of all: that without his help, Delilah would've been dead anyway, the vet would've seen to that.

But he had neither the breath in his body, nor the time to voice them, as Big Col made it clear their conversation was over, pushing himself into a backstroke position, where he could rest enough of Delilah safely on his chest. His first kick wasn't aimed at the water to propel him to land though: it landed as intended, square and flush in Noah's chest.

Noah had no idea how to respond to that. He was too shocked, but as Big Col bobbed further away, the snake coiled incongruously on top of him, the shock subsided, to be replaced by undiluted fury.

How dare he? he thought. *How DARE he?*

Noah could already feel, despite the water, his left forearm burning from where the flames had bit and snarled, and who knew what other injuries he'd sustained. He'd only know that once he was dry and his adrenalin levels had dropped.

At that moment though, he didn't care. All he could see, and feel, was anger. And so he swam furiously in pursuit of Big Col and Delilah.

38

Big Col was no vet. That was evident as he kneeled on the riverbank, chest heaving, Delilah laid beside him as he looked her up and down.

'She all right?' asked Clem.

'Do I look like I know? Can't you see how sluggish she is? She's freezing!' he yelled back venomously.

'I'm only trying to help,' she said, turning her attention briefly to Noah, who was pulling himself from the river. 'Noah. That was so brave,' she said, offering a hand to get him on his feet. 'Brave, but unbelievably stupid.'

But Noah wasn't listening, nor did he accept her help. He'd spent every second swimming ashore letting his anger fester and grow, and it was now at volcanic proportions as he barged past Clem.

'I want an apology from you!' he demanded, as he stood over Big Col.

'You'll be waiting a long time.'

'I mean it,' Noah said. 'What you said out there. It's not right or fair.'

Big Col stopped looking at the snake long enough to shake his head disdainfully at Noah, before ignoring him again.

But Noah wasn't going to let it go. Not like that. He had plenty to say and he was darned if he wasn't going to say every single word of it.

'What is your problem?' he demanded. 'Because I really want to know.'

'Only problem I have at the moment is you dripping all over me and my snake.'

'You know what I mean. For as long as I've known you, which is sadly most of my life, you've made my life a misery. A MISERY!'

'A misery? Don't make me laugh. Because to be honest I've barely noticed *you.*'

'That's rubbish and you know it. Soon as school started you went for me. Always bigger, always stronger, always standing over me, poking and pushing.'

Finally, Big Col put Delilah to one side, pulling himself to his feet so he towered once again over Noah.

But for the first time in his life, Noah wasn't intimidated, or scared. He'd just been onboard a burning boat, just jumped through six-foot flames in order to survive, but more than that, he knew, instinctively, that if he didn't stand up to Big Col right now, then it would always be this way.

And he wouldn't have that. So he stood toe to toe with the boy, chest puffed out.

'I can't help that what I've been given is too much for you to deal with,' Big Col continued. 'That you can't cope with it. So let's finish this now. Because to be honest, it's too . . . easy.' And with that, he pushed Noah, sending him sprawling in the grass.

But Noah didn't retaliate. At least not in the way Big Col expected. He didn't rush him, fists flailing. He knew there was no point. The only weapon he possessed that could pierce Big Col was his words. So he chose them carefully.

'I've decided to change your name,' he said, a wry smile on his face. 'Because that's half the problem. Everyone goes on about *BIG Col*. It's like you were christened with it or something. It makes you someone to be scared of. But I'm not scared of you. Not any more. So from now on, you're not Big Col, or even Col. To me, you're just Colin.'

There was only one person in his life who called Big Col that, and he did it with such regularity and disdain that to hear it from someone other than his father left the boy enraged.

'Don't you call me that,' he hissed, fingers curling into fists.

Noah knew he'd crossed a line. Not because of the

fists. He'd seen and felt them on many occasions already. It was the look on Col's face. Murderous.

It didn't matter that his pet was lying sluggish on the grass, unclear as to whether it would live or die. Big Col only had eyes for Noah. It was as though he were looking at someone else, someone he hated with a passion that far exceeded his feelings for Noah.

But it was too late to take the words back. Noah couldn't, and didn't want to. He'd meant every single one of them, which meant he had to accept whatever came his way.

'Are you sure you want to do this?' Noah said to him, as calmly as he could. 'Because we didn't ask you to come along, but we let you, despite everything you've done to us in the past. But I'm warning you, Colin. This is your very last chance. Hit me one more time and you're on your own. You might make it to the Duchess', but you won't make it alongside us.'

Noah stood proud, not allowing himself to tremble outwardly: not when the boy moved closer, not even when his fist flew back, then forward, leaving Noah sprawled on the ground, nose pouring.

Big Col said nothing. Not a word to either Noah or Clem. All he did was remove his sodden shirt and carefully wrap Delilah up in it, before stomping away and out of sight.

'He'll be back,' said Noah, spitting blood through his teeth.

'You think so?' asked Clem.

'He'll have to. He's walking in the wrong direction,' he said, before frowning up at the sky. 'And anyway, that's the least of our problems.'

For once, Noah was right. They had nothing left to sail, nowhere left to sleep, no water and no way of catching any more food. And to cap off the bleakest of days, the humidity had now reached breaking point and the clouds suddenly burst.

It rained. Biblically. If ever they needed an ark it was now, but it was too late. What was left of *Queen Maudie* was sinking, quickly, into the Thames.

39

It didn't rain for forty days and nights, but it felt like it.

They didn't sleep, not really, there was too much to think about: *Maudie* and what Dad would say, never mind Mum. Big Col and the fact that he hadn't returned, not even to put himself on the right path.

All they could do was hunker under the biggest tree they could find, wearing their pets like furry blankets (though fortunately, for comfort's sake, Samson stayed on his feet beneath the canopy).

While the animals slept, the humans didn't, raindrops landing incessantly on their faces, puncturing what sleep did come their way. They tried to catch the drops on their tongue, to take the edge off their thirsts, but of course it was never enough. Noah even tried to shape the largest leaf he could find into a cup, which again failed miserably. He sat there and cursed, how could there be so much water without there being a way of them capturing it.

The only consolation was that the moisture eased his burns a little, as all night long they remained a searing reminder of how close he'd come to serious injury, or worse.

When the rain finally did stop, the sun was already up, heating the land, making the moisture rise steamily up to the heavens. It would've been an intoxicating sight for both of them had they not been so dog tired, thirsty and hungry.

'At least we don't have to eat fish again for breakfast,' Noah said, trying to make light of Col's absence, though in all honesty, he'd have eaten anything at that moment. Jumping through fire and hammer-throwing snakes in a sack was hungry work, it would seem.

'Do you think he's going to be all right?' Clem asked.

'Colin?' he replied, remembering his vow.

'Well, the snake as well, obviously. It really wasn't moving much, was it? I don't know what Col will do if it gets even colder, especially as he's hardly got a sense of direction.'

'No, but they're not our problem any more,' Noah huffed, pulling himself to his feet, wincing at a burn on his wrist. He looked at the rest of his exposed skin, not quite believing that he'd come through such an event so relatively unscathed. 'We can't waste all our energy worrying about him. All that matters are the animals we have left. First thing we need to do is eat, and the second is get walking. How many miles do you think it is to Windsor?'

Clem shrugged. She hadn't a clue. 'I tried to work it out, but like I said, without a ruler it's a lot of guesswork. All I know is we've just passed Hampton Court and that was about halfway.'

'So what does that mean? A day? Two days?'

'I've no idea, and we don't even have the map any more, do we?' She looked to the river with regret, before sighing. 'I'd say another day if the boat was still . . . well, you know. But on foot? I've no idea. Maybe a day or so if we follow the river. The boat wasn't going much quicker than walking pace by the end, but it could be longer with all the animals to handle.' As she said it, the kittens were terrorising Frank, who looked like he wanted to find a deep hole and hide in it.

Noah winced. How on earth were they going to manage such a journey with no food or water, never mind a map. And what if the police *were* actually looking for them? If they didn't get downriver quickly then who knew how long it would be until someone spotted them and dobbed them in?

'We need to find a shop,' Noah said. He couldn't just sit and fret.

'And leave the river? Is that a good idea when we know that Windsor sits right on it?'

'Just for as long as it takes to find some food. Cos I'm

no fisherman, neither are you, and I can't see any fruit trees or bushes, can you?'

Clem couldn't disagree with that, and besides, the rods had gone down with *Queen Maudie*. So they tied up Samson after giving him a good rub, and set off walking inland, the kittens wriggling and scratching at their arms.

But after only a minute or two, Clem thought of another obstacle too. 'Money!' she gasped.

'Eh?'

'Money. For the food. We don't have any.'

That stopped Noah in his tracks. Winn walked straight into the back of his legs and barked her disapproval.

'Oh.' He rooted through his pockets, but found only soggy linings. 'Best leave that with me then.' Which was exactly the answer Clem *didn't* want to hear. She knew that only meant trouble for all of them, and more pressure on her to rescue them from whatever hole Noah decided to dig next.

So they walked on, Noah distracted, kittens mewing and squirming with hunger, until they hit a town, or a village really, a narrow, cobbled street with shops dotted hither and thither.

It wasn't quiet though, there was plenty of activity, nearly all of it around a large bronze statue of a soldier, rifle pointed, ready, at the sky. It made Noah shiver: a reminder of something he didn't want to talk about.

'Where are we?' Clem asked.

'Not sure it matters.'

As they neared the statue, it appeared that the soldier himself was being readied for war, or protected at least, as piled up to his waist were sandbags, with the mound growing by the second, fed by a human chain of villagers, postmen, bobbies and most importantly, people in aprons – shopkeepers.

Until that moment, Noah didn't have a plan, but this activity gave him a glimpse of hope, as long as he grabbed it quickly. How much longer would it take them to hide the soldier entirely? He couldn't be sure, but with a number of them helping so diligently, he saw his opportunity and went for it.

'Stay here with Frank and the kittens,' he said firmly. 'If the shopkeepers head back towards the shops, give me a signal. Howl like a wolf or something.'

Before Clem had time to argue or question, Noah and his dog were already slinking off towards the nearest shop.

After checking it stood empty, they darted through the door before they could be spotted. Clem sighed. Both the kittens now scratched at her arms, and how on earth was she meant to howl like a wolf without drawing unwanted attention to herself?

Inside, the shop was exactly what Noah needed it to be. It seemed to sell everything, and though he felt guilty about stealing – he knew he had no choice.

He'd have to take as much as he could carry to see them through for as long as possible, but not too much to weigh him down if they were suddenly rumbled.

The first thing he saw that he wanted wasn't even food, it was a newspaper, but he knew he had to have it. Was the story of their disappearance tucked away in there, behind all the war news?

Rolling it quickly, he shoved it down the back of his shorts before turning his attention to the truly important stuff: grub. Apples he found quickly, small enough to ram into his pocket, and bread rolls, which he grabbed in one hand. Damn! He only had one pocket and one hand left, and that wasn't going to get him far, was it?

So, without hesitation, he pulled his stinking shirt over his head, and lying it flat on the floor, started piling whatever he could find on top of it. Tins of ham that came with their own key, condensed milk, a hunk of cheese that smelled just on the right side of sweaty, and biscuits, as many biscuits as he could fit on the material.

Was it enough? Not a chance. Could he carry any more?

Probably not, so folding the material together, and using the sleeves to form a knot, he made for the door with the bundle over his shoulder, like an errant Dick Whittington.

But just as the outside beckoned, he stopped dead in his tracks. *Drink.* He thought. He'd not picked up a single thing to drink! But as he pondered how on earth he could fit it in his sack, his ears were filled with a strange, unsettling noise.

'WHOOOO!' came the cry. What on earth was that? Was it Winn? He looked to his dog, but it wasn't coming from her. So if it wasn't Winn, and it couldn't be Frank – the noise was too throaty and loud to be the ageing dachshund, then who was it?

And then it hit him. It wasn't a dog at all. It was a wolf in Clem's clothing.

The shopkeeper was coming.

He was well and truly trapped.

40

Noah hid behind some sacks of potatoes.

Winn was less happy to do so, then for some reason became desperate to push her nose inside one, lord knows why.

'Quiet girl!' Noah implored, holding her jaw shut gently in case she tried to protest. He did it just in time, as the shopkeeper stomped in, blissfully unaware of the raid in progress.

Noah checked his exit. There was only one door, and to get to it, he had to pass the counter, where the man was now slumped, mopping his brow after his sandbag exertions.

The question was, did Noah think he could outrun the man? Could he reach the door without the man copping hold and dragging him to one of the bobbies outside?

Normally, he'd say yes, every time. But this wasn't a normal time. He had a makeshift knapsack to carry for starters, he'd barely slept in two days, and his arms were raw with burns. It was hardly the kind of preparation that would help him set a new hundred-yard record.

He needed . . . what did he need? Yes! That was it, he needed a diversion. Could Winn provide one? She was easily quick enough to pull the man away from the counter and still escape herself, but would she manage it with so much food around to distract her?

There had to be another way. He surveyed everything, the rows of neatly arranged cans and packets, but saw nothing that could help him escape in anyway.

But as he searched again, he spotted something else. Something they needed, something perilously close to the where the shopkeeper was standing. A map! A folded map. 'The Thames', it declared, and Noah had a feeling it could lead them straight to the Duchess' estate, whether they followed the river, or dared to drift inland. It would be stupid to leave the shop without it, which meant he absolutely HAD to tempt the shopkeeper away from his counter.

Not for the first time, it was Winn who came to the rescue, as her curiosity (and hunger) had overwhelmed her, and she had chewed a hole in the nearest sack, a potato sliding out on to the floor, with the gentlest of thumps.

That was all Noah needed, it sparked his brain to life,

and after pulling a pretend pin from this most opportune of grenades, he lobbed it high to the back of the shop.

'Get ready!' he whispered to Winn, and as soon as the bomb landed, detonating cans and packets noisily all over the floor, they saw the man dash in its direction, forehead creased. That was all the pair needed, and they bolted, Noah whipping the map from the counter as they passed. Adrenalin kicked in and within seconds, they were out the door, eyes straining into the sunlight in search of Clem.

'LEGGIT!!!' Noah yelled, much to the shock of the villagers, who were too stunned to give immediate chase. Clem didn't need encouraging, though it wasn't easy for her to sprint with two kittens wriggling in her arms. Frank looked appalled at yet more drama, but had no option but to waddle stiffly behind them.

By the time Clem caught up with Noah, deep in the wood that led to the river, he was laughing uncontrollably, out of relief as well as gratitude. Now he'd stopped, his stomach was growling.

Clem and Frank tumbled to the grass, the kittens revelling in the freedom to make a nuisance of themselves again, solely at Frank's expense.

'What are you laughing at?' Clem asked Noah, while trying to stop one of the kittens from scratching Frank's left eye out.

'Everything!' Noah replied. 'Your howl, the shopkeeper's face when that spud went flying, and the fact that FINALLY, we can eat something other than fish!' He unveiled his treasure, which delighted the animals, but not Clem.

'You *stole* all this?' she gasped.

'Well, I hardly had time to leave an IOU, did I?'

'But, Noah, that's . . . criminal.'

Noah couldn't believe what he was hearing.

'What's criminal is that they want to put our animals to sleep! Remember? We wouldn't be in this situation if it wasn't for them.'

'Doesn't mean you can just steal whatever you want in their name.'

He reached into the back of his shorts and recovered the crumpled newspaper.

'Got you something to read though, didn't I?'

He watched as her face softened a touch and she snatched the paper from him.

'It doesn't change a thing,' she scolded, in a mother-like fashion. 'You shouldn't have done it. So the first thing you'll do when we get home, is pay him back. Do you hear me?'

Noah hadn't a clue how he was going to do that. His meagre savings had been taken by Mum last month to pay for the window he'd smashed. But it was pointless arguing with Clem. So he nodded, before passing her the map as well.

'Thought this would help too,' he added. 'I know how much you love a good map.'

She took it from him silently, resisting the urge to say thank you. She also looked down at the picnic laid out on Noah's smelly, stained shirt, her stomach waking instantly. The first thing it told her was to forgive Noah. Just this once.

So Clem listened to it, and they all ate.

41

Restraint wasn't easy, but it was necessary.

Neither of them knew how long it would be until their mission was over, and even though Samson could tend to his own hunger, there were still a lot of mouths to feed.

So, with great reluctance, especially on the part of the dogs, the group made themselves stop, bundling up whatever was left back into Noah's shirt.

Now they just needed to find something to drink.

The food was of course, wonderful, a feast given the circumstances, but it did nothing to solve the dryness in their throats. The can of milk had been given to the kittens though all it had done was feed their energy for mischief.

'Every moment I spend herding these darned cats makes me thirstier,' Noah moaned.

'And it's only going to get worse, you know. So we need to do something about it.'

'What do you want me to do? A rain dance? Bit of a waste of time when we don't even have a cup to catch it.'

'I'm not expecting you to do anything. I'm just saying,

I'm thirsty, you're thirsty and we need to do something about it.'

'The animals are fine though.'

'Course they are, because they don't object to drinking dirty puddles. But I don't fancy risking doing the same, do you?'

Noah turned his top lip up. 'Not much. Well, we found one shop, didn't we. We just need to find another, quickly.'

Clem lay back and opened the newspaper. Not surprisingly, most of the pages were dominated by the outbreak of war and the evacuation of children. There were articles too, on the killing of the pets in the cities as well, which did little for their digestion. It wasn't until Clem reached page twenty-seven however, that she found the thing they feared, a headline that read: *Mystery of Runaways and their Pets.*

The article was brief, listing the full names and ages of Noah and Clem, plus the names of the dogs, and the fact that they had been missing for two days. There was no mention of Big Col.

Concern is growing for the safety of the children since their disappearance. It is thought they may have been distressed by the government's proposal to end the lives of animals deemed to be at risk, as well as the prospect of their imminent evacuation. Neither child has relatives living nearby whom they could be heading towards and their mothers are very worried. Clementine is described as being highly intelligent and resourceful, while Noah, according to his mother, is 'young for his age'.

This description did not go down well with Noah. He ranted against the injustice, though it fell on deaf ears, as Clem was too busy revelling in her intelligence.

'You'd better listen to me from now on,' she crowed. 'Cos everyone knows now how intelligent and resourceful I am.' She let the words roll off her tongue several times, and each time they hit Noah like a mallet to his *young* and increasingly offended head.

There was one, key omission from the report however.

'There's nothing about *Queen Maudie* going missing,' pointed out Clem.

'Means we can keep walking along the river,' Noah said.

'Hmm, I'm not sure that's a good idea now,' replied Clem. 'We need water for starters, and there won't be shops on the riverbank. Anyway, just because the boat isn't in the article doesn't mean the police don't know about it. Plus, this would have been written yesterday. A lot could've happened since then.'

'So what you're saying is that we should take a massive

detour just in case?' Noah wouldn't acknowledge it, but his petulant tone *did* make him sound very young, and in Clem's opinion, dim. Which she told him. Which started a whole new argument.

'We wouldn't have even got this far without my ideas!' Noah argued.

'Maybe, but your dad would still have a boat.'

'Don't you *want* to save the animals?'

'Of course I do, and as we have a map now we can see it's quicker if we go inla—'

But at that moment, there was a noise behind them, a snapping of branches, then a second, and a clumsy third.

'What was that?' Noah whispered.

'I don't know, but I don't like it. Maybe someone's followed us from the village. We need to get moving quickly.' And before Noah could disagree, Clem chased down the kittens and held on for dear life. Then she took the path inland, leaving Noah to grumble and curse while peering, over his shoulder.

'Hang on!' Noah yelled. 'You forgot the flipping donkey!' And he dashed to retrieve him.

'Come on, Samson,' he said, grabbing his rope. 'Her ladyship has spoken, hasn't she?'

They made decent enough progress too, thanks entirely to Clem. Her map-reading skills were excellent, never dallying when paths met, or when they found an unexpected junction. She would merely turn the map one way then the other, her head turning counterpoint, before a quick nod and the point of a finger set them on the move again. If she ever got irate, it was simply down to her thirst.

'Have they never heard of shops around here?'

Noah didn't argue. He knew there was no point, despite wanting to remind her they had no money to buy a drink. Plus, he knew they hadn't actually deviated far from the riverbank: most of the journey so far had been through adjacent woodland, hiding them from inquisitive eyes that might greet them on a road.

He did feel uneasy though. And it wasn't a feeling that went away, even after half an hour of walking. Their thirst and the heat didn't help. But he felt . . . watched. Like they weren't the only people in the area. Every so often, he would stop abruptly and turn, swearing blind that on several occasions he saw foliage dance, as if to hide someone.

'It's just your mind playing tricks on you,' said Clem. 'Hardly surprising after everything that's gone on and so little sleep.'

But he didn't think so. His gut, his instinct told him otherwise. So, he thought up a new plan, to set his mind straight. He started tossing sticks behind them into the undergrowth, which sent Winn scampering back to retrieve them.

If there *was* someone or something back there spying on them, then Winn would sound the alarm, with a bark that Noah would recognise as *Danger! Danger!*

It went on for some time. Away flew the stick, and off scampered Winn, ecstatic that finally, finally, she was getting to play her favourite game.

He started to fling the stick a little further, watching Winn disappear completely into the brush, and smiled. If only his life were as simple as hers. But it also served as a reminder to him: that their mission was a good one, and true. His animal, *all* of the animals, they were worth saving. It had to be done.

He waited, still smiling, for Winn to reappear, jaws clenched down on her prize. But she didn't come. Neither did a bark. The forest was still, and quiet.

Or at least, the area behind them was, as the silence up ahead was suddenly broken by a piercing scream. Noah turned on his heels.

Clem was in trouble.

42

'CLEM!!!' Noah roared, as he tore through the brush. The foliage was heavy up in front of him, so heavy that there was no sight of anyone or anything, not even a glimpse of Samson's straw hat. More worryingly, there was no noise now either, and that scared him. A scream was an awful sound, but silence was worse.

'Clem. CLEM!' he yelled, ignoring the branches that whipped at his face in warning, until, he found her. But she wasn't alone.

She was in the clutches of a man. A man in a hat that was too small for him, sat at a jaunty angle on his head, despite the struggle that Clem was putting up.

Noah recognised the attacker instantly. It was the man from the river yesterday, who'd pulled up alongside them in his boat. But this time, he wasn't alone. He had a friend with him. Hatless, this one, with a huge pair of unruly sideburns that bristled upon his red, ruddy cheeks. He had the look of an idle pig, and a mouth just as dirty. In his hands was a grubby sack, like the one Big Col had carried Delilah in.

'This the boy?' he spat, though with a word so blue it threatened to turn the summer to winter.

The hatted man shook his head. 'No, that's not him neither, though don't go running off, boy. Do that and old Jim here will be on you in a flash.'

Noah had no idea what was going on. 'Leave her alone,' he shouted, though of course it was an impotent demand. 'What do you want? Because whatever it is, Clem doesn't have it, I can tell you that . . . but maybe I do.' He was gabbling now, just wanted his friend to be safe, even if it were at his expense.

'Took a while to find you again, it did,' said the man, ignoring Noah's plea. 'Expected to find you on the river still. In that rust bucket you called a boat.'

Noah wanted to punch him into the middle of next week.

'Still, we found you in the end. Quite the hunters us two.' He paused, and looked around. 'So where is he then, the other boy?' the man demanded. 'The big one?'

'Big Col?' Noah said, confused. He couldn't think what use they would have for him. 'He's not with us any more.'

'Don't give me that, boy. I saw the three of you yesterday. Thick as thieves, all of you.'

'I'm telling you he's gone.'

The man was getting angrier, his grasp of Clem stronger. She winced in pain and Noah did too.

'I promise. We had a fight, me and him. So he left.'

The side-burned thug was livid at this, marching up on Noah without warning and twisting his arm up his back.

'That big lad has somethin' we want. Somethin' valuable. And we want it now, you hear me?'

Noah knew instantly what this was all about. Delilah. The second the man had seen her yesterday, he'd known she was special. That there was money in her.

'I don't know where he is, I promise you.'

'Stop LYING!' Noah's arm went further up his back and he shrieked in pain, which started Clem hollering too. She kicked at the man's shins, which appeared to be made of lead for all the pain he was feeling.

'Let us go!' she demanded, again and again. The man just shook her like a rag doll.

But Clem was not for silencing; in fact her protests grew louder and more raucous, each demand spat at the man with increasing venom and fury.

What was she doing? Noah gasped. They weren't playing around these men. And if they worked out that neither Clem nor Noah were actually of use, they would soon tire of them, and who knew what they would do then?

But Clem didn't care. She shook and thundered to the heavens, until finally, her plan came to light, as through the bushes behind her burst a brown blur of fur and teeth and growl.

Now old Frank may have been short on legs, but he was big on heart and loyalty, and it was clear that no one, no one, was going to manhandle his mistress and get away with it. So he bit what he could reach, which was the hatted man's calf, and although the man began a dance which had Frank flying left, right and centre, the little chap refused to let go, which meant of course, that Clem could dart free.

This wasn't to say that the tide had turned though, far from it. It spurred old Jim into a furious rage, and although he released Noah's arm, he grabbed him instead by the hair and dragged him over to where Frank clung on grimly. With a single boot to the belly, the poor dog was sent yelping to the floor. Clem dashed to his side.

'We want that snake – NOW!' old Jim roared into Noah's face, but Noah didn't answer. There was no time, as from the treeline burst a second animal, this one on four hooves and more powerful than Frank. It was Samson, braying in anger, rearing up on his back legs, and towering over the two men and Noah. Noah saw his opportunity for escape, and with every inch of strength he possessed, he drove his fist into old Jim's ribs, his knuckles crunching. It was debatable if Jim let go due to the punch or the sight of a sunhat-wearing donkey charging at him, but it was immaterial. Noah scampered free and sprinted for his friend.

What followed resembled a scene from a Saturday morning Western at the Ritzy.

Samson was a donkey possessed, circling the men, hooves stamping at the ground, digging up the earth like it was sand. The men yelped and waved their hands uselessly, old Jim dropped his sack and instantly tripped over it, but every time they tried to break away, Samson would deftly round them up like a sheepdog. In fact, his actions encouraged Winn to join in, leaving Noah feeling guilty that he hadn't looked for her earlier. It mattered little now, the men were on the back foot and snakeless.

But just as it seemed they might take flight, old Jim spotted a brutal opportunity. As Samson drove them to the trunk of a mighty old oak, Jim tripped over a fallen branch. It was a thick wedge of wood that instantly felt club-like in the man's hands. With Samson's back turned to keep the other thug in check, and Winn's jaws just out of reach, old Jim knew exactly what he needed to do.

Noah and Clem saw it too late to intervene and wished for a long time after that they had never seen it at all. As without hesitation, old Jim swung the wood like a cricket bat, driving it flush on to the back of poor Samson's skull again and again.

43

War would bring many horrors, but to Noah and Clem, this was both a defining and disturbing moment of their childhoods.

Samson crumpled to the ground, all light and life extinguished from his eyes. There was no more braying or pawing of the ground, just silence and stillness from everyone present.

Noah hid behind his hands. He didn't want to risk re-opening his eyes to see the same scene laid out in front of him. Clem though fell on the animal, arms snaking around his neck, face nuzzled into the thick, tangled mane.

'Samson?' she cried, as she tried in vain to lift his head. 'Samson!!'

The only movement came from the hatted man, pulling Clem roughly away with a callous hand. 'It's no good expecting the donkey to help you now. That beast's dead, and you won't be far behind if you don't give us what we want.'

The man was right. Samson was still, a trickle of blood from his right ear marking the hard ground.

There had been so much talk of animals dying in the last week, but until this moment, it had been an abstract idea, not one that Noah could truly picture. But now that had changed. He could see nothing *but* death, and it ate at his insides. He looked at the donkey, not able to comprehend that it was the same creature who had defended them only seconds before. He wanted to stop time, to find a way of catching the life that had left Samson, and force it back inside his body. But he knew it was hopeless. The animal had passed.

Large tears began streaking Noah's dirty face.

'Tears won't 'elp you, boy. Only thing to 'elp you now is the truth. You tell us where the snake is, or we'll start next on the kittens, and then those mutts.'

It was no idle threat, Noah knew that, but he wanted the men to know that he wasn't crying for his own safety, but for the barbarous thing they'd done to his friend.

'How many times do I have to tell you?' he yelled at them, prompting both Winn and Frank to yelp along in agreement. 'I don't KNOW where the snake is, and even if I did, I wouldn't tell y—'

But the sentence was never finished, as it was no longer the truth. Noah suddenly knew *exactly* where Delilah was, as if by some divine intervention, the snake was falling from the sky, or rather from the sturdy branches above them.

Noah thought at first that he had lost his mind, but no, it was happening! The hatted man followed Noah's eyeline instinctively, but as soon as he looked up, the snake was upon him, landing flush on his neck and shoulders, forcing him to the floor with a stunned scream.

'ARGGGGHHHH!' he yelled. 'What is it? What is it? Get it off me!!!'

But there was nobody to help. Noah and Clem were clearly not going to oblige, and even old Jim looked powerless to intervene, eyes wider than if the snake were squeezing him.

'JIIIMMM!' came a scream. 'For gawd's sake, get it off me!!! NOW!!'

Jim made to move forward, as if in a trance, picking up the branch that had done for Samson, but as he came into striking range, he seemed to realise what he was about to do. And the thought process was written large on his face.

Do I really want to take on a python?

It was at that moment, the bully became the coward, as it was clear old Jim wanted no further part in this heist. But as he made that decision, there was another arrival – from the branches above fell Big Col, landing beside them all with a thud that seemed to make the ground shake. He didn't look at Noah and Clem though, he only had eyes for the assailants, or at least for the one who remained – old

Jim had seen enough and was galloping through the undergrowth, falling every few yards, such was his abject fear.

'I hear you were looking for my Delilah?' Big Col said, carefully picking up the snake, savouring and exaggerating the weight and power in her.

Noah looked closely at Delilah. As much as Big Col was trying to make her sound and look savage, she seemed anything but. To Noah's eye, she looked . . . sleepy. She wasn't actually moving at all, the only thing moving was Big Col's arms, manoeuvring her like a puppet.

'Well,' he went on, 'you've found her. So . . . what did you want with her? Because whatever it is, I'm sure she'd *love* to help.' And he thrust his hand forward, again and again as if Delilah were wanting to pounce.

'Get her away from me,' the hatted man gasped. He seemed to be draining of all colour.

'Oh, I can't do that for two reasons,' Big Col replied. 'Firstly, cos she's hungry. Really hungry. I worked out this morning it's been a week since she ate anything, so right now, YOU are the only thing she has eyes for. And the second thing, well, how can I put it?' He seemed to be revelling in the drama, 'Delilah here, she's a wild animal. She won't come to heel just cos I tell her. It don't work like that. Sorry.'

The hatted man was beyond talking now.

'I could try and pull her away though if you give us your word you'll go and never come back.'

Despite his greed, and despite the evil streak that ran in him a mile wide, this was an easy deal for the man to make, and as he fell to his knees he begged, 'Anything. I'll do anything.'

'Then what are you waiting for?' Big Col threw himself forward one final time with such force that Noah wondered if Delilah HAD woken up.

The hatted man scampered, crab-like at first in Noah's direction, which had him pick up the branch and wield it like a batsman awaiting a bouncer. The man grimaced and tumbled away. He didn't run in the same direction as his partner in crime, but Noah doubted either of them would return from any point of the compass.

It was fair to say though, that he felt no relief, as with the criminals gone, the friends were left with the reality of the situation: that whatever happened from now on, they had, in effect, failed in their mission. One of their animals lay dead. And unless Noah was mistaken, Delilah might not be too far behind.

44

None of them were versed in death. None of them had been anywhere close to it before, so at first it rooted them to the spot. The only thing that made Noah move was when the kittens tried to make Samson play with them, running up and down his back. When that got no response they turned to nibbling his ears or pulling at his hat, and when that elicited nothing either, they too grew worried. Joseph mewed repeatedly, while Mary curled herself between the curve of his belly and foreleg.

'Come on,' Noah said softly, as he lifted them up to mournful cries. 'None of that now. Samson's gone. Do you hear me? Gone.'

But as soon as Noah dropped them to the ground they returned to Samson, and the same spots they'd occupied before.

'Leave them be,' suggested Clem. 'For a while at least. We need to work out what to do next.'

Big Col was in no doubt about what needed to happen.

'We have to get Delilah warm,' he said, worry carved deep in his forehead. 'Quickly.'

'What's the problem?' asked Noah, before realising it was the stupidest of questions. His hunches had been right. The snake was cold. Dangerously so.

Big Col rubbed her skin, willing life into her. 'After I left you lot, she went . . . floppy. It was scary, she seemed to weigh twice as much. Couldn't lift her head or nothing.'

Noah and Clem looked at each other. That didn't sound good.

'So why didn't you go and get help? Instead of coming back to find us?'

'I was going to, weren't I? But then, well, I got a bit lost for starters, and then I heard those two blokes coming and recognised one of them from the river. I hid as they passed but they were talking about finding us, about what they'd do if we put up a fight. I could hardly just walk away, could I? When I knew all that?'

Noah and Clem looked flabbergasted. Was this really Big Col speaking? The boy who had made their lives hell back in Wapping. The boy who was now looking grief-stricken at his pet.

'Here, you can wrap her up in this?' Noah said, removing the leftover food from the makeshift knapsack. 'It might help a bit.'

'Won't be enough. She needs a fire.' He stopped and re-thought this. 'Needs the stove at home.'

'Well, we can't give her that,' offered Noah, moving quickly, 'but a fire, we can manage in no time. Let's do it. We'll have her scaring the daylights out of us again in an hour at the most.'

They set to it. The fear of more grief fuelling their movements. There were sticks and dried moss in abundance, and they soon had flames aplenty. Big Col gently laid Delilah close to the fire.

'Right,' said Noah. 'We need to bury Samson.'

'How are we going to do that? It'd take a whole day to dig a hole that big. And we don't even have a spade.'

'I know, but we can't just leave him, can we? Not like this. Where's the dignity in it?'

No one disagreed. Noah looked around, tears close to the surface. 'If we can't bury him then we *have* to give him a proper funeral.'

'What are you suggesting?' asked Clem.

'The next best thing we could do is build him a tomb. Somewhere proper he can rest.'

'A tomb?'

'Yeah, think about it,' he replied, bending to pick up a large fallen branch. 'We've everything we need around us. We just need to gather it up.'

They worked silently. It was tiring work after all, and at the same time, all of them were trying to process what had happened to Samson in their own way. They hit a rhythm, each of them adopting a role. Big Col was the muscle, while Noah started trying to weave foliage together into something resembling a roof. Clem was the architect though, seeing immediately the shape that the tomb would need to take.

They toiled, ignoring the growing hunger that sat alongside the sadness in their bellies, topping up Delilah's fire regularly, and helping Big Col when the branches were too big even for him.

'Thanks,' he said to Noah, as they dragged a bough laden in leaves.

''S'all right,' he replied.

'I should say ... well, you know ... sorry, as well,' he went on, quietly.

Noah stopped dead, with Big Col almost crashing into him as a result. 'Sorry? You?'

'Yeah, you know. For hitting you and for what I said when ... you know.'

'What, when I saved your beloved pet from either burning or drowning to death?'

'Yeah.' Big Col almost looked ashamed. 'It was ... brave of you.'

'Am sure you would've done it if I hadn't dashed in first.'

'That's just it. I wouldn't. I'm not brave. Everyone knows it.' His voice was almost a whisper now. It sounded odd, like a meow slipping from a tiger's mouth.

'Are you kidding me?' Big Col might have been apologising, but Noah wasn't going to let him get away with it easily. 'You go after anybody who dares to even look at you.'

'Don't make me brave though. Ask my—' and he stopped.

'Who?'

There was a beat. Then another deep, deep breath. 'My old man. And my ma for that matter too. Both of them.'

'Why? What do they say?'

'Can't tell you. But it's not just what they say.'

'What do you mean?'

'It's what they do.'

Noah was really confused now. And looked at him in a way that told him so.

Big Col flushed, and a twitch seemed to pass through his entire body. It looked like he wanted to speak, but couldn't find the words. Instead, he unbuttoned his shirt sleeve, rolling it up to the elbow to reveal a bruise that hugged the entirety of his forearm. It was quite unlike anything Noah had ever seen, a hellish rainbow of purples, reds and yellows, yet the anger in the colour was not the most shocking thing about it: even at first glance Noah could clearly make out the shape of four fingers and a thumb.

'Your dad did that?' he said. He couldn't take his eyes off it, as much as he wanted to.

Col shook his head shamefully. 'Mum. You can see where her ring was when she squeezed.' He was right, a vivid purple welt stretched the width of the fourth finger. 'Dad . . . well, he uses his belt. When he's sober enough to be able to take it off anyway.'

I don't . . .' Now Noah was struggling to find the words. 'I don't understand why they would do that.'

'They goad me,' he replied. 'Tell me I'm a coward. That I need to be a man. They want me to fight back, don't know why, because if I do then they only hit me again. It's confusing. I don't know whether to fight or hide.'

It was a lot for Noah to comprehend. He couldn't imagine finding himself in that position, no matter how much trouble he caused. Even when Dad found out about the *Queen Maudie*.

'Well, if it makes any difference, you *are* brave,' said Noah. 'I mean, if you hadn't sneaked back and climbed that tree? Or if you hadn't dropped Delilah on top of that fool, . . . well, I don't want to think where we'd be. So I'm sorry too. If my ideas were daft, or if I sailed us into danger. I just wanted to keep the animals alive.'

'I know,' replied Big Col as he gingerly rolled down his sleeve. 'There's one thing I need you to do though,' he said, his grin disappearing, leaving behind traces of what Noah feared was the old, Big Col.

'What's that?'

'My name,' he replied.

'What about it?'

'It's Col,' he replied, firmly, but without a hint of aggression. 'Not Big Col. And certainly not Colin . . . that's what they call me. Mum and Dad. But Col. Yeah, that'd be good. Please.'

Please?

What could Noah say but: 'Right. Fine. No problem.'

'What was that all about?' asked Clem suspiciously, as Col walked off dragging a bough effortlessly behind him.

'I could tell you,' Noah replied, 'but you'd never believe me.'

And he walked on too. There was an important job to finish.

45

They had no idea if they were doing it right, as none of them had been to a funeral before.

The tomb they'd made was rustic but also magnificent. It hid Samson entirely, the only sign of him being his straw hat, which Noah had perched safely on a twig-made crucifix.

Noah still had concerns though. 'What if someone comes across him and looks inside? They'll be in for a heck of a shock.'

But for once it wasn't Clem who had the answers, but Big Col, who lumbered away before returning with a large flat rock and one small sharp one. Dropping to his knees, with his tongue between his teeth, he scratched at the large stone with the small one, not stopping until he was done.

'There,' he said, a look of pride on his face, despite the spidery writing he'd created.

Here lies Samson. Rest in Piece.

Neither Noah nor Clem felt the need to correct his spelling.

'Perfect,' said Clem.

'It's great. Thanks, Col.'

Col beamed as he placed it at the head of the tomb.

'We should say something, shouldn't we?' said Clem.

'We should,' said Noah.

'Go on then.'

Noah paused.

'Er . . .' It wasn't the most reverential of beginnings. 'We didn't know Samson for very long. But . . . well, we still feel sad about it. Because he was brave. When we first met him, he'd been abandoned, but he trusted us, even when we made him go sailing down the Thames on a boat.'

'He could've smashed the boat apart with his hooves, if he'd wanted to,' added Col.

'But the thing that I'll remember him most for, apart from the hat, was his final act of bravery. If it wasn't for him, those men would have hurt us. He knew we were in danger and that he would be too, but he did it anyway. So, thank you, Samson. And sorry. I feel like I let you down, but I won't let you die in vain. We'll make it to the Duchess', I promise.'

Noah let his head fall, satisfied that he'd said what he could.

As his chin touched his chest, he felt and heard a

rumble. A rumble that quickly grew in noise and intensity. He felt it, they all did, deep in their chests, then increasingly in their ears until it swelled towards a crescendo. But just as the din became almost unbearable, the sky above them split into pieces, and four Spitfires cut effortlessly across the blue. They looked otherworldly, impregnable.

It was a beautiful sight, almost as though they'd been sent to pay a final, wonderful moment of respect to their fallen ally.

The moment wasn't wasted on any of them. They all felt it, and their eyes filled. Col coughed and went to tend to Delilah, who remained pretty much motionless beside the fire.

'If she's warmed up, then we should get walking again,' said Noah. 'There's still a distance to go.' The thought delighted neither Clem nor Noah, but after a deep breath they busied themselves all the same. Col, though, stayed on his knees.

'We're ready,' Noah told him. 'You?'

The big lad shook his head without lifting it.

'We're done,' he said quietly.

'Good. So let's go.'

'No I mean we're done-done.' Finally, he looked at them both. 'Me and Delilah. I'm taking her home.'

46

'Very funny,' said Noah.

'I'm not joking though,' replied Col. 'I wish I was, but I'm not.'

'But you've only just found us again,' said Clem.

'I know, but look at her.' He pointed at Delilah. 'Feel her skin.'

Noah instinctively put his hands in his pockets.

'Go on. Touch her.'

Reluctantly, they did, and although they didn't really know how she was meant to feel, her skin was cold, and slightly clammy. What surprised Noah even more was that Delilah didn't respond to their touch. Not a flick of the tongue or a lurch in their direction. Nothing.

'She's been by this fire for ages now,' Col said. 'But it's made no difference. She's barely moved or shown her tongue. I'm worried if I don't do something now, she's going to be so ill that there'll be no coming back.'

'We're getting closer now though,' replied Noah.

There was a flash of anger in Col's eyes, but it was merely that – a flash – and he replied with a rare calm.

'Are we?' he said. 'I know you want to believe that. And I do too. And I'm not saying that you won't get there in the end. But how long will it honestly take? Can you tell me that and promise it?'

Noah looked to Clem to ask her, but she was already shaking her head.

'I can't,' she said. 'I wish I could, but I can't. Not honestly.'

Col smiled sadly and nodded. 'Thank you. And that's why I have to go home. If I find the road, I can hitch a lift back to London. Gives me a chance of making her well. Take her to the vet.'

'Take her to the vet and you'll never bring her out again!' Noah said.

'Then I'll look after her myself. Get her warm by the stove. It always worked before.'

'Yeah great, but what will your mum say? Do you really think she's just going to welcome you back and tell you Delilah can stay after all? You don't really believe that, do you? They're going to cart you off to Cornwall.'

Col looked flummoxed. Like he was trying to build a bridge out of jelly. 'I don't have all the answers. Not yet. But look at her, Noah. She's dying.'

What could Noah say to that? He didn't want her to

266

die. He wanted *all* the animals to survive, to live the long and happy lives they deserved. But whether he looked down the road to Windsor, or back to London, the view didn't look good for Delilah.

'Then what can we do to help?' Noah said. 'Do you want us to come with you?' The words came out before he could stop them.

'What, and end your adventure? Why would you do that?'

'Because we started this together, and I want us to finish it the same way.'

'So finish it then. You do it your way. And I'll do it mine. The result will be the same. Saving our pets. We just won't be doing it together, that's all.'

Noah sighed. He was out of arguments. 'Just don't let them take her, Col, all right? Don't you dare let them do what they did to all the others.'

Col nodded firmly. 'I won't. I'll fight 'em if they try.' A smile crossed his lips. 'Or I'll join the circus with her. We'd terrify kids everywhere, me and Delilah.'

Noah didn't doubt it, but before he could tell Col this, Clem piped up.

'You know, you could always try the zoo?' she said. 'For Delilah, I mean. They wouldn't be interested in dogs or kittens, but a python? You never know.'

'Won't they be putting animals to sleep too?'

'Maybe. But it's got to be worth a go, hasn't it? There's that woman who lives on Calmly View. She works there. Margaret something. She's a bit fierce, but she must love animals deep down.'

'I'll go there straight off,' said Col, eyes hopeful. 'You always did have the best ideas round here, Clem.' He flashed a look at Noah and smiled. 'I'll be seeing you. And thanks.' He turned to leave, but after a few steps Noah stopped him in his tracks. 'Do you really think someone's going to give you a lift when you're carrying a bloomin' python?' he asked. 'They'll speed up, not slow down.'

'Oh,' replied Col sheepishly. 'Didn't think about that.'

'Just as well old Jim left without that then,' Noah said, pointing at the sack lying on the ground.

Col smiled again, before carefully easing Delilah inside.

'See?' Noah grinned. 'I do have ideas every now and then.'

'Yeah, but this is the first one that was any flipping good.' Col held out his hand. 'I'll see you when you get home.'

'Probably not,' Noah replied. 'You'll be evacuated. Or off with the circus.'

'See you when it's all over then.'

'You will.' He took Col's hand and shook it, trying to match his strength and failing. 'Friends, Col?' Noah said.

'Maybe. Maybe that's why I came back to find you,' Col replied. 'Or maybe we're just *both* terrible at ideas.'

He waved to Clem, she waved back. Then, after carefully placing the bag over his shoulder and looking one last time at Samson's tomb, Col was off through the trees.

Thankfully, this time he was heading in the right direction.

47

They plodded on, quiet for quite some time. Nothing seemed to cheer them up. Noah tried to pretend his misery was down to the endless kitten wrestling, but that wasn't the real reason.

He felt ... sad, confused and guilty too. About Samson, about Col and Delilah. About the raging thirst that seemed to sap him of energy and the ability to think straight.

'Come on,' Clem asked from nowhere. 'Tell me what you're thinking about.'

'The tallest glass of milk in the world,' he replied. 'I'd drink it straight from the cow truth be told.'

Clem agreed.

They walked on, ignoring every bit of beauty in the nature around them. They only stopped to wait for Frank, who might not have been thirsty, but was definitely tired.

'You know you're not entirely responsible for everything, don't you, Noah?'

'What do you mean?'

'Exactly that. All this, it's not your fault. You didn't encourage Hitler to invade Poland, did you?'

'I don't remember that conversation last time we met for tea, no. But I do remember bringing you out here to do this.'

'I do too. But I also remember agreeing to it. I could've said no, Noah. Don't forget that.'

'So why didn't you? Maybe it would've been a better idea.'

'And let the dogs die at the vet's? You don't believe that, and neither do I. So all right, the idea is a bit farfetched, and yes, we don't know exactly how far we are away still, and YES, our mothers will murder us when we finally get home. But do I blame you for any of that? No, I don't. And do I want to go home without really trying to reach the Duchess. NO. I do not.'

'And will we still be friends afterwards?' Noah asked cheekily. 'Even if they evacuate us together and you have to spend the entire war with me?'

'Don't push your luck, Noah Price,' she replied. 'I'd make proper friends with those kittens if I were you. Just in case.'

Noah laughed. That was unlikely. He was beginning to think they had chosen the wrong names for the kittens – Joseph and Mary were far too innocent for them. Trouble and Mayhem would have been more accurate.

Their thoughts turned to what to do next. They had perhaps three hours of daylight left and beyond that map-reading would be impossible. At the same time, Clem believed they had at least seven, maybe eight miles still to walk.

'We're not going to make it tonight, are we?'

'I wish I could say yes,' Clem replied. 'But not at the pace Frank is walking and it'll be dark when we reach Windsor, so to find her house when we don't even know where it actually is . . . it doesn't seem likely, does it?'

Noah sighed. He couldn't disagree, though he wasn't sure he had the energy to work out where they should sleep now *Queen Maudie* was no more.

'Think it's going to rain again tonight?' Noah asked.

Clem licked her finger and held it in the air. 'My finger says there is a fifty-nine per cent chance of precipitation.'

'Really?'

'No, you fool. Why do you think I know the exact answer to everything?'

'Because you usually do.'

'Can I have that in writing?'

Noah pretended to check his pockets. 'Left my pencil at home. Sorry.'

'I do know that we need to find somewhere comfortable for us all to sleep. Not just for us. For these two as well.'

The dogs looked tired. And hungry. Winn loped slowly to Noah, brushing against his knee and thigh whilst whining sorrowfully. It was a move she had mastered over the years: perfected to make Dad or Noah fill her food bowl for a second, or third time that day. Mum never fell for it of course.

'I know you're hungry, Winn. We are too. And I promise you, when we get there, there'll be the biggest bowl of food you can think of. This Duchess probably feeds her animals steak, chicken and strings of sausages longer than Delilah.'

Winn didn't look impressed and lay at his feet. Frank did the same.

'Don't be resting on the job now,' he said. 'Take much longer and the sausages will be all gone.' Winn stood, Frank did not. He looked asleep already.

'Does he need to rest a while?' he asked Clem, feeling that guilt eat at him again.

'We don't have time,' she replied, and swept Frank into her arms.

'I can help you with him,' Noah offered.

'Er, no you can't,' and she nodded at the kittens.

'I'd rather carry Frank than try and tame those two.'

'I'd rather tame *Delilah* than those two.' And they

laughed, until a rustle to their right brought them back to reality.

'What was that?'

'I've no idea.'

'Oh God, it's not those men back, is it? It can't be!' Noah wanted to ball his fists but the kittens made that impossible. What would he do if they *were* back? There was no Col to save them *this* time.

But as the fears started to spin around his head, the noise got louder. It came from behind a proud, thick bush, but before he had time to brace himself, the foliage parted and he was knocked to the ground, a figure falling on top of him. The kittens spilled to the floor and darted away.

Noah readied himself to fight and pushed the figure off him.

He expected to see a hat or unruly sideburns, but found instead the much less threatening figure of a young boy, now rolled up like a hedgehog, shaking.

'What on earth?' Noah said, feeling his burns sting. 'Who are *you*?' His voice sounded harder than he meant it to. The boy was clearly not a threat, but Noah remained on edge, and when the newcomer didn't answer, it didn't help ease the tension.

'I said, who are you?' he asked again.

'Noah? Gently! Look how young he is,' Clem chided.

She'd put Frank down and went to touch the boy's shoulder, only to retreat when he scuttled fearfully away.

'It's all right,' she went on. 'We're not going to hurt you. You just gave us a shock, that's all.'

Still the boy said nothing, though he did look up, his eyes dinner-plate wide.

'What's your name?'

'Matthew?' came the reply, but not from him. 'MATTHEW! For Pete's sake. Where are you? It's not your fault so come back, will you?'

To be fair, the voice *did* sound a little angry, or frustrated at the very least, and when a girl appeared from behind the bush, her face said the same thing.

She was older than them. By a couple of years at least. She wore a long, patched-up dress and an even longer face. It didn't change when she spotted the newcomers, and then her brother, shaking on the floor.

'Matthew!!' She was definitely angry now, though it was aimed at the two strangers instead of the boy. 'What have you done to him? Who are you?' She looked fierce, like she'd put the fear of God into Col, never mind them.

'Steady on,' said Noah. 'We didn't do a thing. He just ran out of nowhere and knocked me over.'

'Did they hurt you?' the girl asked, pulling the boy to his feet. It was the first time they'd got a clear look at him.

He couldn't be more than six. Rivers of tears had smudged the muck on his cheeks.

The girl looked him up and down.

'If he's hurt, it's of his own doing. He can tell you that himself.'

She looked at Noah icily. 'He can't,' she replied.

'What do you mean?'

She didn't answer, taking the conversation instead in a whole new direction.

'He ran off half an hour ago,' she said, still checking him for damage. 'I had no idea which direction he'd gone, but Ma had left me in charge, so I had to find him before she got back from milking.'

Noah heard nothing except the word *milk*.

'You live on a farm?'

'We do, yes. Well, we do at the moment, anyway.'

'What do you mean?'

'Well, there might not be a farm much longer. Can't produce a lot if there's no one to work on it.'

'I don't understand,' Noah replied.

'Dad's going to lose nearly all his workers to the army. Practically overnight. Mum thinks he'll be excused from signing up cos he's too old and folk will still need feeding here. But if there's no one else to do the milking and feeding and mucking out, then the beasts won't last long. We'll be lucky if we're not thrown out by Christmas.'

The girl stopped, looked almost guilty that she'd said so much so quickly: like she'd betrayed someone in doing so. 'Who are you two *anyway*? You're not from round here.'

'We're not,' Noah replied. He didn't want to say anything he didn't need to.

'Well, you'd better keep moving then. Instead of coming round here, upsetting my brother.'

Clem stepped in. She could see Noah's blood rising.

'I'm Clem.' Noah frowned at the mention of her name. 'And this is Noah.'

'Why don't you just tell her everything!' he spat, exasperated. 'Honestly!!'

'It's fine, Noah,' Clem replied calmly, before turning her attention back to the girl. 'We honestly didn't do a thing to Matthew. He just came haring out of the bush from nowhere. He seemed a little . . . upset.'

'Well, he would do,' the girl replied. 'He had a bit of a shock earlier.' She lowered her voice and beckoned Clem closer.

'His rabbits died this morning. Well, not so much died. They were murdered.'

'Murdered?' Noah stepped closer now.

'Keep your voice down, will you?' she hissed. 'Last thing I need is him running off again. Ma would hit the roof!'

'What happened to the rabbits?' Clem asked.

'Foxes got 'em,' she said. 'Shouldn't have been a surprise, I suppose, living where we do. We did pen them in good and proper. But foxes? Well, they're wily, aren't they? They always find a way.'

'Gosh, I'm sorry,' Clem said.

'We only got them to see if it would help him. Matthew's . . . different. He's quiet.'

'Quiet?'

'Well . . . silent, actually. All his life.'

Noah looked confused. 'He can't talk?'

'Well, if he can, he's done a good job of hiding it. The words just never came. He'd find other ways to communicate what he wanted, but then, four months ago, our brother Tom enlisted. It came as a shock to us all. He didn't tell Mum or Dad in advance. And, well, they both hit the roof when he came home with the papers signed. They shouted, he shouted. He cried, they cried. Well, Dad didn't. I thought he was going to blow the roof off the house he was yelling so loud. But the person it hit hardest was Matthew.

'He loves Tom more than anything see. Always has.

Idolises him. Followed him like his little shadow. They'd slept in the same bed ever since Matthew was born. Every night of his life. So when Tom marched off, Matthew just seemed to curl up into himself.'

Noah and Clem didn't know what to say either. All Noah could think of was his own dad marching away.

'When Tom left, Matthew chased after and caught him. We had to prise them apart. Matthew cried, wailed in fact. But then he seemed to close down, wouldn't look us in the eye, picked at his food. We tried everything – toys, sweets, the doctor. None of them worked. Which is why Mum bought the rabbits.' The girl had really hit her stride. She talked nineteen to the dozen, sentences rattling one after another like she'd not spoken herself in a long, long time. Noah had trouble taking it all in. Luckily, Clem worked quicker than he did.

'It must have been horrible then, to find them . . . well, you know . . . dead.'

'He just ran. Bolted like a racehorse. If he hadn't run into you, I don't know if he would've stopped.'

'Oh, so you're thanking us now?' Noah couldn't resist. It earned him a dig in the ribs from Clem.

'Are those two yours?' the girl asked suddenly.

They turned to where she was pointing and there, sitting on the floor, was Matthew. He was no longer looking distressed though. Instead, he wore a smile so wide that no words were necessary to express his happiness. On his lap, lay two kittens. And they weren't raising hell. They were sleeping so blissfully that they actually looked cute, even to Noah and Clem.

48

Noah and Clem were on a mission to save their animals, but not for the first time on this adventure, it was the animals that saved them. Forty minutes later, as darkness fell, they found themselves not hunkering down under the stars, but in a barn.

There had been a lot of explaining to do on the way, much of it against Noah's better judgment, but as Clem told their story and the girl, Esther, listened open-mouthed, it became clear that they had a new, and incredibly helpful ally.

There was only half a roof on the barn, and it smelled awful, but there was straw and enough corrugated tin above them to keep them dry should the rain return. Most importantly, they had water. A bucket of it in fact, brought to them by Esther, who now couldn't do enough to make them happy.

'I'm sorry there's not enough milk for everyone,' she said as the kittens lapped blissfully. 'But Dad's a bit eagle-eyed that way.'

Noah waved her away as he tried to moisten his lips. 'This is perfect.'

Esther had only brought one tin cup, but Noah passed it to Clem, fighting the temptation to drink the water straight from the bucket's jagged rim.

He could have wept when he finally tasted it on his lips, but refused to be emotional now. What would be the point in wasting what he'd just drunk? Instead, they passed the cup back and forth, licking their lips and sighing like they were supping the finest of wines. As ridiculous as it sounded, they felt refreshed, even their hunger abated slightly as their brains whirred back into life. Esther hadn't let them down on the food front either. A folded tea towel revealed two thick doorsteps of bread smeared with the reddest jam, and a large home-baked biscuit broken evenly in two. It didn't matter that the bread came from the crusts of the loaf, it smelled wonderful and as the jam hit his tastebuds Noah worried his head was in danger of exploding, such was his joy and relief. And that was before he even thought about the biscuit.

'This is fantastic,' he spat clumsily, catching the crumbs that escaped before throwing them back into his mouth. He wasn't going to waste even the tiniest amount.

Clem was eating slightly more daintily and, as usual, had important details to think about.

'Are you sure no one will find us here?' she asked. 'We'll be safe until morning?'

Esther nodded her head. 'Dad hasn't been out here for months. Too busy. Mum neither, so as long as your dogs don't give you away, you'll be fine.'

'I don't think there's much danger of that,' Noah replied, smirking at the sight of Winn, submerged in so much hay that only her tail could be seen. 'I don't think we'll hear a peep out of them till morning. Or the kittens.'

Noah hadn't a clue what powers Matthew possessed, but since his sudden arrival, the kittens had been nothing but docile. Gone were the mischief and devilry, to be replaced by a sleepy obedience, even though the little boy obviously hadn't said a single word to them. They had trailed after Matthew on the way to the barn, then laid in his lap and snoozed as he stroked them in tandem, head cocked on one side in adoration.

'Only thing that might give us away,' said Noah, 'is him crying if you try and take him in for bed.'

Esther looked at her brother and shook her head. 'I don't know how a farmer's son can be so soppy about animals,' she said. 'Dad always says they're not pets, they're our livelihood. That we'll get nothing from adoring them. Looking at this, he clearly got it wrong.'

'Will Mathew get upset when you take him inside?'

'Not if I explain he can see them again in the morning. That is all right, isn't it? You won't be leaving before dawn?'

'It'll be early, but it'll depend on the dogs and how they are. Especially Frank. Today was nearly the end of him.'

'Oh, Matthew will be in here as soon as the cockerel crows. So if you can wait that long . . . well, it would make a big difference to him . . . and to me too.'

'Then that's what we'll do,' replied Clem, and even Noah nodded in agreement, realising, as he bit into his biscuit, that they had struck the luckiest of gold when they met Matthew and Esther.

They slept soundly. More than soundly, as not even the cockerel woke them. The first they knew of dawn's creep was the sound of the barn door. By the time they'd wiped their eyes, the kittens were already in Matthew's lap, batting at his fingers and making the most joyful noise.

'Do you think we could take Matthew with us?' Noah yawned, feeling keenly the sting and bite of the burns that lined his wrists. They didn't look the healthiest of colours. Yellowing around the edges and slightly oozy.

'It'd make things a lot easier,' Clem agreed. 'Though I'm not sure Esther would agree to it.'

'Couldn't feed him either, could we? Can barely feed ourselves.'

Eight hours on, their hunger had come racing back, but Noah refused to start the day on a negative note. *Come on*, he told himself, *today is the day when we reach the Duchess'*.

So after waking the dogs, frowning as they saw the stiffness in Frank's hind quarters, they divided up the potted meat and bread roll that remained from their shoplifting, eating like it was the greatest feast ever assembled. Even the water tasted sweeter than normal.

'We can do this,' Noah told Clem, with a smile, 'we really can.'

'I know that,' came a new voice from the doorway. It was Esther, in the same dress as yesterday, but sporting long pigtails. 'But I think I've worked out a way that I can help you.'

'Is your dad going to drive us to Windsor?'

Esther smiled, but shook her head. 'Hardly. But I was thinking about what you told me about the Duchess. It reminded me of something. About this place we went to a few years back, all of us, to a fair at this big house owned by a rich lady.'

Noah sat, intrigued. 'Go on.'

'Well, I don't remember all of it cos it was ages ago. But I know she had a load of animals, this lady. There were peacocks on her lawn and loads of dogs, some ponies and a goat. She had one of those posh-sounding names too.'

'Douglas-Hamilton?'

'I don't know but it was definitely two words together like that.'

'Double-barrelled,' said Clem.

'What?'

'Double-barrelled. It's what you call it when people have two names in their surname. It's a posh thing.'

'Well, yes, this woman had one of those names and she was definitely very posh.'

Clem and Noah looked at each other. It sounded too close to be a coincidence.

'Can you remember where it was?' Clem asked. 'How far it was from here?'

'Not exactly, but it *was* by the river, her garden backed right on to it. And I remember us driving towards Windsor to get there. You could see the castle from the lady's house, I remember that bit clearly. And there was a little church next to it.'

'It has to be the Duchess', doesn't it?' Noah said excitedly. But Clem was still diving into the detail.

'So how far is it do you think? From here.'

Esther frowned. 'Hard to say. On foot as you are? Another eight miles or so, if you stay by the river.'

It sounded like a long way, and Noah thought he heard Frank sigh from his bed. The pair of them frowned.

'Don't look so defeated,' Esther cajoled. 'Because actually, I think I've got an idea that could make your journey there a lot easier.'

She gestured to her brother and the kittens, then back at Noah.

Noah just looked confused, then shocked.

'You're not suggesting we take Matthew to look after the kittens, are you?' He didn't want to offend her or anything, but when he'd said it to Clem he really had been joking.

'I don't think Mum would agree to that. Don't think the police would like it either. Especially if they're already looking for you.'

'Then what do you mean?' Clem asked.

The girl took a deep breath as if nervous. 'Let us take the kittens off your hands. You said it yourself, they're lively. Difficult even. And if you've still miles to go then they're hardly going to sit quietly while you walk.'

'But what will you do with them?'

'I'd have thought that was obvious,' she replied. 'I won't do anything with them, but Matthew here will love them every second of every day. They'll have the best lives imaginable.'

'I'm sorry, but we can't do that,' Noah answered quickly and firmly. Clem looked shocked and as though she completely disagreed.

'Why not?' both she and Esther said together.

'Because . . . well . . . because they're our responsibility. We found them, didn't we? Saved them and made a promise that we'd keep it that way.'

'But they'll be safe here,' said Esther. 'And you can see how loved they'd be.'

'They'd be loved at the Duchess'.'

'Well, yes, but there'll be loads of other animals there.'

'And this is a *farm*!'

'Please, Noah,' said Esther. 'Think about it for just a minute. Think about how little they are, and lively they are.'

'Not to mention how far we'd have to carry them,' added Clem.

'Without proper food,' said Esther.

'Are you two ganging up on me?'

'We're trying to make you see sense,' said Clem. 'I know why you don't want to give them up. It's because of Samson, isn't it? And Col and Delilah.'

'They've got nothing to do with it!'

'Oh, I think they have,' she went on. 'You think you failed them and that by leaving the kittens here you'll be breaking your promise again, but that's not right. In fact, the opposite is true. If we *take* the kittens, then we have less chance of reaching the Duchess.'

'Nonsense.'

'It's not nonsense, it's true. I'm tired, Noah. So are you. And so are the dogs. I'm going to have to carry Frank a lot of the way today, and will probably need your help. And you can't give me that if you've the kittens to keep under control. Please, Noah, listen to what I'm saying to you.'

He *was* listening and the thing he was finally hearing was that she was right. On all scores.

'But what about your parents?' Noah said to Esther. 'What if they don't want the kittens here?'

Esther smiled. 'Dad will barely notice, and Mum will be fine as long as they keep the mice out of the larder.'

'But you can't just turn up with two kittens out of the blue!'

The girl smiled again, coyly this time. 'That's just it, I already mentioned it last night. Told her the farm down the road had a litter needed homes. Told her Matthew fell in love as soon as he saw 'em.'

'So she said yes?'

'She didn't say no,' Esther replied honestly. 'And once she sees how happy it's made Matthew, then she'll never turn 'em away. Not in a million years.'

Noah sighed and rubbed at his forehead.

'Come on, you fool,' Clem laughed. 'They'll have the best life ever here. Mice on tap, fields to prowl in, and a boy who doesn't care how mischievous they are.'

'Please?' said Esther, mock-begging.

'All right! All right!' Noah replied, throwing his hands in the air. 'Anything to shut you both up. Just don't come crying to me if it all goes wrong.'

'I'll have a job,' said Esther. 'I don't know your surname, never mind where you live.'

Once he'd accepted that the kittens were staying behind, Noah could see no point in hanging around, but as much as he'd found them difficult to handle, he didn't want to say goodbye. He still felt that in some small way he was breaking yet another promise.

'Come on now, don't be silly,' Clem told him. 'Remember when you first had this brainwave, we were only trying to save Frank and Winn. And we can still do that. In fact, there's more chance of that than ever.'

'I know, I know . . .'

'Well, try telling your face that!' she said, digging him in the ribs.

In the end though, the thing that got to Noah wasn't the kittens at all. They were hardly going to be interested in a weepy farewell. It was little Matthew and the way he attached himself to Noah with the biggest of bear hugs. For the second time in their short meeting, Noah found himself knocked off his feet with the little man on top of him.

This time though, Noah didn't throw him off. This time he hugged him back and although the boy didn't say thank you, Noah knew with absolute certainty that Matthew was so very very grateful.

'You're welcome,' Noah said quietly, before whispering into his ear, 'Your brother will be home soon. Just like my dad.'

And with that, Noah let the boy go and watched him scurry to Joseph and Mary.

There were now only four of them left.

So they took a deep breath, said a final farewell to Esther and marched purposefully on.

49

Noah spent the morning doing something unusual: thinking.

That's not to say he didn't usually think. He *always* had lots of thoughts. He just had a habit of acting on them before weighing up whether they were sensible or not.

But after the drama of the last few days, the fatigue he felt in his bones and the pain in his throbbing burns, he was happier to live in his head for a while.

He thought about a lot of things, some of which took him by surprise. He thought about having a bath (which was a first) and how nice it would be just to lie there for a few minutes in the old tin tub in front of the fire, with his mum topping up the hot water.

The only problem was this threw up thoughts of Mum, and he couldn't help but picture her, either pacing angrily, or sobbing in fear. It was a horrid thought, the worst, but it wasn't enough to see him stop and walk in the opposite direction back to her.

'Keep going,' he said to himself. 'Keep your promise. Keep it.'

Clem had been pretty quiet all morning herself. Conserving energy in the knowledge that Frank was fading in front of her eyes. It might not have been as hot as the previous day, but it soon would be when her little friend needed carrying. His front legs today were nearly as stiff as his back ones, giving him a strange walk like a clockwork toy, that to other people might have seemed comical but not to her. To Clem, it was simply worrying.

'I'll find you the biggest bowl of food ever when we get there,' she said to Frank, fussing his muzzle. 'I promise.' And that seemed to move the old boy on again, leaving Clem's hands free to navigate the map. She managed to keep them relatively close to the river, which pleased Noah no end. It made him feel like they were moving closer with every step if he caught sight of the Thames, winding its way behind them, all the way back to the city. But by early afternoon, the trees had grown denser, which brought a sense of unease to them both. It could've been their hunger growing, adding to their paranoia, but it felt like there were too many places to hide here, too many opportunities for someone to lie in wait. And battling through all the undergrowth and bushes really slowed down their pace.

'Do you not think we'd be safer and quicker walking the riverbank?' Noah asked.

'I'm sure we would,' Clem replied. 'But we'd also be very easy to spot by anyone sailing down it. We need to keep the river in our sights but we can't be exposed. And look here, if I'm reading this right, then we should be back in the open soon. It won't feel so bad then, I promise.'

So they plodded on, Noah trying to ease his fears by throwing sticks for Winn into the densest undergrowth, in the hope that she would scare away or at least unearth possible assailants. Every bird call or snapping twig had his senses on high alert: whilst the dog's sticks were in his grasp he found himself clutching them like clubs.

But when danger came an hour later, it came from an unexpected place.

'What's that noise?' Noah fretted, his eyes flitting skywards. He stumbled through the last of the trees as a large, fallow field stretched out in front of them.

The sound grew louder and more familiar.

'It's Spitfires again,' he said with relief, though he couldn't see them yet. 'I'd put money on it.'

His eyes scoured the skies in the hope of spotting the planes. He needed something to lift his spirits and these planes never failed. They were magnificent, thrilling machines. But when he finally got his wish, off in the distance, he was surprised to see only one plane, instead of the squadron they'd witnessed earlier.

'Why's that plane on its own?' he asked.

Clem shrugged. The plane flew nearer, lower, noisier.

'And why's it so loud? It's making the noise of four of them.'

It got louder and louder, so deafening that they were soon clutching at their ears.

'Something's not right,' said Noah. The plane was flying lower and lower, too low, and seemed to be dipping further. Its engine sounded more like a tractor than a fighter plane, and it was now spitting out smoke.

'Has it been shot at?' yelled Clem over the din.

'I don't know. Maybe the Nazis have started firing. Maybe they're on their way.'

'We'd have seen them, wouldn't we?'

'I don't know but I don't like this,' shouted Noah, the ringing in his ears so loud that he may well have been speaking to himself. 'It's going to come down. Jesus, Clem, it's coming right at us.'

The dogs didn't need to be told. They sensed it already and bolted away.

'Run!' yelped Noah.

They sprinted as best they could across the field, but it

was a struggle. Noah couldn't help but turn again and again, to make sure they were outrunning the plane, but of course they weren't. So they pivoted, dashing at a right angle, away from its path. But each time they turned, the Spitfire seemed to do the same, as though it were chasing them.

Noah looked again, and now the only thing that filled his eyeline was the propeller, scything gleefully towards him. This was it, he thought. This was how it would end.

As the thunder and smoke reached a crescendo, and they felt the wind whip up a frenzy around them, Noah and Clem threw themselves to the ground, feeling the grass flatten, giving way to hard, rutted mud that pulled at their bare knees.

Noah felt the scream in his throat but could not hear it. He couldn't stop it either, as the Spitfire thundered over them. But even when it passed, he knew the danger wasn't over, because the plane was speeding rapidly to the ground. And when the collision happened, who knew how far the explosion would reach.

Noah cowered, pulled Winn under his arms and braced himself, waiting for the storm to rage.

50

The ground shook, giving way as the Spitfire splintered. One wing flew to the right, the other hung on grimly, though it was broken beyond recognition. Smoke poured from the front, belching into the air, covering them all in the blackest of fugs.

'Clem?' Noah spluttered. 'Are you and Frank all right?' He knew Winn was, as she was burrowing anxiously into his side.

A cough echoed through the fog, followed by a definite but scared call of 'yes' soon after.

'Follow me, then. We shouldn't be this close,' Noah yelled, though he actually had no idea just how far away the Spitfire had landed.

He clambered to his feet, half expecting to feel pain somewhere, although mercifully there was none. With Winn at his side he stumbled to where the light was brighter, constantly calling to Clem so she could follow his voice.

They reached daylight twenty seconds or so later, collapsing to the ground Frank in particular was terrified.

No matter how many times Clem reassured him, the little dog wouldn't have it, scrabbling at her chest as if trying to hide down the front of her clothes.

'Is he all right?' asked Noah.

'He will be.'

After fussing Winn, Noah turned his attention to the wreck. Close up, the Spitfire looked huge, though that could've been due to the wreckage that jutted from the ground in various shards. Smoke continued to pour from the back, but it was the cockpit that held Noah's attention. He didn't want to imagine what shape the pilot, still slumped over his controls, would be in, but he couldn't help it. There was someone in there: a life, someone's son, someone's dad. And that pulled at Noah, made his feet twitch.

'Don't you even think about it, Noah,' said Clem. 'I see what you're thinking and I'm telling you right now, if you so much as take one step towards that plane then me and Frank will rugby tackle you, do you hear me?'

'Yes but—'

'But nothing, Noah. The only thing living in this field is us, these dogs, and that smoke. And who knows how long till it's not smoke any more but flames.'

He knew what she was saying. He'd already thought it himself, but that didn't just mean he could stand by and watch. What if the pilot was still alive? What if his heart was beating as fast as Noah's, what if he was just as scared? He couldn't stand there and watch the man perish.

But just as his brain told his feet to get moving, someone else beat him to it. From their left, some fifty feet away, a figure broke from the treeline at lightning speed. A man. He covered the ground in no time, not pausing or flinching at the smoke or devastation in front of him. He only stopped when he reached the cockpit and pulled at the glass.

'We should help him,' Noah said. He couldn't take his eyes off the man, and his feet began to move. The rest of him didn't though, thanks to the restraining arms of Clem. Not to mention the jaws of Winn, attached to his right sock. How could they be so strong when they were so so tired?

'Don't even think about!' Clem roared. 'How long do you think it'll be before it explodes?'

'That won't happen if I get there quickly.'

'It's not happening at all, Noah. You're staying here with me.' And she gripped even harder.

But before he could wrestle himself free, the plumes of smoke near the tailfin sparked into life like a phoenix: orange, reds and yellows licking into the air. The man, facing the opposite way as he tugged at the cockpit, had no idea.

'We've got to do something!' yelled Noah. But Clem still wouldn't let him go.

So instead they yelled. Noah waving any limbs free of restraint. Even the dogs joined in. The man finally peered over his shoulder as he pulled, and although Noah and Clem were some distance away, they could still see his eyes widen in shock and horror. He had to run, it was clear, but he only did so after one, final abortive yank at the glass.

The children yelled on, warning him, fearing that the flame might only be inches away now from the fuel line, and no matter how hard the man sprinted, they didn't see how he could magic himself away in time.

They were right. For when the explosion came, it brought the mightiest of booms, sending a mushroom cloud of fire high above the trees that ringed the clearing. It chased the man, eating the grass that led to his feet, and when the earth couldn't satisfy its hunger, it blew the man ten feet into the air, his arms windmilling, just as the Spitfire's rotor had as it plummeted to earth.

He fell to the ground, back first, legs hitting the earth like a broken doll.

The children took in what they had just seen, then Noah shook himself free and sprinted to where the man lay crumpled.

51

Sweat poured off Noah' s face. Little wonder. He'd been closer to death in these past twenty-four hours than he had for the entirety of his life, but for some reason here he was again, sprinting in its direction. It was like he wasn't in control of his actions.

Dropping to his knees, Noah went to shake the man, to make sure that he wasn't leaning over another corpse, yet something made him stop, a fear of hurting him.

It turned out this was unnecessary, for although the man's eyes were closed, they didn't remain that way for long. A long slobbering lick to the face from Winn soon woke him up.

'Did he get out?' the man said, attempting to sit up, eyes rolling slightly as he tried to focus.

'Steady on,' replied Noah, as Clem and Frank arrived at his shoulder. 'You flew quite a way when the plane exploded.'

But the man wasn't listening, he was already scrabbling to his feet, and Noah realised that although he *was* older than them, there wasn't a great deal in it. Six years maybe?

Eighteen years old, nineteen at a push. He looked strong, wiry, though he was far from smartly dressed and that wasn't due to the blast alone. His trousers were ill-fitting, baggy and frayed at the hem, held up by a pair of shabby braces that sat on top of a brown, collarless shirt. His hair was thick and brown, seeming to grow outwards rather than down. It had a nest-like quality to it: mossy, whilst tufts stuck out at uncomfortable and untameable angles.

'What happened?' the young man asked, flames reflecting in his widening eyes. 'He got out, didn't he? Tell me he got out.'

They said nothing. It was easier than telling the truth. The man shuffled from foot to foot, back and forth. It looked like he was considering running back towards the burning wreckage.

'There was nothing you could do,' Noah said. 'We saw what you tried to do.'

'The cockpit was stuck fast. Just couldn't shift it.'

'Where did you come from?' Noah asked.

'Home,' the man replied, pointing back to the dense woods. Suddenly a second explosion from the plane shook the ground and had them all cowering once again.

'Are you both all right?' the young man asked. He looked them up and down, like they might be on fire themselves.

'We're fine, fine,' Noah said.

The man was now pacing the ground, brow furrowed as he pulled at one particularly knotted piece of hair.

'Are *you* all right?' Clem asked him. 'I'm Clem and this is Noah.'

The man didn't seem to be listening. He was still distracted, agitated.

'We're going to have to get used to this, aren't we?' He pointed at the wreckage and flames. 'I mean, war hasn't even been declared yet and look, planes are already falling out of the skies.'

Noah looked at Clem, who looked right back, quizzically.

'What do you mean?' Noah said. 'Have you been living in a cave for the last two days?'

The man stopped pacing and stared at him.

'Not a cave, no. But, well, I haven't been listening to the news. I've been . . . busy.' He looked momentarily furtive.

Noah's mind tried to fill in the gaps. How could someone possibly *not* know what had been happening? How could you not find a wireless or read a paper or speak to someone and *know* that the world was imploding? Had the man been in prison or something? Because he had the look of a fugitive.

But despite that Noah wasn't scared of the man. He'd

been up close to bad, bad people on this journey and he just knew this man wasn't one of them. And if he didn't know what was going on, then he deserved to know.

'The Prime Minister,' Noah said. 'Well, he's declared it, hasn't he? We're at war with Hitler. With Germany.'

The man sighed and dropped his head on to his chest. 'It's not a surprise,' he said. 'The only surprise is that it's taken this long. And this death here, this pilot, it won't be the last. There'll be thousands of them, millions even, before it's done.'

Noah found himself nodding. Couldn't believe he'd just witnessed a man lose his life. 'It's already started in the city,' he said. 'There's animals all over London, all over the country probably, being put to sleep. Which is why we're not there any more. It's why we're here.'

He didn't know what reaction he expected the man to offer. Some people were not animal people, after all. But what happened next told Noah everything he needed to know about the stranger. Out of nowhere, a brilliant green bird swooped down: a flurry of feathers thwacking the air, until it landed, squarely on the man's left shoulder. His hand went up to the bird, who rested its head reassuringly on his thumb.

'You'd better tell me what's happening,' the man said. 'Starting with this stuff about the animals.'

52

'Er . . . there's a parrot on your shoulder,' said Noah, as if the man somehow hadn't noticed.

'She isn't a parrot, she's a parakeet called Esme.' The man hadn't taken his eyes off the plane; they glistened with sadness. He still looked like he had half a mind to dash back towards it.

'I can't believe it,' he sighed. 'Well, I can, of course I can. There's people in London, powerful people, who've wanted this war for years. I just don't want to believe they've finally got their wish, that's all. I mean, who's going to tell that pilot's family? They'll never know what really happened, will they?'

'What do *you* think happened? I mean, did someone shoot him down? Do you think the Germans have started to invade?' Noah asked.

'Not today. Sounded like an engine fault. But if what you say is true then it won't be long until the sky is full of planes. And guns. And bombs. Messerschmitts, Heinkels, Dorniers.'

Noah didn't like the sound of them.

The man still looked incensed. The parakeet paced along his shoulder too, back and forth, embodying his agitation.

'Thing that makes me fume,' the man went on, 'is that pilot probably didn't even think twice before joining up. Thought he was doing his *duty,*' he spat the last word. 'Because that's what we're all taught, isn't it?'

Noah was struggling to understand what the man meant. But he didn't have time to ask him, as over to their left came another disturbance, a group of people, six at least, stumbling out of the treeline, pointing the second they saw the flames.

'Police,' said Clem. 'Maybe we shouldn't be here.'

'Why? What you done?' asked the man, though he didn't look too comfortable at the sight of the bobbies himself.

'Nothing really,' Noah gabbled. 'We haven't committed a crime or anything. But they're looking for us anyway.'

'That doesn't make a lot of sense,' said the man.

'It'll be all right, we just need to stay calm,' Noah went on. 'They'll only care about the plane. They're not going to realise who we are. Why would they?'

But as he focused on the new arrivals, he realised that whilst four of the officers were haring in the direction of the plane, two of them were heading in their direction. And they weren't ambling either.

'Oh lord,' said Clem. She'd never had a policeman so much as look in her direction before, never mind run towards her. Just to add to her fear, they were shouting now too.

'You didn't kill no one, did you?' asked the man.

'Do we look like murderers?' replied Noah. He was ready to run, but had no idea in which direction.

'No,' said the man, quickly weighing things up. 'Whatever you did, I don't reckon the law deserves to catch you.'

'What are you saying?'

'If you want to stay free, follow me.'

'Can we trust you?'

'I'm all you've got,' he replied. And before anyone could say anything else, he bolted away from the bobbies, leaving Noah, Clem and the dogs to race after him as if their lives and liberties depended on it.

53

They ran, sprinted in fact, but so did the police. And while the bobbies may have been carrying extra pounds, Clem had a wheezing Frank in her arms, who really slowed her down.

'Give him to me!' Noah shouted.

'Why are we running?' Clem gasped as Noah pulled Frank from her arms. 'What if they don't actually know who we are? Maybe they just want to ask us about the plane.' But she soon accelerated when she heard their names shouted, followed by the word 'STOP!'

'Where are we going?' Noah yelled.

'Nearly there,' the man replied, 'but we need to be quicker or they'll spot us as we hide.'

Noah looked ahead as they picked up the pace, expecting to see a small house or a shack at least, though how they could expect to go unfound in something so obvious, he had no idea.

But there was nothing to see, just tree after tree, punctuated by the occasional bush or thicket.

'Here! Now,' the man hollered abruptly, as he pulled on the brakes, yanking at a bush that sat flush against a tree trunk. Except it wasn't a bush at all, it was a door of sorts made from an old piece of plywood but camouflaged with thick, dense foliage.

'Quickly now!' whispered the man and he pushed them inside. His palms felt rough and calloused as he shoved them into the dark, and he treated Winn the same way, not that the dog seemed to mind. As long as she was with her master, the world was all right with her.

With a quick, furtive look behind him, the man ducked inside too, pulling the lean-to behind him, leaving them all in darkness.

Noah opened his eyes as wide as he could, trying to make sense of where they found themselves, and whether they were actually safer inside than out. But although it remained dark, he felt a sense of space that he didn't expect.

'What is this place?' he hissed, only to be told to pipe down.

From outside, the crack and rustle of twigs and leaves grew louder, until they could hear not just the words of the bobbies, but their panting as well.

'Which way now?' one gasped.

'I don't ruddy know,' another replied, and they felt

something shake above them, like the door was being rested on.

'Well, they can't have just evaporated. Try calling the dogs? See if you can get 'em to bark.'

'What do you think I am, a bloomin' vet?'

Noah felt Winn push her flank into his, and he stroked her tenderly, imploring her not to give the game away. As always, the dog didn't let him down, not even when the immediate danger passed and the footsteps slowly crunched into the distance.

'Have they g—' Noah whispered, only to be hushed by the man again. For once, Noah did as he was told, not saying a word even when the door was wedged slightly ajar, allowing the light to creep inside.

Noah took it all in. This wasn't a tent, though it had the same triangular shape to it. It was certainly smelly and damp, and although he didn't want to look nosy, Noah couldn't help but make a note of everything that littered the floor. There were a couple of threadbare blankets thrown into a bed shape, and a canvas rucksack that seemed to serve as a pillow of sorts, though there was no sign of any other clothes. What there were a lot of were books. Old tattered, clothbound books that should have been on a shelf rather than the forest floor. If their appearance was anything to go by, it looked like they had been read a thousand times apiece. It didn't surprise Noah in the slightest to see Clem's eyes widening, and fingers twitching as she gazed at them.

'Are these all yours?' she asked. The man didn't answer straightaway, choosing instead to snake his upper body into the daylight, only returning when he was convinced the coast was clear.

'So,' he said, ignoring Clem's question. 'Who you been robbing then?'

'No one,' said Noah.

'Well, that didn't look like nothing to me. Spitfire's crashed, man killed in his cockpit, but half the bobbies want to chase you. Doesn't exactly make sense, does it?'

'Show me something these days that *does* make sense?' Noah said. It was a response that sent the man deep into thought again.

'Is it true? What you said, about being at war with Germany?'

They both nodded.

'Then this is not good. Not good at all. I can't be staying round here. Not now.' The man crawled on to his knees and started pulling at his blankets, upending poor Frank from his slumber.

'Looks to me,' said Noah, 'like we're not the only ones with a secret. So here's an idea,' he looked the man in the eye. 'We'll tell you ours, if you tell us yours.'

The man sighed. Then stuck out a grubby, rough hand and shook Noah's firmly.

'Done,' he said. 'I'm Dennis. And if them bobbies catch me, then I'm only one step behind that pilot. Dead before you know it.'

54

'The police can't kill you,' Noah stammered.

'Not directly,' Dennis said. 'But if we're at war, then it's only a matter of time before they come looking for people like me.'

It still didn't make any sense to Noah. 'People like *what*?'

'Does the word conscription mean anything to you?' Dennis said, Clem nodded. So did Noah, but without conviction. He didn't want to lose face by admitting that it didn't.

'People have been talking about it for months,' Dennis went on. 'I mean, if the government is stupid enough to make us fight Hitler, then they're going to need every single person they can to fight him. And it's no secret they're going to come after people like me first, because of my age and because I don't have a wife or children. And the second I agree, I don't just sign up to the army, I sign my own death certificate too.'

'I don't understand,' said Noah. And he didn't. He also didn't like the thought that his own dad might have already done the same thing. Not when he'd promised he'd come back safe and sound. 'That's not true. I know some soldiers will die –' he didn't even like admitting that much – 'but my dad, he's coming home the second the war is done.'

'And maybe he will,' said Dennis; there was kindness in his voice. 'If he's lucky. But I know that won't happen to me. They send me to fight? Then I'll die there. Fact.'

'But you don't know that. How can you know that?'

Dennis sighed, like he was seeing his own demise play out in front of him.

'Because I will never pull the trigger of a gun,' he said. 'I can't and I won't.'

'Not if a Nazi soldier was standing in front of you with a rifle of his own?' Noah interrupted.

'Not even if Hitler *himself* was standing where you are now.'

'But . . . but . . . but . . .' Noah stammered. 'That man is evil. He's killing people all over Europe.'

'He is and it's horrific, all of it.'

'Which is why it needs to be stopped!' Noah couldn't understand what Dennis was saying. His dad, Matthew's brother, men all over the country were joining up. 'So what makes you so special?'

'I'm not,' Dennis sighed. 'I'm far from special, I'm ordinary, and that's why I can't do it. Other people may be able to take a life and live with themselves. But I can't, I know I can't. German? Russian? It doesn't matter where they're from, I know I'd see their faces for the rest of my life. When I'm awake or asleep. They'd haunt me for what I did. And I'd deserve it.'

They sat, silent for a while. Noah hadn't a clue what to say. It had never even dawned on him that it was possible to say no. That you could refuse to fight.

'So what would happen?' Clem asked. 'If they told you to fight and you refused?'

'They'd put me in jail,' Dennis replied. 'Which is why I've been living out here because I saw it coming. And because I don't deserve to be locked up just for being peaceful.'

'You live here? Seriously?' Noah asked the question, though from the blankets and books, he already knew the answer.

'Since June.'

'But aren't your family worried about you?'

'Only family I've got is Esme here, and the bird strutted again on his right shoulder.

'But she's your pet!'

'She's no such thing!' The cross look returned to Dennis's face. 'I don't own her or anyone else. She found me, that's all. I haven't asked her to stay, but she hasn't left

315

either, and the day she does? Well, I'll be sad certainly, but I can hardly stop her, can I?'

'But what'll you do in winter? Two months from now and it'll be freezing. You can't live out here. What'll you eat?'

'Same thing I eat now. The forest will provide. There's berries, fruit and nettles.'

'Nettles?' Noah's face crumpled.

'Well, they're not exactly roast potatoes, but if you mash 'em down into a broth, well, they're not too bad.'

'But you can't survive all winter on nettle soup?'

'Don't you worry about me. I've eaten worse before and probably will again. Anyway, I'll move around, like I always do. Maybe head north, see if I can find a farmer desperate enough for a shepherd to turn a blind eye. 'Anyway, you haven't told me why you're running yet. Something about animals?'

'It's not our fault.'

'Never is, is it?'

Dennis may have been talking playfully, but Noah was serious.

'It isn't this time. We haven't done anything. It's the stupid government's fault.'

'It always is.'

'You won't have heard about it, but they've told

everyone, EVERYONE, to have their pets put to sleep because of the war.'

Dennis burst out laughing, but soon stopped when he saw their faces.

'You're not serious, are you?'

'Deadly. You should've seen the queues back in London. Hundreds there were. Thousands, maybe more. Everyone was doing it . . .'

'Apart from you?'

'Apart from us.'

'Good for you. So what's your plan? You do have one, don't you? I mean, you think *I* won't survive out here, but what about you? This little fella looks beaten.' He pointed at Frank.

'We've got a plan. Had one since we first started out.' Noah tried to sound confident, which drew a cough from Clem.

'What? We have. All right, so it might not have always gone smoothly. But we know where we're heading and why!' And he told Dennis all about the Duchess and her animal refuge, as well as the *Queen Maudie* and the kittens and Delilah and Col and the fire and the thugs and the shoplifting. And of course about poor, dear Samson.

When he stopped and drew breath, Noah looked at Dennis and their surroundings. Late afternoon was upon them: the shadows would soon be lengthening, but that wasn't the only thing. Dennis's smile was also growing.

'That,' he said, firmly, 'is the kind of battle I *can* get behind.'

'Really?' replied Noah.

'Really. And this Duchess' house? Do you know where it is?'

They shared a glance. 'We know it's downriver. Just before Windsor. It backs on to the Thames, we've heard.'

'Well, I think I can get you there then. Though we'll have to be clever about it. Step outside now and there's a good chance the bobbies will nab you. We need to wait a while.'

'How long?'

'A couple of hours or so, I think. Till dusk. There's a boat downriver that we can use. Think you can wait that long?'

'I think so,' Noah replied. His burns were really stinging now, making him feel light-headed and dreadfully queasy but he didn't want to tell the others or admit weakness. 'Do you think the river levels will be all right then, Clem?'

Clem nodded with certainty, though Noah could see that she would have no problem passing time in Dennis' den. Her hand was already moving towards the first of his books.

55

Dusk hugged them close, as did the trees, though the forest floor did little to keep them a secret: there were too many pairs of legs to move anywhere quietly.

'Keep it down,' whispered Dennis. 'You can bet your life those bobbies are still here somewhere.'

'Can you really get us there? To the Duchess?' asked Noah. He wanted to believe it, but daren't.

'Absolutely. There's going to be enough deaths round here without adding your dogs to the list. And besides, it's not their fault, is it? They didn't ask for any of this.'

There was nothing to argue about there, though it made Noah think more about what Dennis was doing, and about his attitude to the war. Made Noah realise there were different kinds of fighting. Dennis might not want to go into combat with a Nazi, but he was happy to sprint towards the fallen Spitfire: more than happy to scrap on behalf of Winn and Frank.

'Not far now,' said Dennis. 'We're nearly at the river.' Though as the words came out there was an almighty crash behind him as Noah lay sprawled on the floor, upended by a tree root.

He was none too pleased about it. 'For goodness' sake!' he yelled. 'Could we not have ten flipping minutes without something trying to kill me!'

'Keep your voice down,' hissed Clem.

'That's easy for you to say. You've not been rugby tackled by a tree.'

'SHHHHHHH!' added Dennis.

'Not you as well. Can you not have a tiny bit of sympathy?'

But there wasn't time, as Dennis's warnings quickly came true.

'Up here!' yelled a voice. 'I can hear them. They're here. Quick!'

That was all they needed to have them away on their toes. Clem swept Frank up from the floor, and Winn was called quickly to heel as their feet pounded the forest floor.

'Don't look back, only forward,' gasped Dennis. 'The river's not far now.'

'How far is far!' gasped Clem.

But Dennis didn't reply. The nearest they got was a rallying squawk from Esme as she dived and dipped above their heads, chivvying them along.

'They're gaining!' shouted Clem. She was floundering at the back of the group now. Frank might have been small, but the days of carrying him were taking their toll, and she couldn't possibly put him down without slowing them all further.

'Then don't let them!' called Dennis from the front. 'Run harder. Catch you and they catch us all.'

That was all Clem needed to hear. She wasn't going to be the weak link in the group. She never had been since the mission started, so she certainly wasn't going to start now. Holding Frank tight by the collar she powered on, lifting her knees, taking Noah by surprise as she gained on him, making him work harder too. The group sped on, leaping logs and sidestepping brambles, until finally, with their lungs burning, they burst through the treeline to find themselves back at the Thames, a small jetty dangling its legs into the still, black water.

'There!' shouted Dennis, relieved. 'Look.'

They spotted a rowing boat tethered at the far end, that looked just about big enough for all of them.

Dennis reached it first, wrestling with the mooring rope as well as trying to hold it steady. 'Get in, quick!' he yelled. Clem and Frank needed no encouragement. Noah leaped in behind them.

But they weren't going to escape without a fight, as the officers had reached the bank now: four of them, sweaty and gasping, and intent on finishing the job.

'Oi!' one yelled. 'Stop. We know who you are.'

That was hardly going to have the runaways surrendering, but as Dennis jumped aboard and pushed them from the jetty, they realised that one of their party had remained on dry land.

Instead of joining the others, Winn had remained on the jetty, and was snarling and growling at the officers for even daring to intervene.

The bobbies drew their truncheons.

'Winn!!' Noah yelled. 'What are you doing? Come on, girl, now!'

But Winn was deaf to his pleas. She had the enemy in her sights and stalked forward, her bared teeth enough to stop a couple of the officers, but not all. One moved left and forward, the other peeled right, truncheons swishing from either side as they tried to negate Winn's threat. The dog wasn't worried, far from it, but Noah was: all he could hear was the noise the truncheons would make if they made contact with her skull. They'd already lost Samson, and he couldn't bear the prospect of Winn being struck down too.

'WINN!' he yelled, with a ferocity he didn't know he owned. He was tired. Oh so tired, and with every second he felt worse, like a fever was sweeping up behind him. But at that moment, Winn was the only thing that mattered. His tone was new to her too, which saw her turn to the boat and lock eyes with her master. As soon as she did that, and heard him call her once more, there was only one thing in her mind. To join him on the river. So with legs a blur, Winn tore down the jetty. She didn't pause or hesitate when her paws hit the end, and she flew, almost as majestically as Esme above her, until gravity pulled her into the river.

She broke the surface with the same momentum, paddling furiously until she was within arm's reach of Noah, who pulled her onboard.

The officers gaped, hands on knees, their final calls to stop and give themselves up a pitiful echo of their earlier demands.

Onboard the rowing boat, the mood was buoyant. Dennis rowed, the children cheered and the dogs barked a farewell.

They were back on the river, with the Duchess' estate within reach.

Nothing was going to stop them now.

56

Night brought a calmness that neither of them had felt for some time. Or perhaps it wasn't night-time at all but the return to the river, or even (though Noah and Clem wouldn't want to admit it) the presence of an adult, even if he were only a little older than them.

Whatever it was, it was working, and it eased the nausea that Noah felt continue to rise. His burns were so very sore now, with an itch that was almost impossible to ignore. All he could do was cool them in the water, which was calm and serene, the moonlight hitting the surface at such an angle that it felt like they were sailing through dark, luxurious ink

Travelling with Dennis added a calmness that Noah needed in his weakened state. He might not have been that much older than them, but his presence made things that would have seemed like obstacles on their own, seem blissfully straightforward. They hit locks again, first at Bell Weir and then Old Windsor, but no one batted an eyelid in their direction, despite the lateness of the hour.

The sound of their breathing gave way to the noise of the oars on water, and soon, the low hum of Winn's gentle snoring as she dozed. The only thing that broke the silence was the sight of something that got Noah's pulse racing.

'Look, look, there!' he yelled suddenly. Even the dogs stirred. 'That's got to be Windsor Castle, hasn't it?'

They all stared into the distance and smiled. It had to be, there were too many grand turrets, it stood too proudly on the skyline, for it not to be the King's castle.

'If Esther was right, then the Duchess' place must be around here soon. We just need to keep looking!' Clem enthused.

'Do you *really* think you can get us all the way there?' Noah asked Dennis. He needed the answer to be yes.

Dennis nodded. 'Absolutely. I was in the school rowing team. I can row for miles.'

Noah sat for a few moments, but he still had questions. He *always* had questions.

'Did you go to school round here, then?'

'Oh no, miles away.'

'So . . . you move around all the time?'

'I have done. Been all over the south this last few months.'

'And you always travel by boat?'

'No. What makes you ask that?'

'Dunno. Was just wondering how you afforded to buy this if you can't even afford food and would rather eat nettles?'

Dennis looked at him dubiously. 'Oh, the boat's not mine, is it? Clearly.'

'So you've nicked it?'

'Nicked it!? You didn't tell us that before we got in.' Clem suddenly looked uncomfortable.

'Would it have made any difference?'

Noah knew he should act all indignant, and could feel Clem's eyes boring into him already, the shoplifting dredged up in her mind.

'It's just another reason for the police to chase us, isn't it?'

'We can take it back if you like?' said Dennis.

Noah didn't want to think about that option. 'Or we leave it exactly where we found it, once we've reached the Duchess. I mean, it's night-time, no one's going to miss it now.'

Noah looked to Clem, who wriggled uncomfortably on her bench before nodding.

'We'll have it back by dawn,' Dennis added, 'no bother,' and he rowed on, easing the boat round the bend as the children looked eagle-eyed for a sign. It was hard to believe now that they were still on the same river, and that the water that stretched out behind them led all the way back to their fretting mothers.

Noah shook the thought from his head, and stroked a dozing Winn.

'What do you know about this duchess then?' asked Dennis.

'Not a lot,' Noah shrugged.

'It's just,' Dennis paused as if working out how best to put it. 'Well, folk with money, 'specially royals, well, they're more known for hunting animals than saving them.'

'That right?'

'Oh yeah, estates like the ones we're looking for, well, they're full of dogs and horses and that, though they use 'em to either chase the foxes up and down the fields or hoover up the grouse they've just shot out the sky.'

Noah felt himself tense, and for the first time wondered if their plan was pure folly. What if this Duchess wasn't all that they hoped?

Fortunately for Noah, he had Clem beside him. And if he didn't know what to think, she did.

'Not this Duchess apparently,' she chipped in. 'She's campaigned for years against vivisection and animal cruelty.'

'Well, all I can say is she's a first,' said Dennis. 'Never met a posh person yet who doesn't see animals as something to own.' Esme chose that moment to jump from his shoulder to the top of his head, as if illustrating the point that *she* was the one in charge of their friendship. 'What you going to say to her then, when you stroll up and knock on her door?'

'Same thing as everyone else, I suppose,' said Noah, who hadn't really thought about it. 'Can you look after our pets till the war's over?'

'You might want to add a please on to that,' said Dennis. 'Cos if what you say is true, then every Tom, Dick and Harry with a rabbit is going to be at her door in the next few days.'

'You don't think she'll say no though, do you?'

'Not if she's the person you say she is. The big question is, what will *you* do? You know, when you have to finally leave the dogs behind?'

This was another thing Noah hadn't really thought about. For days his mind had simply been on getting there without being stopped. He hadn't given a second's thought to what he'd do when it came to actually saying goodbye. So he didn't know what to say. And he couldn't think about it without getting emotional.

'I suppose I'll have to try and say it quickly, won't I? We both will. But it's not like we're deserting them, or letting them down. Standing in that vet's queue till they felt the needle, that'd be letting them down. What we're doing is different. We're giving them a chance, same chance we have when they evacuate us. They deserve that just as much as we do.'

Dennis nodded. 'So that's what'll happen to you then? Evacuation?'

'Suppose so,' Noah sighed. 'The rest of our school's been shipped off to Cornwall.'

'Maybe you should have a word with the Duchess? See if she can put *you* up as well. She'll have *loads* of spare rooms, won't she?'

Noah's face lit up. 'Do you think we should ask her?' he gabbled. 'Do you think we could be evacuated there?'

Dennis waited a beat. 'Not a chance,' he said. 'Even if she does love animals, she won't have time for riff-raff like you. So get that out of your head, quick smart. I was only joking.'

His words were a pin, and Noah would've deflated quickly if circumstances hadn't changed around him.

'Look!' said Clem, shoving a pointing finger under his nose. 'Through the trees there, can you see it?'

Noah squinted into the night. 'What?'

'That house there. To the right. Look at the size of it. It's huge. And it's far enough back from the river for us to know there has to be a big garden too.'

Noah couldn't take his eyes off it. 'Do you think that's it?' he said excitedly. 'Do you think we've found her?'

'I think it has to be,' Clem replied, her eyes now poring over the map. 'There's a cemetery on the map here, look, and if you look behind us, you can clearly see the graves.'

Noah looked at the map then the riverbank then back again, nodding, as Clem pointed to a box next to the cemetery. 'So that has to mean there's a house, and it must be a big one. I just think it *has* to belong to her, Noah. I think Esther was right. We're going to make it, Noah, we're almost there.' Her excitement was tangible.

But Noah wasn't as excited. He should've been, but he couldn't allow himself to be.

Because his eyes weren't on the map, they were peering over Dennis' shoulder, to a series of lanterns being shone in their direction. They may have been a few hundred yards in front of them, but Noah knew who they belonged to.

The police. They were being chased.

He was so so close, but in that instant, he felt a million miles away.

57

'What do we do?' gasped Noah, leaping to his feet, the rowing boat almost capsizing beneath them.

'We sit down, for starters,' replied Dennis, pulling him back into his seat.

'That's not a plan!' said Noah.

'We don't panic then, and we don't get caught. How about that?'

Dennis had stopped rowing, and they could now see that the lanterns belonged to bobbies who were on a boat of their own. A bigger boat, the sort of boat that came with a motor.

'Stay where you are!' a voice shouted through the gloom. 'There's no need to be scared. We just want to take you home. Your pets too.'

Noah, though, knew what this *really* meant. And there was no way he was letting that happen. And neither was Dennis, who dipped the left oar into the river and began to row furiously, steering towards the bank. Noah did the same with his hand, as did Clem.

'Go, go, GO!' shouted Noah once the boat was pointed correctly, but Dennis didn't need telling, arms pumping as the boat dragged its way towards land.

'Soon as we hit the riverbank you need to run, hear me?' said Dennis between gasps. 'If the map is right, then the estate is close. I'll do all I can to create a diversion that gets you there.'

'You're not coming? What if we need your help?' Noah said.

'Don't you worry. You're getting my help,' he replied. 'But if we stick together, chances are they'll catch us.'

And with that, he started unbuttoning his shirt, to reveal a grubby vest.

'Now remember,' he gasped. 'The *second* you're on land, go right. Do it quickly and as quietly as you can. I know it's hard, but try to keep the dogs quiet too. All right?'

'What about you?' Clem asked, worriedly.

'Don't give me a second thought. I've been evading people for a long time. I might make the world's worst soldier, but I'm fantastic at hiding.'

Whatever he had planned, he wasn't giving it away, not even when the nose of the boat bumped against the bank, with Winn the first to jump ship.

Quickly, the others followed, Dennis at the rear, dragging an oar with him, as well as his shirt. Without hesitating, he dashed past them, until he reached the nearest tree. What happened next was unexpected. Gripping the oar like a club, he swung it again and again at the trunk until the paddle splintered and snapped, leaving a short, jagged shard.

Noah knew they should be running, but he couldn't take his eyes off the man as he wound the shirt tightly around the club, before reaching into his pocket and retrieving a box of matches. Holding the club between his knees, he flicked a match into life and set fire to the material, rearing back as it caught and spat angrily. Holding the torch aloft, he turned to face them.

'What did I tell you,' he hissed, as he saw the other boat edge closer to the bank, 'RUN. NOW!'

And without a goodbye or a backward look, he tore to the left, waving the torch wildly in the air, with Esme following him.

Noah watched him go, hearing him yell as he ran. He seemed to be making as much noise as he possibly could, shouting again and again, calling all of their names in turn. Even the dogs'.

Smiling, Noah turned on his heels. 'He's setting a decoy,' he half whispered. 'Let's go,' and with Winn at his heels, he ran, lifting his knees as high as he could without slowing himself down. He couldn't afford to trip and fall, not now. If he banged his burns he'd be sick, he knew it.

Clem and Frank followed, trying hard to strike a balance between speed and silence. Well, Clem did, Frank just struggled, lagging so far behind that before long Clem could no longer hear the rasping in his chest. No one spoke, the only noise the sound of twigs breaking beneath their feet. It was lucky they weren't running in the heart of autumn, or the fallen leaves would have betrayed them in seconds.

The only problem, as they soon discovered, was the growing dark into which they were venturing. As Dennis knew, a torch would be a giveaway, but with the moon hidden by the trees, the blackness soon became both impenetrable and scary. It felt reckless and stupid to run like this, but they had to keep going, reminding themselves that the dangers behind were far worse for Winn and Frank than the ones in front. The shouts and yells in the distance confirmed it. They were louder now, angrier and more persistent, though Noah couldn't tell if they were getting closer or not. It felt like a cruel trick that the trees were playing on them.

What he did know was that he could no longer hear Dennis's decoy calls, nor make out even the faintest glimmer of his torch. What if the bobbies had seen through it straightaway? Or merely caught up with Dennis and shaken the truth out of him? Noah couldn't help but imagine the man being marched off to war against his will.

But Noah immediately had bigger things to fret over. A

noise, some way behind him, a high-pitched yelp of fear and pain that he knew had come from an animal. It wasn't Winn, she was by his side as always. Which could only mean Frank. He ran back, instantly, recovering land he only had time for once.

Had the bobbies caught him? Noah powered on, retracing steps, the darkness intensifying as well as Frank's cries.

'Don't be caught, don't be caught,' he repeated to himself, but as both the dog and Clem hoved into view, he realised the situation was far graver then he could have imagined.

There were no bobbies holding them against their will, only Clem on the floor, cradling Frank in her arms as he yelped in pain.

'What is it?' Noah gasped. 'What's wrong?'

'It's his leg, look, Noah. Look.' She was distraught, so much so that Noah almost didn't want to look.

For Frank hadn't been caught by the police, but by a jagged length of barbed wire that had ensnared his back left leg. His eyes seemed to warn Noah not to touch or try to free him, that it would only cause him the most unbearable pain. And whilst Noah knew this to be true, he also couldn't leave Frank to suffer. They needed him free, but they also needed him free quickly.

'What's it doing there?' Clem cried. 'Who would leave barbed wire just lying around like that?'

'Maybe it's a trap or a snare, I don't know. But we need to get him free, Clem. We haven't much time.'

'I know. But we can't hurt him, Noah. Listen to him. He's in agony.'

Frank's chest rose and fell rapidly. He kept trying to raise his head, to move it towards his leg to lick it, but every time he did so, the pain was too overwhelming. Clem held him closer.

'It's all right, darling,' she whispered, though it was anything but. 'What have they done to you?' The wire's presence made no sense to either of them. It wasn't attached to a fence. Was it a trap or just sheer carelessness? But that was unimportant. All that mattered was getting Frank free with as little pain or distress as possible.

'What do we do now, Noah?' Clem wept.

Noah felt overwhelmed. He knew how close they were, and he knew what he had to do, but he had no idea if he could possibly do it. Pressure built, tears too. He was so weak now, so hot and achy, his burns on fire. He felt like he had hit his limits: like their mission had finally failed.

58

If the chaos in Noah's head wasn't enough, he now heard the sound of voices again, louder, closer. Unless Dennis had taken the wrong path and led the bobbies here inadvertently, his plan must have failed. They were on to them.

Noah didn't know how long it would take them to catch up, but he knew they had minutes at most.

'We need to get Frank free,' he told Clem. 'Quickly.'

'There isn't time,' she replied. 'They're nearly here. Go on. Go on without us. Save Winn!'

'No!' Noah spat back. 'We're doing this together. No matter what.' And he crouched over Frank, fingers readied. But as he moved closer, he found himself hindered by the darkness. He could make out the wire's outline, but not how to remove it. He cocked his head to one side, trying to let the moon's rays through, but they weren't enough, and as his thumb and index finger made contact with the wire, Frank lost all control, muzzle snapping viciously at his hand. It took every bit of strength Clem had to hold her beloved pet down.

'It's all right, pal, it's all right. It'll be over quickly if you just let me help.'

But whichever way he tried, from whatever angle, Frank couldn't cope with the pain. He bared his teeth, he howled at the sky, his body went rigid with shock and overwhelming agony and then he began to convulse uncontrollably.

'Noah!' screamed Clem. 'Do something.'

'It's cut in really deep,' Noah said. 'I don't know how to get him free.'

'Please,' said Clem. 'Think of something. Help him!'

Frank continued to shake and twitch.

'Clem, listen to me. I need you to hold his head tight. Keep him calm. And STILL. The stiller he is, the quicker I can free him.'

'What are you going to do?'

But Noah never told her. For as he reached out once more, his fingers making contact with Frank's leg, he felt the poor dog go rigid with shock. And as he did so, his eyes closed, his chest fell, and it did not rise again.

'Frank?' Clem said, face awash with tears. 'FRANK!' She lifted the dog's head tenderly to hers, seeing his eyes sealed shut, feeling the stillness of his chest. 'Wake up, Frank, wake up. We're nearly there, darling, so very nearly there.' But it didn't matter how long or loudly she begged,

Frank had gone. And there was nothing either of them could do to bring him back.

'I'm sorry, Clem,' Noah sobbed. 'I'm so so sorry. What have I done?' He could feel nothing but sorrow and guilt and regret and shame. So much so that he was oblivious to the noises growing ever closer.

Clem however, was not. 'Noah,' she called to him through her tears. 'NOAH. You need to listen to me, and you need to listen now. You've got to go. Do you hear me? Now!'

But Noah refused to leave or take his eyes off Frank. 'I can't. Not without you and Frank.'

'Frank's gone, Noah, he's gone. And he was old. But Winn isn't, she's young, and you can still get her to safety if you just, for once, do as you're told. So for God's sake, listen to me now . . . and GO!' She shoved at him with her one free hand, which threw him backwards and shocked him out of his reverie.

'But what about you?' he cried.

'What about me? You don't need me. I need to be here with Frank.'

'No, I'm not leaving either of you.'

But Clem could be just as stubborn as he could. 'You are, because when they get here, I'll delay them. Or send them in the wrong direction. You just have to trust me. Just like I've trusted you these last few days. So go on, go. Save Winn.'

Noah didn't want to. He didn't want to move an inch. He was exhausted, and he was tired of running and hiding, tired of trying to work out what to do for the best.

'Please, Noah. Don't let her down,' Clem said, quietly. 'Winn needs you, Noah. Finish what we started. For her.'

Noah moved. Clem had buried her face deep in Frank's fur, out of reach. It felt like he was intruding, like he shouldn't trespass on her grief. So he put one foot in front of the other, and he moved. You could hardly call it running. He'd seen drunkards move quicker. He barely even knew where he was moving to, all he could do was stagger down the path after Winn: hoping that her instinct or judgment was taking them in the right direction.

The moon reappeared from behind the trees and Winn's pace picked up. How she was doing it he had no idea, but he couldn't lose her, not now, so he sped up too. He saw a long, high wall ahead of them, stretching out into the darkness.

It was imposing and grand, with a decorative top section. Could this be it? Feeling giddy with shock, he heard another shout. And for every second that passed, the gap between him and the chasers decreased, the sound of their boots echoing in a menacing rhythm.

'Don't stop, Winn!' cried Noah, ignoring the tears that rolled off his chin. 'Not much further now! That's it.'

He had no idea of course if that were true, but he had to believe it. To think anything else would extinguish whatever waning faith he had left.

But just as it felt like luck had betrayed them, he saw, some thirty yards ahead, what they had been looking for all this time. The first glimpse of the Duchess' house itself. It seemed to rise out of the darkness like a mighty stone giant. It would have taken his breath away had he not been so close to collapse, and it spurred him on, until, finally, finally he saw the metal gates that would lead to its front door.

They stood some twenty-feet high, standing guard, warning him to keep back.

But when had he ever listened?

Instead, Noah and Winn sprinted faster, finding one final gear that neither of them knew they possessed.

It carried them to the foot of the gates, and their lead, if anything, slightly increased.

But not for long.

Because the gates were well and truly locked.

59

Noah pushed, though there was clearly no point.

So he took a different tack. If he couldn't go through, then he would have to go over, and he wedged his right boot into the first iron foothold he could find.

'Stay here, girl,' he told Winn, who looked on, anxiously.

Climbing was not Noah's forte and under pressure, it was like tackling Everest in his slippers. He felt every minute of the last few days in his bones, the pain from his burns screaming at him to stop. He heard every breath reverberate in his ears, as well as the shouts of the officers, moving ever closer.

He tried to speed up, but this accelerated not only his clumsiness, but also an over-riding feeling of futility. It felt unlikely that he would make it up and over the gates, but even if he did, the chances of reaching the house, then rousing and returning with the Duchess *before* the police arrived and took Winn, seemed frankly, impossible.

Despair and exhaustion engulfed him, as did the shouts

of the bobbies. They were close now, too close, they'd be on top of him within a minute, and Noah felt his legs and arms stop moving without realising that his brain had told them to.

How could he get so very, very close, only to see it snatched away? They deserved better than this, Winn deserved better than this. He gripped the bars tightly with his fists and pulled on them again and again, a frustrated wail bursting from his lungs.

'Get down, boy!' came a voice, still far enough away to need to shout. 'You'll break your ruddy neck.'

With arms and legs feeling more leaden with every single movement, Noah descended. It was over. Once back on the floor, he slumped at Winn's side, not even her long, affectionate licks reviving him.

'Leave us alone!' he gasped to the nearest policeman. 'We haven't done nothing wrong, you know!'

'We know that, lad. Though your mother might see things differently. Fancy running off like that with everything else that's going on?'

'We didn't have a choice, did we?' Noah snapped. 'They wanted to kill our pets.'

'It's for their own good,' a second officer replied. 'And for everyone else's. They're only animals, son.'

If there was a moment when Noah knew, *truly knew* that his actions of the last few days were right and just, this was it. And he had no hesitation in telling them so.

'This dog here, and the one back there? They're worth ten of you!' Noah spat. 'Winn's braver and more loyal than any human I know. And even though she hasn't slept, or eaten properly in God knows how long, if I ask her to defend me, she will. Even now. Won't you, girl?'

Noah stood unsteadily, legs apart, fist raised in resistance, and watched as his dog joined him, back arched, teeth bared to each of the bobbies.

The one at the front sighed as he straightened his helmet. 'Come on now, son. Enough of the dramatics. You either come quietly or you come with a couple of thick ears.'

Noah could feel the cold of the metal bars against his back. There was nowhere to go. Nothing to save him.

Or so he thought, for as the game was finally up, and the policeman reached out to take hold of him, from the shadows raced a dog. Not Winn, nor Frank. A dog Noah had never seen before in his life. A long, lean hound that, judging by the barking it offered the bobbies, clearly didn't think much of the law.

Where had it come from? Noah was so tired he reckoned it must be some sort of guardian angel. It didn't seem to belong to anyone. Was he ill? Feverous?

344

But then he heard a woman's voice, which loomed out of the darkness, in clipped, precise tones like the ones that read the news on the wireless.

'Could someone tell me what on earth is going on?' it asked.

60

The woman wasn't tall, Noah thought through tired eyes, no bigger than his mother really, though she seemed to fill the landscape. Through the glow of the police lanterns, he could see that she was wearing a pair of filthy Wellington boots and a long woollen cardigan, buttoned from shin to neck. Upon it sat the contents of a small haystack. Strands were also caught in her wiry, thick hair: so many that she took on the appearance of a poorly maintained scarecrow.

'Madam,' said one of the officers, 'if this is your animal, then may I ask that you call it to heel. This has nothing to do with him, or indeed you.'

This did little to make either the dog or the woman back down. In fact, she marched forward even quicker, positioning herself between Noah and the bobbies.

'Oh, I wouldn't say that,' she said bluntly. 'Given that you seem to be arresting someone on my land.'

Noah felt his eyes widen and his pulse race. Had he heard her correctly? Because if what she said was true, then this was the . . . but it couldn't be? He looked at the woman then back at the house. There could be no way that this person ate and slept and lived in such grand surroundings, not looking the way she did. Even Dennis was better turned out than her. But as he looked at the woman once more, he saw a fierceness and regalness in her stance that offered him hope. She was the Duchess. She had to be.

'M'lady,' he said, though he had no idea if he was addressing her correctly. 'It's you, isn't it? I know it is.'

The woman peered at him confused. 'Are you all right, young man. You don't look well.'

Noah didn't give her the answer she'd asked for. He wasn't well, far from it. One of the burns on his wrist was oozing now, a yellow pus leaking which smelled anything but healthy.

'My name's Noah. Noah Price.' He went to shake her hand then saw the mud and infected blood smeared over it. He wiped it on his vest and offered it anyway. 'And this is Winn. We heard about you from a lady at Battersea Dogs Home.'

'Did you?' she replied, her face a mixture of surprise and revulsion at the hand on offer. 'And what did she say?'

'That we should come to you. And that you wouldn't turn us away.'

The first policeman sighed in irritation. 'That's enough now, boy. Let's get you home.'

But Noah wasn't ready, and the woman wasn't either. 'Let him finish, officer . . . please.'

Noah jumped on the opportunity, as best he could. He felt oh so dizzy and his mouth was parched, but he had to get the story out. Convince her while he had the chance. 'There was more of us before. Loads more. There was Clem, my best friend. And Samson and Delilah. She's a snake. Great big python, she is. But Col took her home cos she was dying. Then there was the kittens, Mary and Joseph, but we left them at a farm for a boy to look after.'

'Is that all?' The woman's eyes suggested she couldn't quite believe what she was hearing.

'No, there was Frank too. Little Frank. Best dachshund ever, and he wasn't a Nazi, no matter what Col's dad said . . . but he died. Tonight. Twenty minutes ago. Back there.' And he pointed, exhausted, ready to collapse, the woman following his finger.

'Is this true?' she asked the bobbies.

'There *is* a girl back there,' one confirmed. 'And a dead dog as well.' He looked sheepish and said no more.

The woman shook her head in confusion as she turned back to Noah. 'Then I can hardly doubt you, can I? Though I'm afraid I really don't understand what this has to do with me.' And she smiled, sympathetically.

'Because you're the Duchess, aren't you? Like the woman said.'

One of the officers laughed. The woman did not. She just looked even more confused.

'The what?'

'The Duchess. Nina Douglas-Hamilton.'

The woman let a sad smile slide on to her face. 'I'm very sorry. But I think you have me confused with somebody else.'

'No,' said Noah, taking an unsteady step towards her, panic rising in him. 'I haven't. You live here, don't you? In this big house.'

'Well, I do, yes . . .'

'Then you're the Duchess. You have to be. Esther's been to your house before. Then Clem found it on the map, backing on to the Thames. Clem never gets these things wrong. I do, but Clem? No chance. She said you'd take all the animals in. She said you wouldn't turn anybody away.'

Another of the officers stepped forward, taking care to move slowly around the woman's dog. 'Come on now, son. You're tired and confused.'

'No. No I'm not.' Noah fought back. 'Go get Clem. I'll prove it to you.'

'Son, you and your pal can swear on each other's lives, but this will never be a Duchess' house. This has been my beat for nearly twenty years, so I know that for a fact. The Duchess of Hamilton's estate isn't anywhere near here. Far as I know it's in Dorset.'

Noah looked at the woman, praying she'd contradict him, but she didn't. Instead, all she could say was, 'It's true I'm afraid, young man. I'm not the person you're looking for. For your sake I wish I was, but I'm not.'

Noah felt the life fall from him. Felt his left knee tremble then buckle, and then sensed Winn at his side as he fell, the gravel biting at his skin.

'I'm sorry, girl,' he whispered to her. 'I let you down, didn't I?'

But Winn wasn't the only one beside him now. The woman was too, her hand brushing Noah's forehead.

'Officer, this boy is burning up. We need to get him some water. His dog too. Help me get him inside.'

'Madam, we really should be getting him home. His mother is worried sick.'

'I'm sure she is. And she'll be even more worried if he returns home with a fever. I have a telephone. We can get her word from here.' She turned back to Noah. 'How far have you come, you and your friend? Where's home?'

'London,' Noah replied. He knew that much. 'Wapping.'

'But that's miles away. How did you get here?'

'On a boat, then we walked. We didn't steal the boat. It was my dad's.'

'*Was?*'

'She sank.'

She shook her head again. 'But why? Why run away with everything else that's going on?'

'Because they wanted to kill them,' Noah said. He wanted to sleep so desperately now, but he had to tell her and make her understand. 'Not the police ... the government, they told us to have them put down. Winn, Frank, Delilah all of them. You should've seen the queues! Wrapped halfway round London they did. They said it wasn't safe to keep them alive, except, well, we couldn't do it, could we? Because they've just as much right to see the end of the war as we have. The government's evacuating us so we wanted to do the same for our dogs. So ... we ran away. Because we had no choice and because we were told about the Duchess keeping animals safe.'

'So you came all this way on your own from London?'

'Well, yes. Wouldn't you? For your dog?'

'On a stolen boat?'

'No, no!' Noah panicked. 'It was my dad's. The *Queen Maudie*. I just ... borrowed it.' He lowered his voice. 'You see, he's fighting. He wouldn't mind. Not if it kept Winn safe. I promised him. We made a deal; if I kept Winn safe, then he'd come back safe too!'

The woman shook her head sadly yet again.

'I promise you, it's true,' Noah pleaded. 'Our animals, they mean more to us than anything. And we just want them to have the same chances we have. And you can do that, can't you? Please. You can, I know you can, because the woman at the dogs home told us. Ask Clem, she'll tell you . . .'

He felt confused and hot again, woozy, like the ground underneath him was made of jelly. A firework went off in his head, or it could've been a gunshot, or another Spitfire crashing into a field. He couldn't tell, he was too tired. He just needed to rest a while, right where he was. Him and Winn together.

61

Noah had the craziest of dreams.

There were arms on him, lifting him, carrying him. Then there was a car. At least he thought it was a car. It may have been a van, he couldn't be sure. Or a Spitfire – engine roaring. Then there was nothing. Except bumps and braking and possibly a siren.

He thought he dreamed of Mum as well. Could hear and smell her, but he couldn't see her. He tried to call to tell her he was here, to explain, but then there was a whole lot more of nothing.

Until he woke.

He had no idea where he was or what time it was. All he knew was that as he moved his hand, he felt fur against it, and relieved, he allowed himself to sleep again.

He awoke to the same thing several times: the only thing that changed was the quality of the light.

When he finally came to for more than a moment, he knew exactly where he was. The smell, the background noise, the feeling of the sheet against his skin, he knew he was in his bedroom, and as he turned his head, feeling pain as he did so, he saw something very familiar in the chair next to him: his mother. Her presence was more of a shock than a comfort, though judging by the wet flannel in her hand and the bowl on her lap, it was clear she'd been there throughout. As had Winn, wedged still at his side.

'About time you woke up,' she said, deadpan.

He looked for the word that he knew he had to say quickly, but his throat and mouth were too parched to force it out. It took a cup, lifted to his mouth by Maudie, to enable him to actually say *sorry*.

Once said, and once his mother had checked his temperature, he braced himself for the inevitable and possibly deserved onslaught.

But his mother surprised him, for instead of strong words, there was only the strongest of hugs that went on so long that he thought it would never end.

'I'm not sure there's enough water in the world to get you clean,' she said, her voice thick with emotion. 'I did try, but even when you were delirious, you still fought me because I had a flannel in my hand.'

Noah laughed, but it hurt. Or more accurately, everything did. From his scalp, to the bandaged burns on his wrists and fingers, to the soles of his feet.

'I'm sorry, Mum,' he said, knowing it was nowhere near

enough, but he had to start somewhere. 'How long have I been home?'

'Well, the war's not over yet. But you've been back three days.'

'Three days?' He tried to sit up, but the mixture of head pain and a forceful motherly arm pushed him back on to the pillows. 'I need to speak to Clem.'

'You'll have a job,' she replied, dousing the flannel and using it to rub at his fingers roughly. 'She's on a train as we speak.'

'She's gone? But what about Frank?'

Maudie sighed. 'We'll talk about this when you're on your feet.' But Noah grabbed her hand and implored her. 'Please, Mum. Tell me what happened to Frank.'

'They buried him yesterday, love.' Her tone was matter of fact, like she needed it to be.

'And is she all right? Clem?'

'Well, she was a lot better than you, that's for sure. She wasn't burnt. Or full of fever. Her mother wasn't so happy though. Neither of us were. Worried us sick you did, the pair of you.' She took a deep breath, like she was burying the rest of what she wanted to say.

'I'm not ready to be angry with you quite yet though,' she said. 'Though I'm sure I'll manage by the time you're clean.'

Exhausted at the thought, Noah closed his eyes and allowed himself to drift off.

His convalescence was quicker than he expected, partially because once he was consistently awake, Mum made it clear that he was to get up and sort himself out.

After batches of her home-made chicken soup and slabs of buttered crusty bread, within twenty-four hours he found himself in the kitchen, in a steaming hot bath, Mum's only words telling him he'd missed a bit when he dared to get out of the water too soon.

It wasn't until he was sitting, wrapped in a towel, that Mum managed to find the words that summed up how she felt. And she delivered them without hesitation or regret, silencing Noah every time he dared to offer a counter-argument. He had no idea what she was most angry about, the running off, the stealing of the boat, the lies, the deceit, they all seemed to add equally to her volcano and he could understand that. All he could do was be as equally honest.

'I just couldn't do it, Mum. I couldn't let them take Winn. I still can't.'

'I know it hurts, Noah. But there's a war on, son. We don't know what that means yet, not really, or how long it will last, but everyone has to do their bit. And there are thousands of people in exactly the same position as you, making a sacrifice.'

'But they aren't the same, Mum.'

'Of course they are.'

'They aren't! Because I made a promise to Dad, didn't I? Swore blind I'd keep Winn with me, and that she'd be safe. We made a deal. And if I don't keep my part, then how do I know that Dad will keep his? How do I know that he's definitely coming back?'

That's when it hit him. All the worry and fear and not knowing, not to mention the tiredness that made his bones ache.

He cried. And he cried because that was the moment that Mum allowed her anger to slip a little, and she pulled him close.

'It's a beautiful thing you promised, Noah. A beautiful, beautiful thing. But it won't have any bearing whatsoever on what happens next. To Dad, or to any of us. There are certain things, I'm afraid, that we just can't control. And this, death, is one of those things.'

'I just want him to come home, Mum. I just need him to come home.'

She held him even tighter. 'We all do, love. We all do. So we have to do our best to stay well and healthy and safe. Starting with you, once you've had some more rest.'

'You're still sending me away, aren't you? Till it's over?'

He saw her head nod slowly. 'There's not one part of me that wants to, but I know it's what I have to do. So you need to promise me, Noah. There'll be no running away or funny business, do you hear? I want a letter every week and good school reports. You need to show your new family that I've brought you up proper.'

He nodded, and tried to make himself relax further into her. But he couldn't, as the same problem remained. He would be evacuated, but what on earth was going to happen to Winn?

He wanted to ask her, he really did. But suddenly, he felt tired again. So very, very tired. So nothing more was said. He just allowed his mum to rock him gently back and forwards, until slowly, his brain unravelled, and blissful sleep pulled him under.

62

Two days later, Noah felt considerably better. Or he did until he opened the door to the kitchen and there was a small suitcase, alongside a gas mask box. Both bore a brown cardboard tag with his name on, written in his mother's best hand.

Noah groaned. He'd known this was coming, but he hadn't expected it quite so soon. He'd tried to speak to her the day before about what was going to happen next: to him, and more importantly, to Winn, but she had remained steely and silent. Which was a deadly combination where Maudie was concerned.

The image in front of him told him everything he needed to know. He would be evacuated, as planned, and he would have to board the train without his two best friends.

Clem might well be waiting for him at the other end, wherever he was heading, but he would still feel hopelessly alone without Winn nestled as usual at his feet.

He knelt to fuss his dog, and she fussed him right back,

but aside from that the house felt empty and lifeless. It was darker than he was accustomed to as well: like autumn had wrestled control overnight without telling anyone to prepare themselves first.

His mother appeared from the back yard, apron tied neatly in place, hair plumped up like Dad was taking her dancing.

'I thought *I* was going somewhere, not you,' he said.

'Watch your lip,' she replied. 'But yes, you *are* going today. I've got you all packed. So eat your breakfast. It'll be a good few hours till you get anything else.'

Noah eyed the steaming porridge on the table, but there wasn't a dirty pot to be seen anywhere else. Instead, the mirror had Mum's full attention, as she stood in front of it, applying and reapplying her lipstick.

'I presume Winn's coming with me then?' he said. He knew he was more than pushing his luck, but he felt he had nothing to lose.

'You presume too much. Eat.' And that was that.

So, he sat and picked at the skin on his porridge with his spoon.

'You've ten minutes by my reckoning. So be quick smart about it. We need to be ready.'

Noah sagged. 'Please, Mum, what's going to . . . ?'

But before he could finish, a car horn sounded on the

street. A long, tuneless toot that had Mum pulling at her apron strings with great ferocity.

'Mum?' he asked, but she was already at the window, pulling rather than twitching the net curtains.

'Tie your shoes, Noah, for goodness' sake,' she replied, before darting through the front door, patting her hair one final time.

Noah wondered if he was actually still asleep and immersed in some elaborate dream, but did as he was told, stumbling on to the street to find a small gaggle of neighbours, gawking at a car parked there.

Cars were rare in their part of Wapping. Horses and carts were bountiful, but this was a proper car – long and shiny and sleek.

His jaw dropped open, and fell even further when he realised his mum was standing by the kerb, as a man in a black suit stepped from the driver's side.

Noah's head span. This couldn't be their ride to the station. They didn't know anyone with an automobile.

He took it all in, how the wing-mirrors shone despite the gloom of the day. The door handles too, glinting like the crown jewels. None of it made sense, not even as the man approached his mum, and after a polite smile, opened the passenger door.

Noah didn't recognise the woman sitting there. She was

wearing a wide-brimmed grey hat that covered not only her hair, but the majority of her face. Her clothing was immaculate, pressed and expensive. Noah saw his mum smooth down her own clothes, front and back. He'd never seen her look so flustered in his life.

As the stranger got out the car, the shadow over her face lifted, and Noah took in her features properly for the first time. He recognised her. Clearly he did – it had only been days after all – but this time there was no hay sticking untidily from her hair.

'Hello, Noah,' she said warmly.

'Hello, Mrs . . .' he replied. He wanted to be polite like his mum had always told him to be, but he realised he hadn't a clue what her name was. Certainly not Duchess Douglas-Hamilton. That was for sure.

Fortunately Mum came to his rescue. 'This is Mrs Donnelly-Brown, Noah.'

'Hello, Noah,' repeated Mrs Donnelly-Brown. 'And hello again, Mrs Price. Let me introduce my husband, David.'

The man held out his hand rather stiffly to Noah, but when he shook it, it seemed genuine enough.

'Pleased to meet you,' Noah said. It all felt very formal, and odd, and Noah wondered if he should bow a bit.

Fortunately, Noah had Winn there to break the ice,

bounding up to the Donnelly-Browns and delivering the friendliest of licks to each of their hands.

'And this, David, is Winn, isn't it, Noah?' said the woman. 'How is she? She looks so much brighter after a good rest!'

'She's ... well,' replied Noah. He wanted to add something about not knowing how long things would remain that way, but he knew his mum was watching him closely.

'Well, that *is* good news. Because I ... *we*,' she seemed a little flustered, 'David and I, that is, we wanted to talk to you about the other night.'

Oh no. What had he done? Had he damaged the gates when he tried to climb them? He hadn't meant to, he was desperate.

He shuffled from foot to foot, fingers scratching at the scabs on his hand as he searched for the right answer.

'Stand still, Noah,' Mum hissed.

'I've been thinking about you, Noah,' continued Mrs Donnelly-Brown. 'We both have, about what you did.'

This did little to ease his nerves. It felt like the preamble to a huge dressing down.

'And what has struck me, is the fact that everything you did, every hardship you endured, if they are true . . .' she fixed him with a stare that could freeze a waterfall, 'you didn't do for yourself, but for your dog. Is that true?'

Noah nodded.

'Speak up, Noah!' said Mum from over his shoulder.

'Yes . . . that's true.'

The lady adjusted her stance, before looking at her husband one final time. 'Then we come to you with an offer. One that you are absolutely free to refuse if you wish. We have a son, Oscar. Older than you. Nineteen. But he's not with us at the moment. Like your father, he's away fighting. And like your father, he will be back soon, I'm sure.'

Her husband squeezed her arm reassuringly, which made Noah like him even more.

'And the thing is, Bramble, our dog – well, he's Oscar's dog really – misses him. Doesn't want me or David walking him. Wants someone who can exercise him properly until the war ends. Which is where you come in.'

Noah leaned forward.

'We've spoken with your mother while you've been recovering, and we have agreed, should you wish, for you to come and be evacuated to us, in our care, while the fighting goes on.

She took a deep breath, which allowed David to speak.

'Now, it won't be a holiday camp, Noah, nor will it be any kind of adventure, despite you seeming to be so very keen on such japes. What it will be is hard work: looking after the dog and our other animals, not to mention your schooling. And should standards drop beneath an acceptable level, our agreement will come to an end. Work hard, listen hard and I think you'll be very happy with us until the war ends, or until your mother wishes for you to return.'

Noah couldn't believe what he was hearing. He looked to his mother, who was nodding vigorously whilst somehow managing to warn him not to mess up this opportunity. He then turned back to the Donnelly-Browns, feeling a surge of confidence swell in him.

'This offer, it's very kind of you, it really is. But can Winn come too?' he asked, feeling his mother's glare burning into him, before adding a very grovelly, 'please?'

'Well, of course!' said Mrs Donnelly-Brown. 'I should have said that. You are *both* being evacuated to us, though we can't have you sleeping in the same room. Humans sleep upstairs and animals in the kitchen. Those are the rules for Bramble, so they're the same for Winn too.'

Noah nodded ecstatically, though he couldn't help but wonder if there might be some bend in that, over time.

'Then . . .' he said, 'I'd love to accept your offer . . . though I'd like to ask you one more favour. If I may?'

He saw his mother tense in fear.

'You can ask . . .' said Mr Donnelly-Brown with a smile. 'We're listening.'

'I was wondering,' Noah said, 'how you felt about snakes. Well, pythons, more specifically.'

But the couple never answered. They didn't have the chance as Maudie cuffed him around his ear, hard enough for Noah to know to shut up.

'You'll get used to his sense of humour, you really will,' she laughed. 'In the end . . . eventually.'

Noah smiled and shrugged. He didn't regret asking the question one bit.

63

The sun shone down on Noah and he allowed it to, tipping his head back so the rays permeated his skin.

The day had started early, just as every day had for almost as long as he could remember now. It didn't matter what time of year it was: Bramble and Winn needed walking, though the distances they had to cover were decreasing as the dogs grew older.

After their exercise there was breakfast to clear up, as well as all the other animals to feed, including the chickens. They'd been Noah's idea, and although Uncle David had been difficult to persuade at first, he didn't regret it now, not when they laid so regularly. It had scored Noah many a brownie point, and saw him get away with some of his other indiscretions.

After chores, there was school, and the Donnelly-Browns had been true to their word on that matter. Noah had to work hard, was given no other option, but as his time at school neared an end, he was reaping the rewards. He had no real idea what he wanted to do with the knowledge he'd accrued, which infuriated Uncle David no end (never mind his mother), but he also knew that he would have choices. That was what hard work had taught him most clearly.

Today though, was an especially good day, as it was Saturday, and he and Winn found themselves walking, pail in hand, towards the chicken coop, which sat beside the gates, where he had first arrived over five years ago.

He often thought about their adventure, had written about it to Clem on many occasions since, though her recollections were often quite different to his.

There were things they both agreed on though, such as how scared they'd been at times, and how brave Col had been, saving them with Delilah like he had. Col never joined in the letter writing, though that wasn't a surprise to either of them. Noah often thought (with a smile) that it must be hard to receive letters when you were part of a travelling circus.

Noah never forgot about Dennis either, in part because of where he was living. Whenever he was walking the dogs in the woods or by the river, he looked for him, hoping that every rustle in the trees might be a wild-haired man, gathering wood for his fire, or nettles for his soup. He hoped to God they'd never found him and forced him into uniform.

'Come on then,' Noah called behind him. 'Let's feed the chickens.' And up trotted his shadow, Winn: her fur a lot whiter at the muzzle now and her legs definitely stiffened by the years of country running.

Noah knew what she wanted, and reached into his pocket for it.

'Here you go. Ready?' he asked, but didn't wait for a reply. Instead, he launched the ball in the direction of the gates, just as he had thousands of times before.

And that was it, Winn was off, practically a pup again as the ball scythed through the air.

But this time was different. The ball landed and rolled to a stop, but Winn did not.

She sprinted on, past the ball, not hesitating once.

Noah loved to see her run at full tilt, but it surprised him, this break from the norm.

Where on earth was she going?

He watched, eyes following the path all the way to the gates, which, unusually, stood slightly ajar.

Winn did not have her eyes on freedom though, but on two figures standing on the path, their own eyes staring up at the house.

Both were smartly turned out. The woman in a two-piece suit and brown hat, with handbag clutched to her stomach. But it was the man who caught Noah's eye.

He was dressed in army uniform, beret tucked neatly beneath an epaulet, polished boots attracting kisses from the sun.

Noah squinted into the light and saw two things.

Firstly, he watched Winn speed up, head thrust forward as she sprinted like a thoroughbred in the newcomer's direction.

And secondly, he saw the man fall to his knees, without a care for the stains that it would leave there. His arms stretched wide in welcome, and as the dog let out a howl of delight, the man released a shout of his own.

'Wiiiiiin!' he yelled. 'My Winn!'

The dog and the man collided, and tumbled on to the grass. There was laughter, and barking, and cries of delight.

Noah gasped and let go of the bucket of feed in his hand.

He was sprinting too, before the pail even reached the ground.

The End

ACKNOWLEDGEMENTS

I'd like to thank the following people who have helped me with the writing of this book, and for their support over the past year.

Tony McGowan, August Sedgwick, Tom Palmer, Chris Mould and Sarah Crossan – for being excellent human beings.

Levente Szabo for creating another cover that takes my breath away every time I look at it.

Dr Jess French and Jim Sells for their expertise in all things reptilian and WW2 respectively.

The booksellers and librarians who have made my tenth year as a published writer the greatest I could have asked for, in particular the Booksellers Crow, Sarah at the Book Corner, Florentyna Martin and Gary Deane.

The teachers who have embraced my work this past year. Your dedication to your students is inspirational.

Jodie Hodges for continually guiding my career with such kindness and dedication. And to Emily and Molly too, I really do appreciate all your help.

My publishers, Andersen Press – Klaus, Mark, Chloe, Eloise, Sue, Kate, Sarah, Rob, Liz, Sarah and Elena – thank you for making me so welcome.

Paul Black – if you've tired of seeing my name ping into your inbox, you've never shown it. Thank you so much for everything, you legend.

And to Charlie – you're a terrific editor, but an even better pal. The finest.

Thank you also to the sales team at Walker, for their expertise and tenacity – Jenny, Ed, Peter, Trippy, Ellie, Jan, Bridie and Conor.

My parents, Ray and Anita, I share this with you.

And finally, to my family on the hill: Louise, Rufus, Albie, Bebe, Elsie and Stanley – thank you for being alongside me for the ride. How lucky am I?

Hebden Bridge, December, 2021.

WHEN THE SKY FALLS

PHIL EARLE

1941. War is raging. And one angry boy has been sent to the city,
where bombers rule the skies. There, Joseph will live with Mrs F,
a gruff woman with no fondness for children. Her only loves
are the rundown zoo she owns and its mighty silverback gorilla,
Adonis. As the weeks pass, bonds deepen and secrets are revealed,
but if the bombers set Adonis rampaging free, will either of them
be able to end the life of the one thing they truly love?

'A magnificent story . . .
It deserves every prize going'
Philip Pullman

'An extraordinary story with
historical and family truth at
its heart, that tells us as much
about the present as the past.
Deeply felt, movingly written,
a remarkable achievement'
Michael Morpurgo

CUCKOO SUMMER

Jonathan Tulloch

Summer 1940. As the cuckoo sings out across the Lake District, life is about to change for ever for Tommy and his friend Sally, a mysterious evacuee girl. When they find a wounded enemy airman in the woods, Sally persuades Tommy not to report it and to keep the German hidden. This starts a chain of events that leads to the uncovering of secrets about Sally's past and a summer of adventure that neither of them will ever forget.

'A ripping wartime adventure and a love letter to Lakeland's farms and fells'
Melissa Harrison